Russian Woman,
A Siberian in New York

X. R. Leblanc

ISBN: 069223439X
ISBN 13: 9780692234396

A Russian Woman Trilogy

Russian Woman: A Siberian in New York

The Boston episode, October 2015
The Los Angeles episode, 2016

R.W. Publishers
New York, NY

website: www.xrleblanc.com
email: xr@xrleblanc.com
facebook: XR Leblanc
twitter: #xrleblanc
instagram: xrleblanc

To my friend Sun

1

OLGA AND SVETLANA

THE CITY OF Krasnoyarsk had been transformed once again following the rise of the oligarchs. During the communist years, the regime had taken great care to erase all reminders of a shameful past. Monolithic, concrete rectangles that served as office buildings and low-cost housing could be found everywhere. Indistinguishable from one another, those boxy buildings replaced a rich and diverse architecture. Centuries-old churches disappeared to make space for administrative offices of the new capital of Siberia, and entire neighborhoods gave way to communal housing complexes, all for the glory of the motherland. Everything changed, however, with the class of the nouveaux riches.

There was a popular theory in the city that Krasnoyarsk was home to the highest number of millionaires in Russia. It seemed logical, given the wealth of resources in the region. Within a one-hundred-mile radius were two of the largest hydroelectric plants in Russia, a few aluminum plants, a great number of iron mines, heavy manufacturing installations, and even some oil fields. Following the collapse of the Soviet Union, all of this had been distributed to the friends of the newly installed regime, and the well-connected had effortlessly become millionaires overnight, thanks to well-placed bribes.

By 2007, the oligarchs had brought back most of the glory of years past and begun to modernize the city: those few historical structures that the communists had spared the oligarchs renovated for new purposes; theaters and museums cropped up in old neighborhoods; world-renowned architects designed modern housing towers; restaurants and nightclubs opened to reflect new cosmopolitan trends; and shopping areas sprang up to the benefit of the new ruling class.

That year, the residents of the Siberian capital had been cheated out of spring. Early June's warm sun replaced the cold rains of May as summer had arrived after another interminable gray winter. In celebration of the warm Sunday, the populace swarmed out. Young men wore tight T-shirts to flaunt muscular bodies built up over the cold season. Young women tucked into their heels and summer dresses, exposing their skinny, pale legs. The elderly, incapable of abandoning their wool sweaters, returned to their favorite benches to exchange the latest gossip.

Just before eleven, Olga parked her car. The tall blonde walked the few blocks separating her from the Sultan Suleyman. Her pace was fast, even in her four-inch heels. It was her first day at work, she was anxious to start, and she did not want to be late. She had been working at another restaurant as a server for the past two years, but the Suley, as everyone called it, was the most prestigious address in Krasnoyarsk.

The restaurant, well known for its cuisine, had become the spot of choice for the who's who of the city: the nouveaux riches, local rugby stars, the politically connected, and the young hipsters. While the well-to-do older customers kept the restaurant very busy during the weekdays, Sunday mornings hosted a younger crowd—especially those seeking refuge after visiting the nightclubs of the area. The unlimited supply of alcohol did, in principle, help people recover from nights short of sleep, and the restaurant owner had adopted the Sunday morning New York tradition with great success. The menu featured an Americanized brunch combined with traditional Russian breakfast fare. Catering to local tastes, he had replaced cheap champagne with true Russian vodka.

The young woman threaded her way along the crowded sidewalk until she stood before the door of the restaurant. She knocked, and it slowly opened to reveal the restaurant manager. "Ah, Olga Kotova.

Welcome to Suleyman," he said. "Come in. I'll introduce you to Dasha. She'll be helping you out."

They walked to the back of the restaurant to the employees' locker room. The man pushed the door open and pointed to another blonde. "Dasha, this is Olga Kotova, our newest server. She's in training this week. She should be ready to handle the Sunday crowd, but I want you to help her out if needed. She's serving section three."

"Of course. The VIP section," Dasha said, nodding. It would be obvious to anyone why the new girl would be given the best section of the restaurant. Olga was tall and thin—like everybody else in town—about five feet eight, and could easily have been a model. She had a symmetrical face with flawless skin, long honey-colored hair, wide blue eyes, luscious red lips, a long neck, and just the right amount of curves for a slim woman. The manager left, and Dasha showed Olga her uniform—a tight black dress with a short white apron. Like all the other female servers, she would wear her own heels. "Once you're dressed, come and see me. I'll help you set up your section."

Olga dressed and joined Dasha in the main dining room.

"Okay, section three, the VIP section, is just these six tables." Dasha pointed at a diagram. "Your first patrons will be at this corner table. Boris Boporesky has a reservation for two at one o'clock."

Boris Boporesky was also known as BeBe. Everyone in Krasnoyarsk knew BeBe. An obvious beneficiary of privatization, he was believed to be the richest man living in the city. In addition to his many business ventures, he had also built a sports arena for the local rugby team. He owned the most luxurious housing tower in the city, Tower Krasnoyarsk, where he had chosen its penthouse apartment as his perfect *pied-à-terre* in the city. He had all the traits of an oligarch: foreign clothes, luxury cars, bodyguards, a private jet, and, of course, interchangeable young women who served as entertainment.

The restaurant opened at eleven thirty. The host opened the doors to the usual crowd of young refugees who had spilled out of bed after a long night at the local clubs. The crowd tumbled in, serenaded by the latest electronic dance music. A second host greeted the young patrons and added their names to the waiting list. The lucky ones, or those sober enough to have made reservations earlier, would be seated within minutes in the few unoccupied tables. The rest would have to wait patiently.

Olga's small section was fully reserved, but the first VIPs weren't due until twelve thirty. She offered to help a few of the other servers in the meantime, but none accepted. She sensed a bit of jealousy from the rest of the wait staff, and assumed that they were disgruntled because the manager had given her the best section on her first day.

She tried to keep busy until her patrons arrived. A few minutes before one o'clock, a red Mazda Miata convertible pulled up in front of the restaurant. A valet ran to the car and opened the door. Two tall, black, high-heeled boots extended gracefully to the pavement, followed by a pair of long, elegant legs in black fishnet stockings. The rest of the lithe body seemed to flow out of the low leather seat, fluidly, like a model in a fashion shoot. The woman was careful not to flash anyone who might be watching. And they were *all* watching. She could hardly go unnoticed, even at the upscale Suleyman, with her short, black leather dress, fire-engine-red leather jacket, black fur scarf, and Louis Vuitton bag. Black designer glasses perfectly complemented her dark hair. She glided into the restaurant, all eyes upon her as she went directly to the host. "I am meeting BeBe at one," she said.

"Your table is ready, but Mr. Boporesky hasn't arrived yet."

"Fine," she replied.

The host escorted the woman to the corner table, helped her into her seat, and then withdrew. Within moments, Olga was there at her elbow. She wondered if the woman was BeBe's girlfriend. "Privet. My name is Olga, and I'll be your server today. Can I get you something to drink?"

"Yes, Olga. I'm Svetlana. Please, could you bring me a bottle of water? Evian. And a bottle of champagne. The most expensive one you've got. Bebe will pay for it, don't worry," she told the young server with a smile.

"Certainly. I'll be right back."

Olga returned a few minutes later the water, a bottle of champagne, and two champagne flutes.

"I've not seen you at the Suley before, but I can see that you're not new to this. That is, you handle yourself very well. I would've dropped everything—except the bottle of champagne," said Svetlana with a smile. "Sacrilege."

"Yes, I've been doing this for a few years. I'm used to it." Olga poured the water into a tumbler. "Should I open the champagne now?"

"Well, of course! BeBe might think he's so important, but not enough to make me wait. He must be busy screwing some bitch."

Olga blushed and Svetlana noticed. "Don't be shy. You know how rich Russian men are. I'm only a friend. I don't fucking care what he does."

Olga listened to the woman politely, and then said, "I'll bring you a menu while you wait." She guessed Svetlana was probably in her forties, and would have been beautiful even without the expensive setting and accessories around her. Olga could not help thinking of her mother. The two women shared the same first name, but were so different. Olga had come from a very poor family, and her mother would never be able to afford any of the things BeBe's friend had. Olga envied this Svetlana, who could clearly afford anything she wanted, and wondered how the woman had done so well.

Svetlana asked, "Are you busy today?"

Olga replied, "This is my first day. I only have six tables. No one has showed up yet, so, I'm not busy just now."

"Good, I really don't like being alone. Talk to me. Where are you from?"

"Well, I'm from Krasnoyarsk-13," Olga said. "I came here to study at the university. I now live in Krasnoyarsk Tower."

"How old are you?" Svetlana asked.

"I'm twenty-three."

"Boyfriend?"

"I've been married for nine months now."

It was not unusual for Russian women to get married as early as eighteen. Any woman who had not found a husband by the time she reached twenty-five would be written off as too old or, even worse, as someone with a "problem." Most people assumed that Olga had married a rich man who had set her up at the luxury apartments.

"Is he rich?" Svetlana asked.

Olga just smiled, tired of hearing the same old question again.

"I left Krasnoyarsk at eighteen to go to Moscow and become rich," said Svetlana. "That's where I met Boris. He still has an apartment there, of course. He was married, but I didn't care. He gave me things when I asked. He introduced me to an American agent who got me a job as a model in America. Later, Boris helped me buy that modeling agency—which I still own. Just recently, he bought me a house in Miami, and that is where I live now. Have you ever been to America?"

"No. I've never been outside of Russia."

"Your husband never takes you anywhere? What a shame. Come visit me in America. Your husband must be rich, no? Have him pay for the trip, but don't bring him. I'll find you a nice, rich American man."

Not accustomed to extended conversations, especially personal ones, with her patrons, Olga stood slightly away from the table, shifting uneasily. Still, she was intrigued. "Is it difficult to become a model?" she asked.

Svetlana took a sip of champagne. "Not really. Why? Do you want to be a model? Or do you just want to go to America?" Svetlana said, looking Olga up and down with an appraising eye. "Either way I can help you. You just need to get a visa to America."

"Really? I could go to America?" Olga asked.

"Why not? America is a paradise. It's always warm and sunny in Miami. All the people are beautiful, famous, and very rich. My friends have everything—cars, maids, private chefs, and yachts. I tell you, it's a paradise," she said with a smile. "But I see there are other diners here now, so I will let you go. Otherwise, your customers will complain."

The idea of leaving Russia mesmerized Olga. She could already imagine herself as one of those wealthy people who could afford anything. That was exactly what she wanted—a life of wealth in America. She wanted to hear more, but her other tables were filling up with VIPs. "Yes, you'll have to excuse me. Do you need anything more before Mr. Boporesky arrives?" When Svetlana shook her head, Olga retreated to introduce herself to the other diners in her section.

A few minutes later, a black Mercedes-Benz S550 pulled in front of the Suleyman. Before the valet had time to approach the car, the driver emerged dressed in a black suit with a white shirt. More than six feet tall and all muscle, he could easily have been an American football player. Scanning the surroundings with the practiced eye of a long-term bodyguard, he walked to the back door of the car and opened it. A short man slowly eased his bulk out of the car. Boris Boporesky.

BeBe was a bland-faced, slightly balding man with a large belly and small features. The rest of his appearance was far from ordinary. The custom suit, crisp shirt, sparkling watch, and soft Italian shoes cried wealth. His bodyguard ushered him to the restaurant, opening the door for him and then returning to the car. BeBe headed directly for the VIP section and the corner table without bothering with the host.

"I'm sorry, baby. I hope I didn't keep you waiting for long."

"Finally! I'm guessing a woman kept you away from me again?" Svetlana stood and hugged the portly man, bending slightly at the waist to keep from pressing her breasts into his face. She smiled. "Not too late, BeBe. You just missed one glass of champagne," she said.

Olga stepped discreetly to the table. She smiled at the man and handed him a menu, which he waved away. "Hello. My name is Olga. May I pour you some champagne?"

Boris devoured the young woman with his eyes. "No," he replied with disdain. "Bring me a bottle of vodka from my private stash. The bartender will know. Two glasses with ice. Lots of ice."

"Of course. Anything else I can get you?"

Before BeBe could answer, Svetlana replied, "Thank you."

The moment Olga left the table BeBe said, "Hmm...young and fresh."

"That young and fresh girl is married, so behave," said Svetlana.

BeBe smiled. "Of course, baby. Of course."

The restaurant buzzed with activity. Olga's six tables of VIPs kept her moving. As soon as one set of patrons left the restaurant, she cleared the table and readied it for the next set. As she bustled from one table to another, she kept a close eye on Svetlana and BeBe. They lingered for hours, seemingly enjoying themselves.

The day shift ended at five o'clock. Olga sat in front of her small locker, massaging her feet. Her first day had been eventful. She had been busy most of the day, and made more tips in eight hours than she used to make in a few days at the other restaurants. The best part of the day, however, was meeting Svetlana. Olga had thought about leaving Krasnoyarsk before, as her prospects remained limited in the city, but she hadn't thought about leaving Russia. Meeting Svetlana was a good omen. She would call her mother when she got home. Her mother always provided good counsel.

When Olga returned home, her husband greeted her at the door. "How was your day?" he asked, as he stepped close to kiss her.

At five feet eight, Olga was of average height among women in Krasnoyarsk, but she towered over her short and portly husband, especially in her high heels. She leaned down to reach his lips.

"It was fine," she replied.

"Good. Anything interesting happen?" he asked.

"No, not really. Just busy."

"You know you really don't need to work."

He had said this many times, and Olga always gave the same answer. This time, however, she couldn't keep the slight edge of irritation out of her voice. "I've told you many times, Vladimir. I'm alone here all day. You leave early in the morning and come back very late at night. I want to meet people and talk to them," she said. "I can't stay here alone like a…like a prisoner. I don't want to talk about it again. Leave me alone, please. I've got to call my mother." She left the boudoir and went into the study.

OLGA HAD GROWN up in Krasnoyarsk-13, a dormitory town that housed thousands of the local industrial workers and was located in the middle of the Siberian forest, about one hundred fifty miles from the Siberian capital. Like the other workers, her parents had been required by the party to move from Moscow to Siberia for the glory of Mother Russia. Her father was an electrical engineer at one of the local hydroelectric plants and her mother was an elementary school teacher.

Life during the communist era had been difficult for Olga and her family. As a young girl in the 1980s, she had experienced firsthand the hardship of the communist regime. She could still remember fidgeting in the long lines with her mother at the local store. After hours of waiting, they might be able to buy a pound of sugar, some soap, and maybe a "brick" of fresh bread on a lucky day; a few days later there might be butter and light bulbs, but no bread. A small community garden helped feed the family during the long winter months. Her father frequently hunted in the forest; rabbit and deer were common on the Kotova table. Olga's clothes were nearly always hand-me-downs from her sister, or dresses she made with their grandmother's help. Store-bought toys were only something she wished for, a wish occasionally granted on Christmas. More often the holidays brought some practical item and an orange, a great luxury during the cold Siberian winter.

Even after the collapse of the Soviet Union, nothing changed significantly for the Kotova family. The promises of a better life never materialized. Slowly, all the simple luxuries of years past—food, clothes, electronics, toys, and cars—were theoretically available to the populace, but realistically out of reach for the Kotovas, whose limited income denied them access to the new abundance. Olga grew up resigned to that reality. Then, as a teenager, she had visited her grandparents in Moscow, and her world view totally changed. She discovered that life could be better. Everything seemed different in the capital. Wealth was omnipresent. There was a sea of luxury cars, beautiful people with fabulous clothes, and foreign designer stores. Everyone seemed rich to her. That was the life she wanted.

Olga had moved to Krasnoyarsk five years earlier to escape the dreaded and dismal future she knew awaited her in her hometown. Deciding to study at the local university in the hope of making a better life for herself, she chose to follow in her mother's footsteps and become a teacher. Upon her arrival in the city, Olga had taken a job as a server at a local restaurant to help pay for her college expenses; her family, after all, could not support her. It was at work that she met

Vladimir, a regular customer who had finally asked her out. He was unhappily married, he told her, but she made it clear that she would never be his mistress. He wasn't very attractive, and he was old—in fact, he was just one year younger than her father—but his wealth made him desirable. She had always dreamed of marrying a very rich man who could give her everything she wanted.

She resisted his advances for a few months before finally agreeing to go out with him. Vladimir understood that the young woman was less interested in him personally than in the attention and the benefits that came with being with him. He took her to the best restaurants in the city. He showered with expensive presents. He tried to satisfy her ever-growing obsession with shopping. Even with all that, she didn't give in to his sexual advances.

Vladimir had been seeing Olga for four months when he decided to change his life for her. He moved out of his house, filed for divorce, and moved into a luxurious apartment in the Krasnoyarsk Tower, all in the expectation that Olga would come to him. Vladimir told Olga he wanted to be with her. He wanted to marry her as soon as his divorce was final. Before answering him, Olga had called her mother, seeking much-needed counsel. She was very close to her mother, and she always relied on her advice before making any major decisions. Her mother knew of Vladimir, as her daughter had shared some of the details of their relationship. Her mother was always very practical. She had strongly encouraged her daughter to consider the offer.

"He's rich," her mother said. "He doesn't mistreat you. You might grow to love him. This would be beneficial for you and your family."

And so Olga married Vladimir.

⸺

OLGA ENTERED THE boudoir and closed the door slowly, dialing her mother's number. She wanted to talk about the day's events, and she didn't want Vladimir to hear any of it. Her mother answered the phone immediately, and listened patiently while Olga told her about the restaurant, the standoffish employees, and the generous tips she had made that day. She explained how she had met the famous BeBe and described the exciting conversation with Svetlana.

"That's very interesting," her mother said.

"Mama," Olga said, "I really need a change. I finished college a year ago, and I've no real future here. I make more money as a server than I would as an elementary school teacher. And Vladimir…" She stopped, knowing that her mother already knew what she was going to say. "Maybe this is a sign of something to happen. I can feel it."

"Olga, you're twenty-three. You need to be happy. I know things with Vladimir didn't turn out as you expected. But America? You'd be so far from me!"

"Mama, I'd miss you, too, but…there's nothing for me here. *Nothing*. I'll never be able to help you and Papa as I want. I'll never make enough money here. I'll never be happy here."

"You're probably right. Maybe America would be better for you. If this is what you want, I think your father will agree."

Olga was happy to hear the words of support. Strengthened by her mother's implicit approval, she decided to try to go to America, the paradise where everyone was rich and beautiful. Olga knew little of the country beyond what she had seen in movies and on television, but she was certain that America was a dreamland where people could make names for themselves and become rich and famous. Svetlana had confirmed that dream life—so very far from Olga's current life. In Russia, everything came down to who she knew; nothing else really mattered, and Olga didn't know anyone.

It was time for a change. Olga was determined to do something with her life.

2

US VISA

ONE WEEK AFTER meeting BeBe's friend Svetlana, Olga found a way to America. A local travel agency had advertised in the newspaper and presented its long list of services: airfare, lodging in all major cities, proposed tours, and travel visas. Olga knew a US visa could be difficult to get, but the travel agency claimed a 99 percent success rate. She called the agency on Monday and scheduled an appointment for nine o'clock the next morning.

The day was sunny and warm. Olga walked to the drab old building, a relic of the Soviet era. Though the stairs seemed like a safer option given the general state of the building, she decided that five floors would require too much effort and pushed the button to call the elevator. The door opened immediately. The antiquated elevator climbed the five floors, screeching the entire way. As the door opened, the agency's sign directed her to the left to office number 509.

She knocked on the door, waited for a few seconds, and opened it. The agent sat behind a metallic, rectangular desk piled high with paper. He got up to greet the young woman. "Ms. Olga Kotova, I assume. I'm Sergey Grobikov. Nice to meet you."

"*Privet*, Mr. Grobikov. Nice to meet you too."

"You can call me Sergey. Sorry for the mess. We've had a lot of new clients since we posted the ad last week. Please, sit down.

I'm sure we'll be able to help you," he said. "So, you want to go to America. You're married. Your husband owns an apartment. All good. One thing…have you ever been outside Russia?"

"Never."

"Mmm. It will be much easier for you to go to America if you get a tourist visa to Europe for a couple of weeks first. A visa to Europe is much easier to get—a formality for someone like you. You should travel somewhere on the continent and come back, to show the American consulate that you're not looking to stay in the country illegally. After you do that, I'll apply for a visa to travel to the States."

He described in detail the application process and answered her few questions.

"Where do you want to go in the United States? Miami? Los Angeles? Chicago?" he asked.

Olga listened to Sergey reel off the highlights of several major American cities, but she knew already where she wanted to go. She'd been awakened that morning by an old song on her alarm radio. Olga spoke English, so she understood the lyrics.

"Start spreadin' the news: I'm leavin' today.

I want to be a part of it…New York, New York."

She could still hear the song. "Maybe…New York! Yes, New York!" The song had been a sign. A series of events was slowly directing her to New York.

"New York. Good. We've a good number of contacts in Brooklyn. As I explained before, we'll be providing you a nice place to stay upon your arrival. There's a large Russian community there," said Sergey. "They can help you find things you might miss from home, like certain foods. That's *if* you ever miss home." He smiled. "I'll take your documents to make copies. I assume you brought the one thousand US dollars for the deposit?"

She opened her purse and pulled out the documents and an envelope filled with cash. She handed him all of it.

"Good. My fees are nonrefundable, to be clear."

She nodded.

"I'll get started, but you need to plan a trip to Europe soon. After that, I'll submit your application to the American consulate in Moscow. You'll need to go there for an interview."

"Do I really need to go to Europe first?"

"A trip to Europe will ensure that you get an American visa. The consulate wants to make sure that young women like you aren't planning to stay illegally in America. If you go to Europe and come back, they'll see that you aren't fleeing Russia, and they'll give you the visa easily. Without a trip to Europe, I can't assure you'll get it. Your chances are probably fifty-fifty."

"I understand. How long does it take to get the visa?" she asked.

"Once you come back from Europe, I'll need to see you again to collect a few more documents. I'll especially need your passport again. I'll file the application, and you could get the interview within a month of submission. If all goes well at the interview, they'll issue the US visa in a few days. For the European visa, we can get everything done here."

"Understood. I'll start organizing a trip to Europe. Thank you." After a few seconds, she asked, "How long is the American visa for?"

"Two years, but you can never stay more than three months at a time," said Sergey. He rose and shook her hand. "Thank you, Olga. I'm sure you'll be very satisfied with our services."

Olga left the office disappointed. Suddenly America seemed unattainable. *Europe? I have no interest in going there now, but…New York! I need to find a way to go to Europe.*

AFTER JUST A few weeks of working the Sunday shift at the Suley, Olga was pleased. By her calculations, she was on track to make close to five hundred dollars in her first month—more than double the salary she would have made as a full-time schoolteacher.

Around four o'clock, things started to slow down. The morning crowd, fully satisfied, had dissipated. Three tall men came in, and the host directed them to one of Olga's empty tables. Their leather jackets in the colors of the powerful local Krasnoyarsk rugby club, the Krasny Yar, caught everyone's attention. Conversations hushed. Women smiled, hoping to attract the attention of the players. Men tried to identify the players by name. Krasnoyarsk was the powerhouse of Russian rugby, and Krasny Yar players were always treated like heroes.

After the host had seated the players, Olga walked over to their table, eyeing them as she approached. She thought the one with black hair, a short, black beard, and piercing blue eyes was very handsome, and she smiled at him.

"*Privet.* My name is Olga. I will be your server. And you are with Krasny Yar. Right?"

The handsome man replied in Russian with a heavy accent. "*Privet,* Olga. Yes, we are. My name is François. This is Richard and Jacques." He pointed to the other players. "We are from France, and we came here for the rugby season."

Olga could not restrain herself from looking at François. "France? How nice."

A Frenchman from Europe. I need him for my trip.

"Your Russian is very good," she commented. Her hopes of a trip to the United States came back to life. She might have found her ticket to Europe.

He smiled. "Thank you. I took some lessons before I came. I think my English is better. Well, we all took lessons. As for my friends, they speak just a little."

"English?" she replied, switching to English. "Are you from Paris?"

"No, we're from Marseilles, in the south of France," said François. His English was clearly better than his Russian. "So you speak English, too! Not as many people learn English here in Russia as in Europe."

"You're correct. We are taught some English at school, but not much. I was lucky. My mother is an English teacher. She made me read, watch TV, and speak in English all the time. So I'm not too bad."

"We're in an exchange program. A few Russian players will go to Marseilles next year," said François.

"That's so exciting! I've never been to France before."

"It's the most beautiful country in the world."

"Well, maybe after Russia," she replied smiling.

"Now I *know* that you have never been to France. But Russia does seem to have the most beautiful women in the world."

Olga blushed, not knowing what to reply. After a few seconds, she said, "Can I get you something to drink while you look at the menu?"

"Yes, three beers."

"Pikra Kupecheskoe? It's brewed right here in Krasnoyarsk."

"Perfect."

The moment she left the table, the three men began chattering about her like little boys in a candy store. Jacques, who had been silent, said, "Shit. I should've paid more attention to my English lessons."

"No fucking worries," said Richard. "We've got money. The Russian bitches are only looking for that. Plus we're French. French with money? You'll get pussy."

François said, "Come on, guys. There are some normal women looking for normal guys."

"François, you're such a pussy," said Richard. "You know Russian women. They want something. Always. There's always an agenda with them."

Maybe, thought François. One hour later, the three men had finished their meals, and Olga brought them their bill. François said, in English, "Olga, thank you. I think you should give me your phone number. I would like to take you out this week."

"Well…" She hesitated only a moment.

"Well…maybe? Well…yes?"

"Okay." She pulled out a pen and a piece of paper and complied. As she gave him the precious piece of paper, he said, "À *bientôt, ma chatte.*"

Olga blushed. "What did you say?"

"See you soon, baby."

"Yes. See you soon, Frenchman," said Olga.

As they were leaving, Richard spoke in French, as he knew no one would understand. "François, did you see how she looked at you? Lucky bastard!"

François acknowledged the comment and turned around to catch a last glimpse of Olga.

Olga woke up at eight the next morning. Vladimir had left the house a couple of hours before to head to an early morning business meeting, leaving her alone in bed. She enjoyed those moments when she could be lethargic and get up slowly. She would take over the entire bed, stretching her body across its queen-size width. She was without her husband and happy about it.

It was a beautiful Monday morning. The sun pushed its light through the bedroom's shades. It was time to get up and start her day—a morning visit to the gym, a stop at the grocery store, lunch with a friend, and a trip to the nail salon. A text message interrupted her morning thoughts.

François: Bonjour, Olga. This is François, the Frenchman. How are you this sunny morning?

She read the message to make sure she clearly understood all the English words. After a few seconds, she smiled and replied.

Olga: Fine. You?

François: Great. Are you available this week? I would like to take you out for dinner so we can practice our English ;)

Olga: I am working Thursday and Saturday evenings and Sunday morning. Maybe Wednesday?

François: Wednesday works for me. I will text you tomorrow. Is there somewhere you would like to go?

Olga: I will think about it! ;)

François: Great. Have a fabulous day. TTYL.

Olga: TTYL?

François: Ha ha. Talk to you later.

Olga: OK! ;) TTYL.

Olga smiled. She had found her ticket to Europe.

3

THE FRENCHMAN

OLGA SET THE date with François for Wednesday evening at Retro, a newly opened Russian restaurant mostly visited by young hipsters. She had selected the location for the atmosphere, but she was also certain that they would be unlikely to encounter her husband or any of his numerous friends. She and Vladimir had long since grown apart, and she didn't want to reignite the sort of confrontations they'd had in the past, when the reactions of her jealous husband began to frighten her. Like many Russian men, he did not hesitate to use physical violence to get his point across. She had tasted his fury a few times since their marriage, although on only one occasion had he totally lost control. That happened after he had seen her talking to a young man at a local café and had accused her of cheating. That "confrontation" had landed her in the hospital for a week with a concussion.

On Wednesday, Olga left the apartment shortly after her husband had left for another late business dinner. His dinners were frequent and predictable, and she knew he would be back very late. She felt at ease to enjoy her evening. She arrived at the restaurant a few minutes late to find the Frenchman at the bar patiently waiting.

"*Privet*, Olga. I'm happy to see you," he said, kissing her once on each of her cheeks.

"Hello, François." She tried to pronounce his name correctly.

"I asked in my bad Russian if the table was ready. I think it is."

"I'll ask," she replied and smiled.

Olga walked to the host and quickly returned. "Ready?" she asked François. The host guided them to their table.

Olga was happy. The time with François flew by. Dessert was coming, and Olga knew she would need to go home shortly. When the bill came, François grabbed it. She simply smiled and let him.

They left the restaurant together. François walked Olga to her car. As she stopped and turned around to thank him, he took her in his arms, pulled her close to him, and kissed her slowly. Her body shivered with pleasure. After a few seconds, he pulled his head back just enough to see her eyes. "I had a great evening, and I would like to take you home," he told her.

"I'm not that kind of girl. This is our first date."

A bit surprised, François replied, "I respect that. Good night then. I would like to see you again. Yes?"

"Yes."

"Soon?"

"Maybe."

"Good night."

"Good night, Frenchman."

He opened the door, and Olga slipped into her sports car. He stayed on the sidewalk and watched the car leave. *She is a great catch,* he thought as he turned around to go to his car.

FRANÇOIS HAD BEEN on six dates with Olga and he was starting to doubt his seductive abilities. Olga was really playing hard to get. All the other Russian women he had met were much easier. After a couple of dates, he took them to his apartment, and sex was a sure thing. After six dates, all he had gotten from Olga was a kiss.

"It was nice to see you again, Olga," he said as he walked her to her car.

"I don't think it's time to say good night yet. Do you?" she replied. François was perplexed and did not answer.

"My husband's away for the rest of the week, and I took a few days off," she said. "Maybe we can go to my place?"

"Of course," he replied. He was somewhat surprised by the invitation.

"Go get your car. I'll wait for you, and you can follow me. My apartment is in the Tower."

He turned around and walked quickly to his car. *Finally*, he thought, *my patience is paying off. Her husband is away? She didn't tell me she was married. I have a two-day break from the team, though. Perfect setup for a great night of sex.*

As he drove, he could only think about the moments to come. He hadn't been with a woman for more than two weeks now. He didn't care that she had a husband. He only wanted to touch this beautiful woman. François started imagining all the positions they would experiment with together.

At the apartment building, he parked next to her. "Wow. I've only seen the Tower from far away. It's really nice," he said.

"It's comfortable. Let's go up."

She grabbed his hand and led him to the building entrance. François understood that this was probably a bit delicate since she was married, and he purposely avoided talking about it. She passed the guard, who greeted her without looking at François, apparently understanding that he should ignore the presence of the young man. At the elevator, Olga said, "One second. I need to take care of something."

François was surprised, but quickly understood the purpose of this intermission. Olga walked to the desk of the guard, put her hand in her purse, pulled something out, and gave it to the man. Only then did she walk back and press the elevator call button.

While they waited for the car to arrive, François felt a bit uncomfortable with the situation, but once the doors open and they stepped in his guilt began to subside, outweighed by thoughts of what was to come. It was still early in the night, just past ten, so she obviously cut the night out short to have more time alone with him. It was clear to François that he would be spending the night with her.

When the door opened to a hallway, they walked down a few doors to apartment 21-F.

"Come in," Olga said, and she unlocked the door.

A few steps into the vast apartment, he expressed his amazement. "Wow! This is really a great apartment."

"Thank you. It's my husband's house. I'm lucky, I guess."

The last comment puzzled him, but he knew better than to ask too many questions. His intentions were simple—sex. Nothing else mattered.

She walked to the kitchen. "Open this, please." She handed him a bottle of champagne.

"*Bien sûr,*" he said. Quickly he translated into English. "Of course."

She pulled out two glasses and put them on the counter. "I'll be back in a few minutes. Make yourself comfortable in the living room. Put some music on. There are a few jazz CDs that would be nice. I'll be right back."

He headed to the living room and selected one of the CDs conveniently arranged on the coffee table. He opened the bottle of champagne and poured two glasses, and then sat down on the long leather couch, excited about what was coming. As the minutes passed, he started getting anxious. *What is she doing? How long does it take someone to get ready? I'm already ready. So ready,* he thought.

A few minutes later, he heard heels clicking the hardwood floor as if they were following the slow rhythm of a clock that seemed to follow his pulse. Olga finally appeared from the long hallway. She stopped for a few seconds at the entrance to the living room for effect, her left arm raised to caress the wall. She smiled at him. Then she walked slowly toward him, crossing her legs as if she was walking down a runway.

He could not take his eyes off her. She was stunning. She was wearing white lingerie—a lace bra that showed off her dark nipples, a thong that tightly wrapped her vulva, white stockings that embraced her long, thin legs, and elbow-length satin gloves. She stood on towering black pumps. He was ready. *I am so lucky,* he thought.

She came to him. He tried to stand up to hug her, but she pushed him back onto the couch with one hand. She slowly bent over, put her left hand behind his shoulder, and grabbed the top of the couch to keep her balance. She slowly blew in his ear and gently kissed him on his cheek. Her right hand slowly stoked his other cheek as she continued to kiss him.

This was so unexpected that François was frozen to the couch. He wanted to participate, but she had paralyzed him. She had taken full control of the situation, and he has happy to oblige, enjoying every gesture and touch. He knew it would be his turn very soon. Her right hand swirled around his neck, and she softy blew on his neck. Then her hand came back to his cheek and slowly descended, gliding like a butterfly along his body. She kissed him again, and she grabbed his chest and then finally found her way to his penis. She started slowly stroking him. He pushed his hips toward her so he could feel more pressure on his erection.

Unexpectedly, she stopped. She pulled herself up, stood in front of him, and offered him her hand. She whispered, "Come to the bedroom."

THEY BOTH LAY on the bed, naked and staring at the ceiling. After a few minutes of silence, François turned his head toward Olga. "That was amazing."

"Yes, it was. I like you," Olga replied.

He knew exactly what to say, as he wanted more of her. "I like you, Olga. I always have fun with you."

That was the opening she had been waiting for. She had been thinking of that moment for a few days, and she, too, knew exactly what to say. After a few seconds of silence, she said, "You'll be leaving soon for France. I'll miss you so much."

"Yes. I leave in July, and I'll be there three weeks. All the Russians players are competing in the nationals in preparation for the championship next summer before the Beijing Olympics." He paused. "I'll miss you too."

There was a brief silence.

"Maybe I could go, too? I could meet you in Paris! I've never traveled outside of Russia. It would be perfect to see France with you. You could show me around."

The request surprised him, and he replied hesitantly. "Well, yes. Of course. I'm sure we could set something up."

"You make me so happy." Olga put her head on his chest. "Really happy," she added.

He felt obliged to answer. "That's great."

She kissed him on the cheek. "François." She paused for a few seconds. "I need to tell you something."

"Yes." He was a bit afraid by what she might say.

"Well, I just want to tell you that…" She paused again. "I have only been with three men, including you. This was really wonderful. I have never felt this way after sex."

François smiled. *I* was *good*, he thought. He pulled her toward him, and she nuzzled her head against his chest.

4

GETTING THE US VISA

WHEN SHE RETURNED from her trip to France, Olga returned to the travel agency. Sergey was in his office. It was messy, as usual.

"Olga, how nice to see you again," he said as he opened the door. "How was your trip? Summer is a great time to see Paris, I'm told."

"It was a good trip."

"Happy to hear it. Now, about your trip to America. I'll need the final amount of two thousand three hundred US dollars. Then I'll make copies of your stamped passport, and send everything to the American consulate in Moscow. You'll need to go to Moscow and wait for them to set up an interview. It'll take about two weeks, maybe three. We'll try to do it quickly."

"I understand."

"Before you go to Moscow, we'll prepare you for the interview. I can give you an idea how it works."

Olga nodded. "Okay."

"For example, they will ask why you want to go to America. What will you say?"

"I want to go see the cities I've heard about."

"Okay. Good start. Which cities would you visit and when? You can think about it, and we'll help you. They will ask how you will pay for your trip."

"I have some money, but I can always work if—"

"No! No! You can't say that," Sergey cut her off. "You'll have a tourist visa. You're a tourist, so you can't work. You need to show them you already have plenty of money for your trip. I would say about one thousand dollars per week. What does your husband do again?"

Olga never knew how to answer this question, but for most Russians the typical answer sufficed. "He is a businessman."

"What kind of business?"

"Well, you know. Business."

Sergey knew exactly what that meant. Her husband was part of the apparatus that was benefiting from connections to the right people.

"Americans won't understand that," Sergey said. "Find a business for your husband such as retail, hotels, oil, or something like that. They need to think you're telling the truth. If they don't believe your story, you'll get rejected, and you'll never go. When we get the notification from the consulate, we'll get you fully prepared for the interview. I think you understand how it works. Take a look at the map, and decide which cities you want to visit. You don't actually need to go to those cities; it's only for the consulate."

"So I could stay in New York?"

"If you choose. When you arrive, we'll arrange your ride from the airport and take you to one of our rooms. You'll like it a lot."

"Okay. I understand."

"Great. I'll take your documents now, and I'll get everything ready for you. You should go to Moscow in the next couple of weeks."

Sergey stepped into a rear office with her documents. Olga waited in the chair in front of the metal desk, smiling. She would be in New York soon.

After her meeting, Olga returned to her empty home. Vladimir had left again for two days. She dropped her bag and grabbed her phone to tell her mother.

"Mama, I've made the arrangements. I'm going to America."

"That's great news. I'll tell your father tonight when he comes home. When do you leave?"

Olga explained the process and timing in detail.

"I'm so proud of you," her mother said. "You're such a determined woman. You've been like that since you were a little girl. Nothing ever stopped you."

Olga knew her mother was right. When Olga had something in her mind, she made it happen.

⸺⧉⸺

OLGA ARRIVED IN Moscow a few days early in preparation for her interview. She was confident. Sergey and his team had done a great job preparing her. After passing through tight security, Olga was directed to a waiting room, where she joined about a dozen people, all waiting for a chance to go to America.

Olga's appointment was for ten o'clock. She was still waiting at 11:40 a.m. Her name was on the monitor, but there were five people in front of her. The agents came out and called one name at a time. Olga thought of François. She had chatted with him many times after she left him in Krasnoyarsk. She missed him, but she was conflicted. She liked him, but her mother did not approve.

A young woman burst from the interview room in tears. The room fell silent. An older woman, probably the girl's mother, tried to comfort the crying woman. Olga, just a few seats away, heard the young girl whisper to her mother, "They said no."

For the first time, Olga felt nervous about the interview. The consulate might reject her visa request.

"Olga Kotova."

Finally. It was her turn. Olga got up and followed the consulate officer. As they entered the interview room, the man turned around and asked Olga if she spoke English. She replied affirmatively.

"Please sit down," he said in English, sitting behind his desk. After flipping a few pages of her file, he asked, "Are you married?"

"Yes," she replied in English.

"Will your husband be traveling with you?"

"Not this time. He's a very busy man."

"You own an apartment in Krasnoyarsk?"

"Yes."

"What do you do for a living?"

"I am now working as a server, but I want to be a schoolteacher. A Russian language teacher like my mother."

"Okay." The consulate officer continued to study the file. He pulled out her passport and took a quick look at the stamps from France and the Czech Republic.

"What does your husband do?" he asked.

"He's in the oil business in Krasnoyarsk."

"Where will you be going?"

"America."

"I mean what cities are you going to visit?"

"I want to go to New York, to Florida to see Disney World, and to Hollywood."

The agent paused again to look at the file, "That is a lot of travel for…how long will you be staying?"

"About one month. I want to be home in Russia for the New Year."

"And where will you stay?"

"I have a room in New York. I will get hotel rooms in the other cities."

He looked at her file for one long minute, and then raised his head, staring at her intensely. "All of this is very expensive. Are you planning to work?"

She looked at him and blinked nervously. She could feel her heart racing, but she smiled, and said, "No, it's a vacation. My husband is rich. He's giving me all the money I need."

"Your husband does what again?"

"He's in the oil business. He manages some of the oil fields for Lukoil, a big oil company."

The agent paused, flipped a few pages of her file. Olga could feel a bead of perspiration tickling her temple, and hope it didn't show. The consulate officer studied her face, and she thought for sure he suspected her of lying.

"What's his title at Lukoil?"

"Director, oil operations, Siberia."

"The room in New York. Are you staying with friends?"

"No, I'm renting a room from a Russian family."

"Okay," he said. "How much money will you have for your trip?"

"A little over four thousand American dollars. One thousand for each week."

The consulate officer looked down at the paperwork for what seemed like forever. Olga stared at the top of his head and waited anxiously. *Did I answer correctly?*

"Everything seems in order. I'm going to keep your passport for now, and you'll get your visa tomorrow. The visa is good for two years and can be renewed. Note that you can't stay in the United States more than three months at a time."

"Thank you."

He got up. "Let me walk you to the door."

She heard him call the next applicant, but within moments of leaving the consulate she had forgotten all about the other hopeful faces she'd left behind. She had made it happen.

Start spreadin' the news…

Her dream was coming true. She was headed to America, and her future looked fabulous.

5

OLGA'S PARENTS

ON HER WAY back to Krasnoyarsk, Olga decided she should visit her parents in her hometown. She would be leaving in three weeks, and she wanted to see them before her trip to the United States. As always, she took a bus to make the two-and-a-half-hour trip to Krasnoyarsk-13, excited to see her mother and her sister. Her sister, Ekaterina, had also married a much older man who, like Vladimir, was a local businessperson with ties to the old regime.

At the city gate, a security agent boarded the bus for the usual passport inspection. The agent walked up to Olga and said, "Papers."

She handed them over.

"Reason for the visit?"

"I am going to see my parents. I have registered with the local office," Olga said.

"Where do they live?"

"On Second Avenue. Near the Boulevard of the Great Victory."

"Fine," said the agent. He returned her papers and moved on to the next passenger.

Such control was very common for a town like Krasnoyarsk-13, a vestige of the Soviet era when free travel had been a privilege of only the few. Even Moscow still had some restriction of movement, mostly to control the flow of incoming citizens into the capital. For

Krasnoyarsk-13, the control ensured the security of the town, built during the Second World War for the workers of the mining, heavy manufacturing, and oil industries in the area. At least, that was the official position of the local government. Olga didn't understand why the controls were still necessary. She found it very annoying. Krasnoyarsk-13 was not in a foreign country. It was no longer a secret city. It was just a quiet Russian town. Nothing ever happened there.

When the bus came to a stop beyond the gates, Olga stepped out, taking great care to maintain her balance while going down the steps in her high heels. She walked the three blocks to her family's apartment. They lived in one of the numerous monolithic apartment complexes along the boulevard, a seven-story building that held seventy nearly identical apartments.

Olga arrived at a familiar building and walked up a flight of stairs to the family's apartment. It was small by any standard. Olga had shared a bedroom with her older sister; their two single beds barely fit into the tiny room. Her parents' bedroom was only slightly bigger. The living room included a couch, two chairs, and a black-and-white television set. The apartment had only one bathroom. Storage was very limited, but that was not an issue since they didn't have much. It was a humble home, but the family was thankful to have somewhere to call home for so many years.

Olga knocked on the door and her mother flew out to greet her.

"Olga! I'm so happy to see you!" She took her daughter in her arms. "Yuri, Olga's here!"

Olga's father came into the hallway to greet his daughter. Extremely muscular and about six feet tall with a military posture, he had serious brown eyes, trimmed dark hair, and a long black beard that reached down to past his shoulders, like a storybook pirate.

"Welcome, Olga," he said coldly. He never demonstrated any loving emotions toward his daughters. For as long as she could remember, Olga had wished her father had been more expressive. He never hugged or kissed her. He never showed her any signs of affection or pride.

The three of them entered the tiny kitchen and sat down. "You'll stay for the night, yes?" her mother asked. Olga nodded. "I'll make a stew. Your father went hunting yesterday and brought back a few rabbits."

Olga was not surprised. Her father was a rugged man who enjoyed the outdoors. He always found great pleasure in any activity that took him deep into the Siberian forests, and often left home for two or three days for hunting trips. He liked to camp in the middle of nowhere and feed himself off the land.

"I'll help you. But I'll be going out soon after dinner. I promised to go see Katya tonight. I haven't seen her in months," said Olga.

"Of course you can go see her. Right, Yuri?" her mother said.

"You need to be back by eleven. No later," her father said in a flat voice.

Olga knew there was no point in arguing with her father. She could have reminded him that she was old enough to decide when she could come back—that she was a married woman and able to make her own decisions—but she didn't. Such arguments would have been lost on her father, and merely angered him.

"Yes, Papa. I'll be back by then," Olga replied.

"So, you have your visa now. What's your plan?" asked her mother.

"I will go to New York in October for a few weeks, but return here for the holidays. Then I will go back to New York in March. The tourist visa is good for two years. It was easy to get because I'm married and have money. And after two years...who knows?"

Her mother understood exactly what that meant. Olga shared just about everything with her mother. Olga's relationship with Vladimir was no longer working, and Olga had decided she would find a way to leave him. The trip to the United States would be a good way for her to start over again, and maybe even find a better husband. The prospects for a young, divorced woman in Russia were relatively limited.

"I want to be here in Russia to see in the New Year. I'm sure 2008 will be a great year. I want to start it here with my family." Svetlana smiled. "After that, I'll see what happens in New York. I will find a way to get a job there and help you out."

"We always appreciate your help. Come, help me cook dinner."

After dinner, Olga left to see Ekaterina. Her mother kissed her good night before she left. "I'm sorry I won't be up when you return. I'm a bit tired," Svetlana said. "I'm going to bed early."

Yuri just nodded. He sat the kitchen table, facing the bottle of vodka he had opened at dinnertime. He was slowly taking care of what was left; the bottle was already nearly empty.

He'd started another bottle when Olga returned at a few minutes before midnight. When she entered the apartment and locked the door behind her, he stood up and lurched toward her. She knew exactly what would follow. As she opened her mouth to explain her delay, her father slapped her across the face. She lost her balance and stumbled against the walls.

"This is my home, and you follow my rules. Eleven means eleven. Not later."

"I'm sorry," Olga cried out loudly.

In a vodka-fueled rage, Yuri was unmoved by her apology. He was raising his right hand to hit her again when Olga's mother came out of the bedroom, screaming.

"Yuri, stop it! You drunken brute! Stop it, you bastard!" Yuri spun to face his wife, fury in his eyes. "You can't beat her anymore. She's married now. She's not a little girl!"

Yuri turned around with his fist still raised, and then headed to his bedroom in silence. Svetlana hugged her tearful daughter. They did not speak. They never did after any of Yuri's outbursts.

Olga whispered, "That's why I got married, Mama. To get away from *that*."

Svetlana took her daughter's head in her arms. "I know. I'm sorry. Go to bed now. I'll check on your father."

"No, Mama. He'll hit you now. Stay in my room tonight. When I get a job in America, I'll take you with me."

"Okay. Let me go to the bathroom, and then I'll go to your bedroom."

Olga walked into her bedroom and closed the door. She pulled a small mirror from her purse and looked at her cheek. The hand of her father was stamped as if tattooed on her face. She sat on her bed, crying, remembering all the pain her father had inflicted on her over the years. He had beaten her regularly for any reason he could find, real or imagined, until she was sixteen and Svetlana finally stood up to him. Olga's mother had finally found the courage to stop the abuse of her daughters and pulled a knife, saying that she would kill him if ever he dared touch one of them again. That act of courage changed Olga's view of her mother, earning her respect. The events of that night, though, were a sad reminder that her father would never change.

OLGA WOKE TO the sound of her alarm at seven. She was planning to take the eight-thirty bus back to Krasnoyarsk. She got out of bed and went to the kitchen. Her mother was preparing breakfast.

"Good morning," said Svetlana. "Your father left already. I think he was ashamed of his actions."

Olga had no response.

"Do you want some breakfast?" her mother asked.

"I'm not really hungry. Don't prepare anything for me. Just coffee."

"Okay. Come sit down for a few minutes."

"Yes, Mama."

"Now that you are back from your trip, what will you do about the Frenchman?"

"Well…I still want to see him."

"So, you *like* him?"

"Maybe. Is that bad?"

"Yes," her mother replied in a stern voice. "He's not the right man for you. For your future."

"I know, Mama. I know."

Svetlana confirmed what she had deciphered from her last call with Olga: the trip to Europe had deepened her daughter's feelings toward the Frenchman. Olga was infatuated with the rugby player, and Svetlana did not like it. Her daughter needed an established man, not a Bohemian with little ambition. "I want to give you something," Svetlana said, pulling a bag from under the table. Olga took the bag and pulled out a forest green velvet dress. "You left it here. It'll be cold in New York. This is a beautiful dress and it's warm. Take it with you."

Olga hugged her mother. "I thought I'd lost it! Thank you, Mama. Thank you."

It was the last dress Olga had made with her grandmother before the old woman passed away, and was a reminder of how difficult life was in Russia. Since the family had rarely been able to buy new clothes for their daughters, a determined Olga had started making her own dresses at the age of ten. She still remembered fondly the hours she had spent with her grandmother by the sewing machine—some of the happiest moments of her life. The two women looked at each other and started crying.

"I love you, Mama"

"I love you, too. I want to hear from you every day, promise?"

"Promise. Let me get ready now."

When Olga left her mother that morning, she decided that she would leave Russia forever. She would arrange for her mother to join her as soon as possible. *No man—not my father, my husband, or anyone—will hit me again*, she thought. *I will be a rich, powerful woman, and men will honor and fear me.*

6

OLGA'S HUSBAND

AFTER BREAKFAST OLGA thanked her mother and left for the bus stop. It was a balmy summer day. She called Vladimir to ask him to meet with her when she returned that afternoon. She needed to tell him about her big trip. After the call she sent a text to François.

> Olga: Baby, on my way home ;) I
> want to see you tonight.
> François: Where? When?
> Olga: Around 8. I can't wait to see you.
> Will text you later. Missed you
> François: Miss you 2 ;)

Vladimir was waiting for her at home, as they had agreed on the phone. She explained she was planning to go to the United States for a few weeks.

"What?" Vladimir asked.

"I'm traveling to America. I saved my own money for the trip."

Vladimir approached her and grabbed her arm. "Fucking bitch. Is this why you wanted to work? Who are you going with? You're running away with another rich guy, aren't you?"

Olga replied calmly, "No, don't you remember? I told you about the woman I met at the Suley, the one who owns the modeling agency.

She lives in America, and she invited me to come and see her. There is no one man but you."

As she finished her sentence, Vladimir slapped her face. Olga purposely fell to avoid being hit a second time. She screamed, "Stop! I'm your woman. I'm yours. Only yours." She continued yelling, loud enough for her voice to carry beyond the apartment. She knew it was the only way to stop the beating. On the floor, she rolled herself in the fetal position and cried out, "Stop! Don't beat me."

Vladimir got ready to hit her again, but he held back. He turned around and left the apartment, leaving Olga on the floor.

Olga slowly got up. Frazzled, she went to the bathroom. Once again a man had left a mark of his rage on her. She took a couple of deep breaths. Pulling her compact out of her purse, she carefully applied blush to erase the second bruise on her face. Slowly the handprints disappeared under a thick layer of makeup. *François will not notice*, she thought.

Olga knew she had won. Her remorseful husband would now do anything to be forgiven the next day, as usual. She had already decided what she would ask him for this time—money for her *next* trip to America.

She sent a text to the Frenchman as if nothing had happened.

> Olga: I will be ready earlier. 7:30.
> Can you come then?
> François: K.
> Olga: Text me when you are here.
> François: K.

—⸞⸝—

François arrived at the Tower and texted Olga as she had requested. She texted back, telling him to meet her in the lobby.

Olga smiled and left the apartment as soon as she got the text. She needed to be comforted. She wore a red pencil dress with her usual black heels. François, as agreed, came into the lobby. She approached him, hugged him, and kissed him. The uncharacteristic public display of affection, especially in her building, confused him.

"Hi. Good to see you."

She grabbed his hand and looked at him. "Let's go, *babitchka*."

He remained silent until he got to her car. "What happened? I thought you wanted to be careful because of your husband."

"Maybe I don't care about my husband. After I came back from seeing my parents, I realized it was time to talk," she replied. "I want to celebrate. I want to go out. I want to make this a special night with you and me as a couple."

Olga's marriage had always given him some comfort. François had no intention of fully committing himself to her or any woman in Russia. He firmly believed in his ability to charm women, and being tied down with one was not something he was ready to do. Nevertheless, he said nothing for the moment.

After dinner, they headed to the Havana Club, the best night-club in the city. Though the summer night had cooled, the couple decided to take the short walk from the restaurant to the club. Olga grabbed François's arm. She was simply happy to be with him, and she needed to be comforted that night. She wanted to feel safe. All of the attention humbled François, but her strong feelings made him uncomfortable. He had counted on her marriage to slow her down.

When they arrived at the club at just past midnight, there was already a long line. "I made a reservation, so we don't have to wait. Let me talk to the bouncer." Olga stepped forward and conversed briefly with the bouncer, then turned around and said, "François, follow me."

They entered the club, escorted by a large man and an attractive server. The pounding music and thick crowds made it almost impossible to talk. It was difficult to imagine that more people could actually be let in. François and Olga pushed through the crowd and arrived at the VIP section of the club. The server turned and let Olga know by pointing at her wrist that the host would need to stamp them to enter the VIP section. After receiving their identifying marks, they climbed the steps into the special section. They walked past a few tables where young, attractive women were dancing while their men sat drinking vodka.

The couple finally arrived at their destination—a small, isolated room with red velvet curtains that would provide some privacy from the rest of the club. The U-shaped couch could easily seat about ten people. In the middle, a table had been set up with a large bucket of ice, four bottles of different juices, and a dozen glasses. Though the music was still loud, it was still quieter than other parts of the club. They would be able to talk. They sat down, and Olga ordered a bottle of champagne.

"Do you like it?" she asked.

"It's perfect."

"It'll get better, my baby."

The server brought in the bottle of champagne, opened it, and served the couple. She asked in Russian, "Do you need anything else?"

"*Niet,*" Olga replied. "Just privacy."

The server understood. She walked out of the room and closed the curtain.

Olga looked at François. "To us, baby. To us."

François replied, "Cheers!"

Olga put her glass on the table. She kissed François softly, and then with more vigor. Her tongue was in his mouth. Her hand made its way to his pants. Olga looked at him. "I'm going to take care of you."

She kneeled in front of him, unzipped his pants, pulled down his boxers, and grabbed his manhood. She slowly stroked his erection with her hand, and then plunged headfirst. Her mouth wrapped his hard pole. She slowly moved it in and out, while her hand played with his sac. She sucked a bit faster, feeling him getting harder. Her pace accelerated. She could feel his hips moving back and forth, following her rhythm, and maintained the fevered pace until he climaxed. She captured all his juice without letting a drop spill, pulled back, and then swallowed. She grabbed her glass of champagne and took a sip. She sat down, and he pulled his pants up. She took another sip and kissed his cheek. She whispered in perfect French, "*Je t'aime, mon amour. Je t'aime* François."

"Me too." He said it uneasily, and he wasn't sure what made him say it at all—love or lust—but he knew he would continue her game as long as she wanted to do that to him.

7

Olga in America

THE COLD OCTOBER morning brought the first signs of winter to Krasnoyarsk. Light snowfall changed the color of the city from a drab gray to a clean white. It was the day Olga had been waiting for. She was finally leaving for America. She had packed the night before, bringing as many things as she could fit in her large suitcase. The last item she placed into the suitcase was the forest green dress, for good luck.

She walked out of the building. The doorman followed a few steps behind, a large suitcase in tow. He carefully put the large bag in her car. Olga got in and drove off to pick up François so he could drive her to the airport.

"Thank you, *babitchka*, for driving me," Olga told her Frenchman.

"My pleasure. Thank you for letting me use your car while you're away."

"No problem. No girls in this car."

He smiled. "Of course not."

"I'll keep in touch via Skype and email."

"Great. When are you coming back?"

"I'll see how it goes. I'll be a simple tourist. I'll be back by the end of November."

"My season ends soon, but I'll wait for you before I go back to France."

"I need to go. I don't want to miss my flight."
They kissed and said good-bye.

⸻ ◦◦◦ ⸻

THE TWENTY-HOUR JOURNEY seemed to last an eternity. Olga left Siberia in the morning, had a five-hour layover in Moscow, and then boarded another plane for the eleven-hour flight to New York. The flight had been brutal. The limited space had barely accommodated her long legs. The uncomfortable coach seat made sleeping nearly impossible, and talkative seatmates had shown too much interest in her. She found some solace in knowing she would be in New York soon.

The plane finally landed. Like the other passengers, she was anxious to leave the plane after the long flight. She was exhausted, but knowing that someone from the travel agency would meet her there was comforting. Sergey had organized her voyage, and he had done an excellent job so far. After he helped her get her tourist visa, he had taken care of the plane ticket and found her a room. She would be staying at one of the Russian guesthouses in Brooklyn where the agency sent people all the time. Sergey had shown her pictures of the room. It looked small but clean and comfortable.

She walked out of the security area, towing her large red suitcase with one hand and trying to manage her other two bags with the other. She spotted a man holding up a sign bearing her name in Russian, which made her smile. He wore a black suit with a white shirt and looked as if he was going to attend a funeral.

They conversed in Russian. "I'm Olga Kotova."

"Welcome to America. My name is Anton. How was your flight?"

"Long, but I'm happy to be here."

"I'm sure. Let me take your luggage, and we'll walk to the car. I have a sandwich and some water for you. I'll drive you to your guesthouse, and you can relax. We're going to Brighton Beach in Brooklyn. From there you can get to Manhattan easily."

Anton opened the back door of a black limousine for his passenger. Olga was impressed. In Russia cheating and lying were common, so she was surprised that the agency had actually delivered on its promises. Sergey's services had thus far been worth every extra penny she'd had to spend.

While Anton navigated out of the airport, they conversed more in Russian.

"Sergey told me to provide you with a list of close-by stores for things you might need, such as a cell phone," said Anton. "Brighton Beach is very nice neighborhood—lots of Russians. You'll not feel far from home."

He was friendly enough, but she was too mesmerized by what she was seeing to pay much attention to him and did not hear a word he said. It was dark, so she mostly saw lights, buildings, and cars. She focused on the road, trying to compare Krasnoyarsk and New York. It was too dark. She could see only cars. Within minutes they arrived in Brighton Beach. After a few stop signs, the driver stopped the car in front a large apartment complex. He opened Olga's door.

"Here we are. I'll get your bags."

"Great. Thanks."

Anton removed her luggage from the trunk and carried it to the door of the building. He buzzed the apartment and waited for someone to answer. A woman asked in Russian, "Who is it?"

"Anton."

Olga heard a buzzer that unlocked the security door. They walked into the building. The lobby was clean. It left a good first impression. They took the elevator to the tenth floor and found the apartment.

Anton knocked, and the door opened. A conversation followed, in Russian.

"*Privet*, Olga Kotova. Come on in. My name is Elena. Thank you, Anton. I'll take it from here."

"Hi. Nice to meet you," Olga said. She turned and thanked Anton. The man left and closed the door.

"Let me show you to your room," said Elena. "This is a small apartment, but it's very comfortable and convenient. We're close to the subway if you want to go to Manhattan. We're also close to Brighton Beach Avenue—the shopping area. You can find anything you need. Here's your room."

Olga entered her room. Slightly larger than her parents' bedroom, it was furnished simply, with a single bed pushed against one wall and a small desk against the opposite wall. A door opened to an empty closet. Across from the door was a small window. The decor was modest. The white walls were empty. A little, discolored rug was pushed against the bed. The covers and curtains were plain white. It reminded her of parents' place. She had hoped that she would find greater luxury in America, but at least it was clean; just then, that was the only thing Olga really cared about.

"This is okay," Olga said.

"One of my other roommates, Masha, should be back soon," said Elena. "Why don't you get settled in? When she returns, I'm sure she'll take you out. It's Saturday, after all. Two young, attractive Russian women should go out."

"Maybe. I'm tired, but I'd like to go out. After all, I think it's morning in Krasnoyarsk." Olga was certainly tired, but she was excited to finally be in New York. She felt reenergized. Everything was going well so far. She was especially happy about the apartment.

"I'll let you get unpacked. Come and see me when you want to take a shower, and I'll show you the rest of the apartment."

"Thanks."

Olga felt good about her host. Elena was a very attractive platinum blonde in her midthirties, with long, manicured nails and the right amount of makeup. Her body was very fit and curvy, with long legs and large breasts. She would have attracted a lot of attention from men in Krasnoyarsk.

8

RUSSIAN WOMEN IN NEW YORK

OLGA AND ELENA had been talking for about an hour when the door opened and Masha came into the apartment. Soon she joined the two women in the dining room.

"Masha, there you are. This is Olga Kotova, our guest from Siberia," Elena said in Russian.

"*Privet.*"

"Nice to meet you, Masha."

"Masha," Elena asked, "did you eat? We just finished, but there is some food left."

"No. I'm not hungry," Masha replied.

"Why don't you take Olga out tonight?" Elena said.

"I'd love to. I'm going out in two hours, and it would be great if you came along. Can you be ready by ten?"

"Yes, of course. Thank you. I'm so excited to see New York," Olga said.

"Drink some coffee," Elena said. "Sometimes I think it really is 'the city that never sleeps.'"

Olga smiled. "Good idea. I'll make some and drink it in my room while I get ready."

"You know where everything is now," Elena told her. "But I'll make some this time. I'd love a cup, too.

"Thank you. Do you have a computer I can use?" Olga asked. "I would like to e-mail my parents." She wanted to tell her mother she had arrived safely.

"Yes, of course. There's a computer in the living room. You can use it whenever you want."

Olga walked to her room, closed the door, opened the freshly filled closet, and looked at her clothes. She pondered the eternal question—what to wear. Getting dressed for a night out on the town in Krasnoyarsk was always complicated enough, but in New York, she had no idea. Olga caressed the forest green dress but left it hanging. *Another day,* she thought. She decided on her sleeveless red pencil dress. She wanted to be sexy. It was François's favorite dress, so she knew it would get some attention from men. She put on her black pumps and took her black purse. She applied red lipstick to match her dress. She looked at herself proudly in the mirror, pushing up her small breasts, and then joined the two women in the living room.

Elena said, "Not bad for a woman who just got off the boat."

Olga looked puzzled. Elena explained in Russian. "Don't worry. It's an expression for new people arriving from the old country. You look fabulous."

Olga blushed.

Masha stood and said, "Ready? Good night, Elena."

"Where are you taking her?" Elena asked.

"I think we'll go to Tatiana. It's not too far, and Olga will feel at home there. We'll go to Manhattan tomorrow," Masha replied.

"Good idea."

"I'll call a taxi." Masha left the room to use the phone in the kitchen.

"Olga, let me write down this address. That way, you can take a taxi back if you get tired before Masha. And if I know Masha, she may not get tired enough to come back until tomorrow, if she comes back at all." Elena lowered her voice. "She's looking for an American husband. She sometimes disappears for nights."

Olga smiled.

Masha came back. "Olga, you might want something to cover your shoulders. It's a bit chilly. Oh, don't forget your passport—you'll need ID. The taxi will be here in a few minutes. I'll be downstairs. Come on down when you're ready."

Olga stopped by her room, grabbed a black sweater, and joined Masha. "Good night, Elena."

"I've been living with Elena for two months," Masha said. "She's very protective. That is why I call her *mother* sometimes. But I can tell she likes you. You're lucky. She didn't like the last girl. A real bitch. Elena kicked her out after ten days." Olga cringed at the possibility of losing her room so quickly after her arrival. She could only imagine how difficult things would have been without Sergey's help. Coming to another country was difficult enough, but with no support or friends it would have been a trying experience.

Olga was sure she had established a good relationship with Elena. Although her host was Ukrainian, and therefore someone whom most Russians would consider inferior, Olga thought Elena was smart and articulate. Over the past few hours, Olga had already started to like her.

Elena had come to the United States in hopes of finding a better life, which was something Olga could understand. Shortly after her arrival, Elena had met an American man of Russian heritage. They married after a few months of dating, but divorced after just three years. She had no children and seemed to have abandoned the idea of having any. Since then she had been dating Russian men from Brooklyn, which was why her English remained rudimentary.

The girls arrived at Tatiana, a glitzy Russian nightclub in Brooklyn that had adopted the format of many hip spots in New York: it was a restaurant until around eleven at night, and then the dining tables disappeared to open the space up for dancing. Olga followed Masha into the club and immediately felt as if she were back in Russia. Everything and everyone was Russian. The decor was similar to some of the restaurants in Krasnoyarsk. Red and gold dominated, and communist era symbols prevailed, with portraits of Lenin, Stalin, and a few Russian czars on the walls. The DJ played the latest Russian pop songs, and the restaurant served all Russian specialties.

Masha found her friends' table and started introducing Olga in Russian. One of the women said, "We're having dessert. Do you want anything?"

Masha answered, "No, thanks, but we'll have vodka."

Olga looked around the table. On their way to the nightclub, Masha had explained that the four women she was meeting up with had all come to New York that year with the same goal—finding a better life.

Ksenia, from Moscow, attended college in New York. Nataliya, from Odessa, studied English. Yulia, from Saint Petersburg, was there on a tourist visa. And Katia, from Vladivostok, had just obtained her green card. Katia's story was not very clear, but Olga gathered that Katia had been able somehow to get her documents after a very short stay.

Olga understood the importance of documents. Sergey had explained all about the common US visas, so she knew that all visas were temporary, unless the Russian traveler married an American citizen.

While Masha chatted with her friends, Olga looked around. She found it amusing she had flown all the way to the United States, only to find herself in a miniature Russia. Had the restaurant been in Krasnoyarsk, it would not have been much different. She listened to these girls' stories and anecdotes about their relationships and thought, *Different country, but the same stories of men.* These young women were all looking for love and a future.

The waiter brought a bottle of vodka and poured it into the glasses. Masha raised her glass. "To the most beautiful women in the world—Russian women."

As the glasses clinked, all the girls started laughing. The rest of the evening seemed like a blur, especially after Olga had downed a couple of glasses of vodka. The jet lag finally hit her. She stopped talking and tried to focus on staying awake, realizing that she had been too enthusiastic; the lack of sleep was catching up with her. She decided that she had to go home to catch up on much-needed sleep.

Masha noticed Olga was fading. "Olga, are you okay?"

"I'll be fine. I'm just more tired than I thought I'd be."

"Well, I'm sure you're tired. Let me know if you want to go. I'll get you home. It's really close."

"I think I should go now," Olga replied.

"Okay. You had two glasses of vodka. You owe thirty dollars."

Olga raised her eyebrows but pretended it was fine. Thirty dollars in Krasnoyarsk could buy six bottles of good vodka. She pulled her cash from her purse and gave it to Masha. New York would cost much more than she had expected. Even with the additional thousand dollars her husband had given her, remorseful after his last outburst of rage, she would have to manage her travel budget closely. She realized that she would have to stay very friendly with Vladimir in case she needed more money. The last thing she wanted was to cut her trip short because of a lack of cash.

Olga got up and said good-bye to the girls, and Masha told the girls that she would be right back. The two women made their way out of the club and grabbed a taxi.

"Masha, if you can just help me with the taxi, you don't have to come with me. Really, you can stay."

"All right. But rest up—tomorrow we're going to Manhattan to see some of the sights."

OLGA WOKE UP just before nine the next morning. She e-mailed her mother, Vladimir, and François. Olga remembered her plan to maintain a good relationship with her husband in case she needed additional financial assistance during her trip. She knew Vladimir would, if asked, provide her with more money. As for François, she wanted to keep in touch with him. She would be returning to Siberia for a few months, and she wanted to spend that time with him.

The next day she e-mailed her mother again to tell her about her adventures. Olga had spent Sunday with Masha in Manhattan visiting some of the major landmarks of the city: the Empire State Building, Times Square, Ground Zero, and Central Park. She and

Masha had walked down Fifth Avenue, passing so many designer stores that Olga gave up counting. When she looked at the store windows, she was reminded of her dream of becoming famous and rich so she could afford everything in these stores. For the moment the two women were just happy to gaze at the beauty presented in the windows.

Olga had been tempted to add to her note home that she wished her mother was there with her, but she didn't, fearful that her father might read it. The last thing she wanted was to induce anger that would ultimately turn against her mother. Just before noon, Olga joined Elena in the kitchen.

"Good morning, princess. I guess you needed some beauty sleep," Elena said as Olga came in slowly.

"Good morning. Maybe I did need to catch up on sleep," Olga responded.

"Sit down. I'll get you coffee. Are you hungry? I made some blini."

"Blini? That's my favorite!"

Blini reminded Olga of her mother, who prepared the thin Russian pancakes every weekend. She served them for dinner, keeping whatever was left over for breakfast in the morning. Her mother's evening meals also included smoked salmon, sour cream, onion, and a few other things—all Olga's favorites.

Masha came in. "Good morning, Olga. Caught up on sleep?"

"Yes."

Masha had clearly been up for some time. She was fully dressed and freshly made up, ready to leave the apartment. "Olga, I'm taking you out tonight. We're going out to Mari Vana, the best place to hang out in Manhattan on a Monday. We'll meet a few of my friends, have dinner there, and stay for a little while."

"Sounds like fun," Olga replied.

"We'll take a taxi because I don't like taking the subway at night. We'll leave at seven and be there by eight. There's always a lot of traffic between Brooklyn and the city. I suggest we stay in Brooklyn today, if that's okay."

"Masha, you're very nice to take care of me like this."

"It's okay. I know how it feels to be in this country for the first time."

Olga's first two days in the United States had been truly fabulous. She had already seen some of the city and she had met two good women. Masha was becoming a good friend, and Elena was becoming like a big sister to her.

Olga spent a slow afternoon in the apartment. She sent a few private Facebook messages to François, writing, "I'm having a great trip, and so far there is only one thing missing—YOU!" She went to the Russian equivalent of Facebook, VKontakte, or VK.com, to provide updates to some of her friends and post pictures of the landmarks she had visited the day before, adding comments for each image she uploaded.

She quickly got responses from her friend Oksana. Olga smiled at the response. "I love it!" was followed by other short messages: "Having fun, I see!"

Olga replied, "Great trip! Miss you! You should be here with me." Olga was thrilled to share some of her trip with her friends. She knew her mother, who was still worried about the trip, would be checking Olga's page. Olga sent her a private message. "Mama, everything is perfect! I will call you later this week! I'm having a great time. Love you. Olga."

Olga was well rested and in a great mood. She had a plan: she would stay for one month, go back to Russia, and quickly come back. In the meantime, she would try to figure out how to become rich and famous.

Olga started getting ready for the evening. That night would be special—her first night out in Manhattan—and she was very excited to see the nightlife in the part of the city where all the action, the best restaurants, the museums, the theaters, the clubs, and the rich people were.

Masha came out of the bathroom and, after stopping by her room to get a short leather jacket, joined Olga in the kitchen. Masha had chosen a red, tight, short dress, a pair of black high heels, and a small purse. She picked up the phone on the kitchen wall, called a taxi company, and gave their address to the dispatcher.

"Olga, we have to go now. The taxi will be here in a few minutes," said Masha.

"Okay," Olga said, applying a last touch of lipstick. She walked out of her room wearing a sleeveless little black dress. She had decided to wear black silk stockings since the night was a bit chilly, along with black leather pumps and a small black purse. She wrapped herself with a large, black wool scarf to keep her small body warm.

Olga joined Masha in the kitchen. "Ready."

"Very nice," Elena said to the two young women before they left the apartment. "Have a good night, girls."

The two women walked out of the apartment building into the chilly evening.

"I hope the taxi gets here soon," said Masha as she shivered. They were not dressed warmly enough to be outside on a cold night, but they would be indoors nearly all night. "We've got time to smoke. Want a cigarette?"

"Yes, I'll take one."

Olga looked up in the sky as she smoked her cigarette. *No stars,* she thought. *Strange.* It was a clear night, but she couldn't see a single star. In the Siberian countryside, stars always filled the sky. Even in Krasnoyarsk, a large city, a good number of stars was always visible. Here there was nothing—not even a little speck of light.

"We're going to meet a few friends in Manhattan—girls from Moscow who've been in the city for a few years. We'll have fun for sure," Masha said.

Olga nodded. She was pleased to be part of Masha's circle. Finally, the taxi arrived. The two women threw their cigarettes onto the sidewalk and got into the black car. Masha gave directions to the driver in Russian. Olga thought, *Russian again! It's everywhere.*

The car slowly made its way to the city. The traffic on Ocean Parkway was heavy, even heading into Manhattan on a Monday evening. Olga was lost in her thoughts when the New York night skyline finally appeared in the night. She brought her head a bit closer to the window. The spectacular view fascinated her. She could distinguish the Statue of Liberty near the horizon, standing proudly in the middle of the Hudson River. The city was simply magical. Thousands of lights were reflected in the calm river, which had become a mirror on that clear night. The Empire State Building bore orange, yellow, and red lights like a tree with changing autumn leaves. Olga smiled.

"This is so great!" Olga said. *How happy Mama would be to experience all of this!*

"Yes, it is. I've been here for a few months, and I still find it beautiful. Especially tonight," Masha replied.

Olga looked out the window. The beauty of the city simply amazed her.

The car plunged into the Brooklyn-Battery Tunnel, making the city disappear. After a few minutes in semidarkness, the car emerged in Manhattan. Traffic was heavy, and yellow taxis competed on the street for each little open space. It was something like a ballet; each car seemed to move just right to find its place at the right moment. The black car headed north on FDR, then cut west. After about fifteen minutes, the car stopped on Twentieth Street between Park Avenue and Madison.

"We're here," Masha said, and she pulled out her wallet to pay the driver. "The usual?" she asked.

The driver answered in Russia. "Yes."

"Thank you," Masha replied. "Let's go," she told Olga.

The girls got out of the taxi. Masha stopped Olga. "You'll pay for the taxi when we come back. It's fifty dollars."

"Fine," Olga replied, reminded once more how expensive New York was.

"Let's have a cigarette before we go in," Masha said.

The two women smoked, and then Masha threw her cigarette away and reached into her purse. She pulled out a small Russian doll keychain. The two women took the few steps to the restaurant door. Masha showed her keychain to the guard, who opened the door. He smiled and saluted both women in Russian. Masha, leading the way, spotted her friends at the bar. She walked past the host and went directly to her friends.

A beautiful woman got up and came to Masha. She screamed in Russian, "Masha! Baby! I'm so happy to see you." She hugged Masha and asked, "Do you remember Yuliana and Darina?"

The other young women got up and kissed Masha's cheek, and Masha turned to introduce her new friend. "This is Olga, the girl from Siberia I talked to you about. Olga, this is my friend, Anna, and her friends Yuliana and Darina."

As she and Masha sat down, Olga looked at the three women. They were all very attractive and looked so similar that they might have come from the same mold. They were thinner, taller, and more attractive than most American women, and all were dressed very well. Darina was just a bit taller than Olga. She had excellent taste, judging by her clothes. She wore a short-sleeved bronze dress covered with black lace that showed off her perfectly fit body. *Clearly a very expensive dress,* Olga thought. Famous designers made everything Darina wore, from her black Chanel bag, matching pumps with the distinctive red soles of Christian Louboutin, a silver Gucci bracelet, and a set of diamond earrings. Her friend Yuliana was also beautiful, a platinum blonde, tall, and model thin. She wore a little black dress with designer accessories. Anna was the shortest of the three. The brunette wore a tight red dress that exposed her long, tanned legs. She was someone who loved the sun. Olga envied all of them. She wanted to be like these women.

Olga sat just beside Anna, who started the conversation. "Masha told me you're visiting. How long are you here for?"

"I arrived a few days ago. I'm planning to stay for a month and then come back again early next year. I'd like to stay for good."

"We all want to stay after we come here. We just need a way to do it," Anna replied and smiled.

"I have only been here for a short time, but I see things are better here."

"Yes. You'll be here for Halloween?"

"Maybe. When is it?"

"The thirty-first, but we're celebrating on the twenty-seventh at a masquerade party at my friend's apartment. He likes to have beautiful girls around." She smiled again.

"Masquerade?"

"Everyone wears a mask. The guys are usually in suits, and the girls wear sexy outfits."

"It sounds like fun."

"You have no idea. I'll make sure you and Masha are on the guest list."

9

ROBERT

THE ADMINISTRATIVE ASSISTANT put her head in the doorway of the private office and said, "Robert, can you please go see Charley in his office?"

"Sure. I'll be right there," Robert replied. He went to his boss.

Charles Gorman, or Charley as he was known, was a man from an older generation. He clung to old habits developed over the years, so he did not walk around among the offices. He rarely interacted with his staff. People went to his office only when invited. He was Robert Thompson's superior, and though he was very respectful, the old man clearly enjoyed his status as one of the founding partners of Brewster & Associates—a thriving, midsize brokerage firm based in Boston. Although much smaller than its New York competitors, Brewster had been able to forge a great name for itself, especially in foreign currency trading. It had gone public a few years before, following the path of larger investment banks. This gave it the necessary credibility in the market to be considered a serious financial institution.

Robert walked to the corner office, knocked on the doorframe, and walked in. "Charley, did you want to see me?"

"Yes, please close the door and sit down," Charley replied.

Robert sat down as instructed. He had been in the office many times; his boss invited him on a regular basis to discuss business. Robert had joined the firm after graduating from Harvard Business School, and he had rapidly risen through the ranks during those eight years to become one of the top three revenues generators of the firm. Charley had quickly recognized the young man's intelligence and great business judgment, and Robert had become his trusted advisor.

"Robert, I brought you to my office because I wanted to talk to you about something. You've helped us make the Boston office very successful. As you know, we performed better than our New York and London offices, and that's mostly because of you. This year will be our best year yet, and people have noticed. I know you've talked in the past about doing something different, and I want you to think about going to our New York office to lead the foreign bond desk. If you're interested, we'd like you to be there by late November or early December—just after the end of the fiscal year."

Robert was surprised. "Well, that's great. I want to thank you for the offer. Can I have a few days to think about it?"

"Of course. I know things have been challenging for you personally. I thought you might want a change of scenery. We need someone top-shelf there, and you, of course, are my first choice. Business is thriving, as you know."

Robert replied, "Yes, certainly. Charley, I truly appreciate your confidence and everything you and the firm have done for me. I will give you a definite answer by the end of this week."

"Okay. Friday will be fine. We can discuss the logistics—salary, bonus structure, start date, apartment, moving, and everything else—when you're ready. We'll be very fair to you," the old man replied with a smile.

"Thank you," Robert said, rising.

"Robert, I know a change will do you good. Can I suggest something? There are times when you need to talk to someone. Doing so might help you move forward, if you have not already done so. Maybe you can find someone who will listen. Just a thought."

"Thank you. I'll think about it." Robert appreciated Charley's last words. Charley was a very tough businessperson, but he was also a very decent human being.

Robert walked back to his desk and sat down in front of his three computer screens, which he ignored.

New York? Why not? he thought. *I do need a change.*

❦

ROBERT WAS EXCITED about this new beginning. Accustomed to the good-old-boy insularity of Boston, he enjoyed the hustle and bustle of New York, with its sidewalks filled with streaming pedestrians, streets choked with yellow cabs, buses, and the occasional car, and air alive with sounds and smells and promises. What he didn't like was returning at night to an empty hotel room. He wanted to find an apartment as quickly as possible.

The realtor referred by his firm was just a fifteen-block walk from the office, a pleasant stroll on a bright October day. He entered the office and greeted the receptionist. The woman lifted her head and looked at him.

"Hi, my name is Robert Thompson. I have an appointment with Natalie at one thirty."

The young woman behind the counter replied, "Yes. I'll let her know you're here. Please take a seat, and she'll be right out."

The agent emerged within a few minutes. "Robert Thompson?" she asked, holding out her hand.

She took a good look at Robert. She liked to get a sense of what her new clients were all about. Thompson was of average height, slender but toned, with a full head of hair, dimples, and a square jaw. He was very handsome and dressed in a blazer, dress shirt, designer jeans, and just-shined, black, Italian shoes. *Not bad for a guy from Boston,* she thought. He had style, and she liked it.

"Yes," Robert replied.

"Let's get going then. Your office gave me pretty detailed requirements, which makes my job of finding the right apartment for you easier. Our agency, Bear Real Estate, is one of the best known in the city. We cater mostly to the upper end of the market. So you're in good hands."

Robert smiled at the infomercial. Charley had spared no expense to make sure his transition to the city went well. He appreciated that.

Robert held the door open for Natalie, and she noticed. *A true gentleman. Another plus for the handsome man,* Natalie thought. She had gotten used to New York men who disdained any kind of chivalry. She raised her hand to hail a taxi as they reached the sidewalk on Lexington Avenue. After just a few seconds, a yellow cab stopped, and they got in. Again Robert opened the door for the agent. That was not such a great idea this time, as she needed to slip down the backseat, and that required some agility in her pencil skirt. The door closed behind Robert, and Natalie instructed the driver, "Twenty-Ninth and Park Avenue please. And let's stay on Lexington. Thank you."

Robert understood she was clearly a New York woman just by the way she had addressed the driver. She was direct and self-confident. He found that attractive.

Natalie turned her attention to her client. "Is this your first time living in New York?"

"Yes."

"Do you rent or own in Boston?"

"I live just outside of Boston. I was planning to move into the city, and had recently bought an apartment in a new building in the South End, an up-and-coming neighborhood, but I just put it up for sale. The market is a bit crazy. I sold it in one day at a 15 percent profit without ever having lived in it."

"The market is relatively similar here. The best apartments sell quickly. We'll find you a great place. I've got three fantastic apartments to show you today. Based on your assistant's request and your company's budget, we can find you something very nice. Your firm is very generous. I'm sure you'll be happy with the choices you have."

Robert simply smiled.

"It's a beautiful fall day. Are you staying in the city tonight?" she asked.

"Yes, I'm planning to."

"You should enjoy Halloween in the city. I've lived here for over ten years now, and the Halloween festivities always amaze me. The city goes crazy. Everyone dresses up. It's always a fun time."

"Sounds like it."

The rest of the cab ride was filled with Natalie pointing out landmarks until finally she directed her attention to the taxi driver. "Near the corner on Twenty-Ninth please." She turned back to Robert. "We'll be there in a few minutes. The apartment is between Park Avenue and Madison—a great area—and we're going to see the penthouse apartment. The owner bought it after the building was completed one year ago, but now he's in the middle of a messy divorce. He just put the apartment on the market. It's a rental with an option to buy once his legal issues are resolved." She smiled and added, "In New York, that could take a bit of time. I'm sure you'll love the view from the fifty-sixth floor."

The real estate agent stopped talking long enough to pay the cab driver, and then returned to selling mode. "Nice neighborhood. Lots of restaurants. A few of my favorite restaurants are down the street on Park Avenue—Barbounia, Chez Jacques, Sushi Samba, and a few others. This is a penthouse apartment with fabulous city views. About two thousand square feet. Fully furnished. Two bedrooms. Washer and dryer in the unit, of course. There's a gym on the premises that is just okay. I can help you find another one. Twenty-four-seven security. It's simply a great apartment for the asking rental price."

After a short walk, they arrived at a high-rise building and entered the lobby. The agent checked in with the concierge, and the guard gave her the apartment keys. When the elevator arrived at the fifty-sixth floor, the door opened onto a small lobby.

She said, "There are four to six apartments on each floor, except for the penthouse, of course. Here there's just the one."

Robert followed her into the penthouse and immediately thought, *Yes.*

As they toured the apartment, she gave him a detailed description of each room. He didn't hear a word. He was in trance. *Wow*, he thought. There was no need for him to see others. This was it. The penthouse had a spectacular view of the city. He could see New Jersey from one side and all of the midtown view with the Empire State Building standing majestically in the middle of city from the other side. He liked its modern, simple furniture. He was happy to have found such a place so quickly or, more precisely, for his firm to have arranged for this be available for him.

Natalie saw him smiling. "So what do you think?"

Robert had become more cheerful. "When can I move in?"

She smiled. "I guess that's a yes. Great choice. We just need to take care of the paperwork. In your case, it'll be relatively simple, as your firm is paying ahead of time for the first year's rent. I really don't see any issues with the owner. Realistically we should be done in a week."

"One question. How much will the owner ask for it?"

"You mean to buy it?"

"Yes."

"I'm guessing about five million. Maybe six. I'm not sure when he would be able to put it up for sale, though. I know he can't put it on the market until the divorce is settled."

Robert did some quick math in his head. *Doable,* he thought. He could sell all his company shares, and he would have enough money to cover the maintenance costs.

"Hmm, I see. Well, I'll be very interested if it goes on the market. One more question. How much is the rent? Just curious about how much my firm is paying."

"It's twenty-two thousand dollars a month. Utilities, furniture, and everything included."

"Okay," he replied, confirming that he would be able to afford the apartment on his own next year.

"Are you sure you don't want to see the other apartments?"

"Yes, I'm sure. This is fine. Actually, it's perfect. Thank you."

"My pleasure. That was easy. I believe you start your new job on Monday, December third. That means you have over a month to get ready to move on Saturday, December first. Hopefully this gives you time to settle in and explore the city."

"I'm looking forward to it. Maybe I should take you out for a drink to thank you."

"I'll think about it." She smiled back at him.

As Robert smiled, he finally noticed how beautiful she was. He had been with her for at least an hour, and he had only now realized. *New York will be a really good change.*

10

THE MASQUERADE PARTY

ROBERT WALKED THE short distance from his hotel, the London, to Milos, one of the best seafood restaurants in the city, to meet a couple colleagues from the New York office for dinner at nine. He was touched that on a Saturday night two single guys would take time away from their personal lives to take a colleague out on the town. He had met them a few times over the years through the firm. They had been there much longer than he had, though, and he understood that it was part of the internal process to make sure the New York team welcomed him.

Stephen Parrish, the senior of the two, stood well over six feet tall, which made him very noticeable in any crowd. A Harvard graduate like Robert, he had more personality than most of the other bankers in the firm, and was instantly likable. He had grown up in Cincinnati and came from a humble background.

In contrast, John Reynolds had been born and raised in New York City. He was slightly overweight and much shorter than Robert. John never stopped talking. He had stories and anecdotes to fill entire evenings. He had graduated top of his class at Wharton—one of the best MBA schools in the world, as he always tried to remind everyone around him. When he became a successful broker, he didn't hesitate to emphasize his accomplishments. One of his specialties was dropping names of former presidents, senators, and other wealthy individuals to whom he had gained access through his very wealthy family. Robert was not fond of John, but he thought he would get used to him.

Robert entered the restaurant a few minutes before nine and found his two colleagues settled in at the bar. The two men wore custom-tailored suits, but had left their ties behind. Robert was not really surprised. They were wealthy and seemed to enjoy showing that fact off.

"Robert, you made it," said Stephen, flashing a grin.

"Nice to see you again," said John, extending a pudgy hand.

"Stephen, John, thank you for invitation," Robert said.

"No problem. Our table will be ready shortly," John explained.

"John knows everyone in the city. If you ever need a table at the best restaurants, he's your man," said Stephen.

"I'm not sure if you had plans tonight, but we have an invitation to a party later if you'd like to tag along," said John.

Robert replied, "No plans."

"Well, Robert, it will be a great introduction to New York. The party is being hosted by one of our clients, Lenny Rothstein. He's a hedge fund guy, but he's also an old guy who knows how to party! He's got this two-story penthouse apartment—the place is huge—and when I went last year, it was wild. All the girls were models. Open bar and music. One of the best parties I've ever been to."

Robert smiled. "Sounds interesting. I don't have a costume, though."

"No problem. All we need are masks. We're stopping at my place after dinner to get ours, and I have one you can wear."

The host came to get the three men. "Mr. Parrish, your table is ready. If you have a tab open at the bar, can you please settle it?"

After Steve took care of the bar bill, the three men followed the host to their table. The manager of the restaurant walked up as the three men sat down.

"Mr. Reynolds, it's so nice to see you again. I'm sorry about the confusion. It wasn't our intention to make you wait," the restaurant manager said.

"No problem," John replied.

"Can I offer something? Maybe a complementary bottle of champagne?"

"That would be perfect," John said.

As the manager walked away, John said triumphantly, "I fuckin' love it. I knew we wouldn't have to wait. I called the owner when the host told me we'd have to wait forty-five minutes for a table."

"Well done," Stephen said.

Robert nodded without enthusiasm. He disliked John's pompous attitude and sense of entitlement. It was just one of the many things about John that grated on him.

The waiter brought a bottle of champagne. After pouring the three glasses, he took the food orders.

"Cheers, guys!" said Steve as the waiter left.

"Lots of alcohol, great food… The only thing missing is a few willing models, but there'll be plenty of bimbos at Lenny's," said John.

Robert cringed.

After dinner, they stopped at John's apartment as planned and picked up masks. They took a taxi to the party. Robert and Stephen followed John, who walked to the building concierge to check in.

"Good evening. Can I be of assistance?"

"Good evening. We are guests of Mr. Leonard Rothstein."

"Very good. IDs, please?"

The three men pulled out their wallets and dropped their driver's licenses on the counter. After comparing the names to the guest list, the guard returned their IDs. "Mr. Reynolds, here are your bracelets. Please put these on. You will be asked to show them at the door. Apartment 40-PH."

Interesting, thought Robert. *I got a red one, but these two guys got blue ones.* He wondered if there was any difference.

The elevator opened onto a small hallway and the three masked men walks to 40-PH. A man with the physique of a linebacker stopped them. "Bracelets, please." The trio showed their bracelets, and the bouncer opened the door to the apartment. "Have a great evening."

The party was well under way. The apartment seemed packed, the music was blaring, and the alcohol was flowing. The crowd seemed diverse, but clearly young, attractive women outnumbered the men.

John led his two companions in a slow march toward the bar that had been set up in the vast living room. He pushed some of the guests aside as if he was hacking his way through a tropical jungle. He was on a mission. He turned around and announced the goal of his expedition. "Once we get our drinks, I need to find Lenny and say hi."

Robert was the last in line of the three and was in full observation mode. Lenny had a lot of sexy lady friends. *Money,* he thought, *can buy everything. Even beautiful women.*

They finally reached the bar after a few minutes of navigating the dense crowd. John turned to his two friends. "Martinis for everyone?"

The other two men shrugged, and John told the bartender, "Three martinis, please."

The bartender served the three glasses. John took the glasses and distributed. "To our friend Robert. Cheers." The trio raised their glasses. John continued, "Okay, I'm off to find Lenny. I'll see you guys in a few."

Stephen turned to Robert. "So, what do you think?"

Robert replied, "I've heard about parties like this, but I never imagined I'd be at one. It's like in a movie. We have parties in Boston, but this is… over the top."

"If God organized a party, this would be it."

Robert smiled. Stephen was right. Stephen looked around and decided to explore.

"I'll be back in a few minutes," Stephen said. "I need to find a restroom."

"Okay," Robert said.

Robert turned around and asked the bartender for a glass of Cabernet.. When he was getting served, a young woman approached the bar. Robert couldn't look away. In her early twenties and thin—actually, she was skinny—she was as tall as he, though she did wear high heels. She was stunning in her little black dress. He noticed that she wore a green party bracelet.

She asked the bartender for a glass of champagne, and then she turned around to Robert. "Having fun?"

She had a foreign accent he could not identify. "Yes. So far, so good. We just got here."

"We? Did you come here with friends?"

"Yes, they're somewhere around here. How about you?"

"Same. My friends are over there. How do you know Lenny?"

"I don't know him, but my friend knows him well. Our firm does business with him."

"Hmm. You're a banker."

"Yes."

"Nice." She raised her glass. "Cheers."

"Cheers. I hear a slight accent. Where are you from?"

"A *slight* accent?" she said and smiled at him. "You're kind. I'm Anna. I'm from Moscow."

"Nice to meet you, Anna." He smiled back. "My name is Robert. I'm from Boston."

"Boston?" she replied with disdain. "You don't live in New York?"

"Not until next month."

"Okay."

"What do you do for work?"

"I'm a model, but I want to be an actress."

"How long have you been in New York?"

Her BlackBerry vibrated. She pulled the phone from her purse and read a text. "Sorry. I need to go find my friends now."

"Okay. It was nice meeting you."

"*Ciao!*"

As the young woman left, Robert noticed her green bracelet again. The colors must have some meaning. *I should have asked for phone number. She's hot,* he thought. Anna joined four other very attractive women close to the bar. She turned around and looked at him, smiling as she talked to a blonde. At that moment Stephen came back.

"I see you're enjoying the crowd," Stephen said. "Was she Russian?"

"Yes."

Stephen laughed. "Do you still have your wallet?"

Robert looked at him, puzzled.

With a wide grin, Stephen said, "My dear friend, have you never dated a Russian woman?"

"No. Why?"

"There is one rule with Russian woman: don't trust them. They're very good at presenting themselves as innocent ladies, but they're *far* from innocent. Here's how it usually goes. On the first date, she'll size you up—figure out what you do for a living and how much money you have."

Robert nodded.

"On the second date, she'll go out with you and probably have sex with you."

"And that's a problem?"

"Wait. On the third date, well, she'll 'fall in love' with you." Stephen paused before completing his speech. He lowered his voice. "That is, she'll say she's in love with you, but she'll really be in love with your wallet. High-maintenance women, my friend, high maintenance. The good news is, we can afford it, and the sex is usually very good. The more she wants your wallet, the better she will perform." Stephen took a sip of champagne and looked at Robert. "Got it?"

"Got it."

"Just be careful."

Robert smiled. He was always careful.

ANNA HAD BEEN with her friends for a few minutes when Olga asked, "Is that one of your friends?"

"No. I just met him at the bar. He's a banker from Boston." She turned around and waved at Robert. She put some emphasis on word *banker*.

Olga did not understand the significance of the word. "Banker?" she asked Anna.

Anna explained that there were a few lines of work that were very lucrative, and one of them was banking. "Bankers make a lot of money. They have great lives—the best cars, homes, clothes, and parties. In New York, bankers are kings. A banker is a great catch...if you can get one."

Olga looked at Robert. *Handsome and rich,* she thought. *Nice combination.*

Stephen decided to go find John. "Okay, let's see if we can introduce you to Lenny. I'll text him now." He pulled out his BlackBerry.

Stephen: Where are you?

John: Upstairs. In the BLUE room.

Stephen smiled. "I see. I know where he is." He led the way. Again he and Robert forced themselves through the crowd. When they reached a large room, the trek became a bit more challenging, as it had been transformed into a nightclub. The DJ perched on an elevated structure, rousing the crowd by pumping his fists in the air. A complex set of lights and lasers followed the rhythm of the music. The music was so loud Robert could hardly hear himself think. He could feel the rhythm of the music thumping in his bones.

They finally reached the other side of the room and found the stairs to the second floor of the apartment. As they started their ascent, a bouncer stopped Robert and said in a loud voice, "You can't go up."

Robert barely heard the large man due to the loud music, but he understood.

Stephen had already passed the bouncer when he noticed the large man had stopped Robert. He walked back and asked, "What is the problem?"

"He can't go up." The man pointed at Robert's bracelet.

Stephen understood immediately what that meant. "Robert. Let me go ahead and find John and Lenny. I'll meet you back at the bar. It shouldn't be too long. I'll text you."

"No problem."

Robert turned around and walked back down the stairs slowly. As he headed back toward the bar, he thought *all this intrigue is worthy of a spy novel,* he thought. As he passed through the crowd, he noticed the color of the bracelets. Most of the men's bracelets were red. A few were blue. For the women, most wore yellow ones, and a few wore green. Now he understood that the bracelets allowed selected people access to certain sections of the party. He assumed that the second floor was the VIP section. Anna's bracelet was green, so she must have been on the VIP list, like his two colleagues.

He returned to the bar, got another drink, thinking about the VIP room. What a great setup for a single, wealthy man with a large entourage of hot, sexy women. He imagined a movie scene playing out upstairs—a secret society of rich men holding regular orgies with young and attractive women. Whatever was happening on the second floor, Robert was intrigued.

So far, though, he could only *imagine* what was going on in the Blue Room. He decided to stay at the bar to use the opportunity to meet a few other women. He was handsome enough to attract a fair number of the attractive women who kept coming to the bar for drinks. With the ratio of men to women at the party overall, the odds seemed to be in his favor.

A woman approached the bar. She started talking to Robert while she waited for the bartender to take her order. "Hi. How do you like this party?"

Robert turned around to her. *A very attractive woman*, he thought. Her dark hair, extremely muscular body, and thin frame caught his attention. She wore high heels like all the other women, but Robert could not help but notice her strong calves. "I like it. You are a very graceful woman. You must be a dancer," he said nervously.

"Actually, I am," she said, smiling.

"Are you a ballerina?"

"Indeed."

Robert could not help but think about the various sexual positions that would be possible with this obviously extremely fit and flexible woman. "I've always wanted to see a ballet. If you're free this weekend, let's go. I'll buy the tickets."

Another art illiterate, she thought, *but he is kind of cute*. "The season starts in the spring," she said, "but that doesn't have to stop you from meeting me this weekend."

Robert liked her direct approach. She was clearly a New Yorker. "That will work. What's your name?"

"Vanessa."

"Robert. Nice to meet you. Where are you from?" he asked.

"Seoul, Korea. You?"

"I'm from Boston."

"I enjoy visiting Boston. I have a great friend who lives on Comm Ave. Where do you live in Boston?"

"Well, I don't live in Boston. I live in Andover, outside of Boston."

"Andover? That's not even close to Boston, is it? I guess it's like people from New Jersey say they're from New York City."

He blushed. She was another New York snob who believed nothing existed outside the city. He would have to get used to that New York condescension.

"I'm just teasing. I saw a movie yesterday, and one of the characters, a girl, told the man who was trying to pick her up at a party that Queens was *not* New York City. That's why I said that. It's a funny movie; you should watch it."

Robert smiled. He found her too attractive to be annoyed by her snobbish attitude. "Let me start over. My name is Robert. I'm from the Boston *area*. I live in Andover—a prep school town thirty minutes north of Boston. I'm moving to New York for work in a month."

Vanessa found him cute, so she played along. "Nice to meet you, Robert. My name is Vanessa. I'm from Korea, and I live in New York currently." Vanessa paused. "Robert, I like your sense of humor. I can't stay out late tonight, though. I have to get up early tomorrow. I've to be on my toes in the morning—literally."

"I see, but we agreed on a date this weekend. Can I have your number?"

She replied without hesitation. "Sure." She reached into her small, black purse. "Here's my card."

Robert took it. "You teach ballet? That sounds grueling."

"Yes, I teach in the off-season. Have fun with the rest of your night."

Robert smiled. She had a good sense of humor. He liked her. He gave her a kiss on her cheek. "Good night, Vanessa."

The classy, stylish woman turned around and disappeared in the crowd. *This is a great night.* He had been able to talk to a few interesting women and he got their phone numbers so easily. Robert was especially happy that he had met Vanessa. *This is much better than Boston. The women are more attractive and easier to approach.*

He looked around and saw the blonde who had been talking to Anna. *Another sexy woman.* She seemed alone, so he decided to walk the twenty feet to talk to her. "Hi," Robert said. "I think you're one of Anna's friends."

The woman replied in English, though with a strong Russian accent. "Yes. My name is Olga."

"My name is Robert. Where are your friends?"

"Somewhere," she replied. Olga quickly shifted the direction of the conversation. "Are you enjoying the evening?

"I think it's a great party. Interesting crowd," he said in a sarcastic tone, "How about you? Are you enjoying yourself?"

"Yes, fun. I like it. Where do you work?"

"I work in banking." Robert remembered his earlier conversation with John. He couldn't believe how right his friend had been about Russian women. *She is really trying to size me up.*

"Nice. Where do you live?"

"I live in Manhattan. Not too far from here. I have a penthouse apartment."

"Oh, that sounds lovely," Olga said, brightening.

"Can I offer you something to drink?"

Olga had been alone for most of the party, and the attention from this banker pleased her. "Maybe."

"Come with me to the bar."

When they reached the bar, another Russian woman approached Olga. She spoke urgently to Olga in Russian. Olga's face showed concern. She said something to the other woman, and then turned to Robert. "I have to go now. It was nice to meet you."

"Already?"

"Yes. I'm sorry."

"Okay. Could I at least—here, take this." He handed her his business card. "My number. It was nice to meet you, too, Olga. Another time, maybe?"

"Maybe." She put the card in her purse with great care. He was one of the bankers Anna had described. She thought the card might come in handy when she came back to New York.

The two women left the bar area in the direction of the main room. Robert found a comfortable spot at the bar and ordered another glass of champagne. His BlackBerry vibrated with a text.

Stephen: Coming down. Done for the night.

Robert looked at his watch. It was close to 2:00 a.m. He replied.

Robert: Me 2. Meet me at the bar.

Stephen: K

The two men finally came back to Robert. John offered his apologies. "Sorry about leaving you alone. Lenny wouldn't let us go."

"I was fine. I had fun." Robert wanted to ask questions about the VIP room, but he decided to ask another time.

"Well, this is going to last all night, but I'm done," said John. "Ready to go?"

"I am," said Stephen. "How about you, Robert? Did you enjoy yourself?"

Robert understood the underlying question. "Yes, I did. Lots of interesting people. But I'm ready to leave."

"Great," John said, and the trio found the exit.

11

BACK IN RUSSIA

OLGA'S MONTH IN New York flew by. Too soon, it was time to return to Russia. She was just about out of money—her own savings and her husband's guilt money. Even though she did not care for him, Olga still had some control over Vladimir, but not enough that she could afford to extend her stay.

She had mixed feelings about leaving. She had fallen in love with the city, but she was anxious to go back home. Nevertheless, the trip had more than exceeded her highest expectations. She had been fortunate to meet Anna and some of her friends. She loved the hip city clubs and the spectacular masquerade party. Sushi had become her favorite dish. She had enjoyed her stay in the comfortable home in Brooklyn, where she'd grown close to the motherly Elena and the effervescent Masha, who had been her guide during her whole trip.

Yes, she missed Russia, but this was New York. She knew that soon she would be back. And she would stay for good.

12

ROBERT IN NEW YORK

THOUGH IT WAS still early December, Robert already found himself thinking about how pleased he was with the changes in his life. Everything seemed new: soon he would be ushering in the New Year, celebrating his new life...in New York. His new apartment was nothing less than spectacular, and he couldn't wait to buy it once it became available. Even his job was new, although it was the same company, and he already felt very comfortable in his new work environment. At the office, he was seen as a hero, preceded by his reputation as the broker who set the firm's record for generating the highest revenue in a single year by an individual. Everything should have been perfect, but he had no feelings at all. He was neither happy nor sad. He was simply numb. He thought he might be depressed, but if he were, wouldn't he feel sad? Sadness required caring, and he really didn't care. He had just stopped living in the present. He kept reliving past moments, yet he wanted nothing more than to forget those dark days in Boston. Work became his only escape. Nothing else mattered. He was depressed. He needed help.

That weekend, he searched for a doctor in his health care provider directory. He typed in a few keywords, although he wasn't quite sure what he wanted or needed. *Psychiatry? Psychology? Therapy?* He knew he could ask around—everyone he knew seemed to have a therapist—but he didn't want to talk to anyone about himself or his feelings. Instead, he just tried to approach the search logically. He thought a male therapist would be better, as he knew he would feel more comfortable with someone of his own gender, and he wanted someone close by so he could book appointments right before or after work. He found five therapists who met those criteria and wrote down their names and numbers so he could call them on Monday.

Robert had always been an early riser and had never really liked to sleep in. Sleeping was a waste of time. There were always many things to do. He had a very disciplined approach to life. He enjoyed routines such as waking up at the same time every morning, taking the same road to work, performing the same tasks at the office, going to the same bar for drinks, and eating the same food at familiar restaurants. He didn't consider himself boring or without imagination; he just liked predictability in his life.

On Monday, he got up just before six, as usual, so he could be at work by seven thirty. Before leaving for the office, he made calls to the five prospective therapists and left voice messages asking for callbacks that day. He decided to set up an appointment with the first one to return his call.

Robert was at work monitoring the three screens in front of him when his cell phone rang. The ID showed an unfamiliar New York number. *One of the therapists,* he thought. He closed the door to his office and answered. "Robert Thompson speaking."

"Robert, this is Carl Ahearn. I believe you called me earlier this morning."

"Yes, I did. I would like to see you as soon as possible."

"Is this an emergency?"

"No, no! I'm just anxious to get started," said Robert.

"I see. Have you seen a therapist before?"

"No. One of my friends suggested I find a...someone to talk to, though."

"Okay. I have openings for Monday or Thursday evenings or early morning Tuesdays."

"This is Monday. What do you have something tonight?"

"I have an opening at five thirty."

"I'll take it."

"I'll see that you're booked. My office is at 21 West Tenth Street, apartment 6-D. Ring the bell, and I'll buzz you in. When you come to the apartment, use the code one three to open the door to the foyer."

"Okay. Thanks." Robert hung up, feeling a bit relieved. He had hoped that the meetings with Carl would finally move him forward.

Robert ended his workday at five, as he had done most days in Boston. He took the subway to the Astor Place and walked the remaining four long blocks to Carl's office. He was somewhat familiar with the area, as he had walked all over the city after work, figuring it was the best way to explore the area. Walks were also therapeutic. They gave him time to think about his state of mind and try to make sense of some of the events from the past few months. Unfortunately, he had not found the solace he sought, and he hoped Carl would be the answer to his quest for peace.

He welcomed the fifteen-minute walk after the long day at work. He crossed Broadway and made his way along Eighth Street and slowed to see some of the local stores, taking mental notes. A few stores were intriguing enough that they might warrant a future visit. At Fifth Avenue he turned north for the two short blocks to Tenth Street. The environment had totally transformed in during the walk from an urban, commercial, somewhat dirty streetscape to a tree-lined, quiet, residential area. It was surprising how quickly the city scene could change.

Robert arrived at the destination, walked up the few stairs, opened the door, and found the number 6-D. He rang the doorbell. Almost immediately, a buzzing sound signaled that the door was open. Robert walked into the lobby and found an elevator. He got to the apartment after a slow elevator ride. He pressed the code, turned the knob, and let himself into a foyer, where he found a door slightly open.

A man in his early sixties opened the door. "Robert? I'm Carl."

"Yes. Nice to meet you."

"Please, come in," said Carl. He closed the door behind Robert.

Carl sat on one of the two chairs and looked up at Robert. "Please, sit down. We can do the intake paperwork at the end of the session."

Robert took a quick look at the small room as he sat in the chair in front of Carl. Like the rest of the building, the room was clean but in need of some restoration. It was warm and welcoming, its setting well thought out. Robert felt as though he was visiting a friend's living room, not sitting in the office of a therapist. Five bookshelves, filled mostly with psychology books, lined two walls. The square seating arrangement—a couch and two chairs—was designed for focused conversation. Silk plants filled the fireplace, giving the impression of a green fire. Remarkable paintings adorned the walls. Robert studied the one above the fireplace; it showed a man sitting on a beach under dark skies, looking out at the ocean. A lonely man. Robert connected with this image.

Carl's sixty-odd years had taken their toll. Though he was not bald, his thin hair barely covered his head, and deep wrinkles had been sculpted into his forehead. His back was slightly hunched, although he was slender and appeared to be in relatively good shape. He dressed like a casting director's idea of a college professor, with a brown wool sweater several sizes too big for him, a plain coffee-colored shirt, beige khakis, and brown shoes.

"So, Robert. Can you please tell me a bit about yourself?" said Carl.

"I'm originally from outside of Boston. I was born, raised, and educated there. I recently moved to New York for work."

"And what do you do for work?"

"I work at the trading desk in a midsize boutique brokerage firm. I'm basically a banker."

"A stressful job, I assume."

Robert smiled. "Yes. Sometimes."

"Are your parents in the Boston area?"

"My mother is."

"And your father?"

"My father left my mother when I was ten. I never heard from him since."

"I see. I'm sure we will talk more about that later. Siblings?"

"No. Just me."

"Thank you. I forget if I already asked. Is the first time you've seen someone professionally?"

Robert understood that *someone* meant therapist. "Yes."

"And what brings you here today?"

Robert took a few seconds. "Something happened a few months ago, and I can't get over it. I'm just so mad. I can't stop thinking about what I did or didn't do or should've done. I think I just need to talk."

"That's what we do here," said Carl with a quick smile. "Please, feel free to share. I'm here to help."

"Where do I start? I was engaged. About a month before the wedding, I found out that my fiancée was having an affair—cheating on me with one of her ex-boyfriends. I called off the wedding." Robert stared out the window for a minute. "I've been mad at her and at myself for not seeing the obvious signs."

After Robert regained his composure, Carl spoke. "I imagine anger is just one of the things you're feeling. That must have been a stressful experience for you."

"Yes."

"Have you considered the positive side, which is that this happened *before* you got married?"

"Yes, that's true. But still I can't get over it. I'll never forgive her. I hate her."

"When did this all take place?"

"This past July. We were planning to get married in late August."

"So, very recent. You said you were mad. Can you tell me about that?"

"I'm just mad at myself. How could I be so naïve? The signs were everywhere. I knew in my gut something wasn't right, but my heart took over."

"I see. So you've felt anger since July. What have you done about your emotion?"

"I've been working like crazy, but that hasn't solved the issue, of course. That's why I'm here."

"Have you felt any other emotions lately? Anything else at all?"

"No. Not if you mean wanting revenge or vengeance. I believe in karma. She's done something bad, and karma will get her back."

"Were you in love with her?"

"Yes, Nicki was the love of my life," said Robert. "At least, I thought so."

"Nicki."

"Tell me more about your relationship with Nicki."

Robert told Carl about the first time he had met Nicki, at a bar in Boston. He had found her very attractive, and he couldn't keep his eyes off her. He had walked up to her, started talking, and asked for her phone number. She said no, but asked for his number.

Robert felt comfortable with Carl, and for the next hour, he started opening up about the events that had led him to Carl's office. Carl interrupted Robert. "Our fifty-minute session is just about over. I can see that there's a great deal to talk about. I think I can help, and if you feel comfortable with me, I'd suggest that you come at least once a week. More often, if you feel the need, but the important thing is to come regularly to ensure progress. Together we can help you better understand your feelings and learn to manage them."

Robert replied, "I'm interested. I think I need to talk about this, but also about other things."

"I have five thirty available on Mondays. Would you like to make that your weekly appointment time?"

"Yes, that works for me."

"If you're paying the whole thing out of pocket, the fee is one hundred dollars per session, payable by cash or check at the end of each session. If you're using insurance, they'll determine the co-pay. Before you leave, please fill out these papers and leave them on the credenza." He handed Robert a clipboard and a pen, and Robert pulled his money clip out of his pocket and gave Carl a one-hundred-dollar bill.

"I'll pay it all personally."

"Very well. See you next week," Carl said.

"Thank you."

Robert left Carl's office and walked down the stairs. Robert hadn't been quite sure what to expect, and he was surprised that he had been able to open up in front of a stranger so quickly. It was the first time since the treachery that he had truly talked about the events in any great depth, and he felt as though a great load had been slightly lifted from his shoulders. It gave him hope that he might be able to move forward. He felt a bond with Carl and was looking forward to his next session.

It was just past six thirty when he left the therapist's office. Walking home, he stopped by one of the local restaurants he had spotted on one of his evening walks. He liked exploring the city, and he was ready to start living. The Mediterranean restaurant he chose, Barbounia, was busy on weekends, but Robert quickly discovered that it—like almost every place in New York—was quiet on Mondays.

He found a seat at the bar. The man behind the bar walked up to him. "Hi. My name's Leon. What can I get you? Just a drink, or would you like a food menu?"

"I'll take the food menu. Give me a glass of Cabernet, your best one. Also, can I have a glass of water?"

"Yes. I don't think I've seen you here before."

"I just moved in around the corner. I'm from Boston. I'm looking for a spot to hang out."

"This is the right spot. Mondays and Tuesdays are usually quiet, but it gets busier."

"That's great. Any suggestions for food?"

"Of course. The chopped salad, the hummus, and the tuna are all excellent."

"I'll take that."

As the bartender walked away, Robert pulled out his BlackBerry to check his e-mails. After a few minutes of browsing, he decided to contact Vanessa. He had been so focused on his move that he had forgotten about her. He knew it might be a long shot to contact her after over a month, but he figured he had nothing to lose. He sent a text.

> Robert: Vanessa, this is Robert. How are you?
> Vanessa: Who is this?
> Robert: We met at Lenny's masquerade party
> around Halloween. I'm the banker from
> Andover…not Boston. I am now in NYC.
> Vanessa: LOL! How are you? Not
> too lost in the big city?

Robert: Well. Would you like to meet this
weekend? Saturday? Drinks? Dinner?
Vanessa: I could do Saturday. Let's
confirm later this week.
Robert: K. Will text you Thursday ;)
Vanessa: ;)

Things were already getting better. Moving to New York was going to be a good thing—new job, new environment, and new friends. This was the first time since he cancelled his wedding that he had even asked a woman out. The New Year was just around the corner, and this was going to be his year.

ROBERT'S FIRST SESSION with Carl had given him hope that he could finally move on with his life rather than just throwing himself into work to forget his pain. When he arrived at Carl's for his second session, he felt hopeful for the first time in many months.

"How are you today, Robert?" Carl asked.

"I'm fine. Maybe better. I think last week was helpful. I felt comfortable talking about Nicki with someone else for the first time," said Robert. "I was actually looking forward to this session."

"So, you feel that it's helped. Do you want to talk some more about Nicki?"

"No, not today anyway. We talked a lot about her last week."

"Fine. Maybe you'd like to tell me a bit about your childhood."

Robert had vague memories of his early years: some painful events between his parents...his father's heavy drinking...the day his father had abandoned his family after a particularly violent eruption. Everything else was blurry. He had no specific recollections of living with his father—not birthdays, family vacations, or anything else.

Robert's happier childhood memories came from the years after his father left, when he lived with just his mother. Maybe to compensate for his father's absence, she had celebrated his birthdays with great fanfare and lots of cake, balloons, silly presents, and friends. Christmas also took on great importance. Their house was always fully decorated for the season, and his mother always put up lights outside and wreaths on the doors to inspire holiday spirit. Every December they scoured the Elks Lodge parking lot for the perfect tree, tied it to the top of their car, and took it home to decorate together. Vacations were mostly camping trips on Cape Cod, which was just a couple of hours away from where they lived. Robert felt loved and knew his mother did her best to provide him with a normal childhood, even though she always struggled financially.

Carl listened intently, barely interrupting his patient's monologue except to occasionally guide the conversation. "Robert, can you please tell me more about your mother? Did she have someone special in her life?"

"My mother had many boyfriends. She was a smart, funny, good-looking woman—she still is," he replied and smiled.

"Did you get to know any of these men? Did you like them?"

"I remember my mother's first boyfriend, Tony. They were together for about three years. I liked him a lot. He took me to Red Sox games—he was a big baseball fan—and we played catch. He taught me a lot about the game, like how to keep the scorebook, strategies, that sort of thing. He smoked a lot, though, and when he quit it made him short-tempered. I thought he'd get over it, and go back to being the guy I liked hanging out with, but then one night I found my mother crying. I tried to comfort her, find out what was wrong, and she said she's just broken it off with him. She said, 'I'm never going to let anyone yell at me again. Never again.' I hugged her, and pretty soon she was smiling again."

"So, you took a somewhat protective role with your mother?"

"Yes, I guess so," said Robert. "Let's see…after that, she really didn't date any one guy seriously. They'd be around for a month or two, and then she'd just move on."

Carl glanced at the clock. "Our time is just about done for today."

Robert was surprised time had passed so quickly. "Okay. Then I guess I'll see you next week, same time." He handed Carl a check. Thank you. Really."

And he meant it.

CARL DIDN'T LIKE to take notes during the sessions, but he had an extraordinary memory for details, and the moment his patients were out the door he jotted everything down. Robert Thompson's recollections of his childhood, especially of his mother, gave Carl a much better understanding of his patient. The man clearly loved his mother. As a young boy, though, he might well have felt that she constantly abandoned him for other men—and men to whom she felt no particular attachment, at that. The loss of his father at a young age and his mother's serial dating might have created the abandonment issues that seemed to be at the heart of his devastation over a garden-variety betrayal. His childhood experiences, combined with the recent episode of the cheating fiancée Robert claimed had been the "love of his life," had left him with profound trust issues. Robert might not understand that yet, but the connection was something Carl would delve into further in future sessions.

THE NEXT DAY, after stopping by his apartment after work, Robert headed out to Barbounia to meet Stephen for dinner. A creature of habit, Robert felt comfortable returning to the same restaurants and bars. When he walked into what his thought of as his new local hangout, Leon saluted him from behind the bar.

Robert sat the bar and ordered a drink, and then pulled out his BlackBerry. He started reading the interminable stream of e-mails from Asia with the latest currency updates. As a trader he needed to be continuously aware of what the market was doing. Charley, his mentor from Boston, called it the hedge. Robert had to consider things no one else thought about, and spot market directions almost before they took place. *If the market continues to be good,* Robert thought, *I'll make a killing this month.*

"Robert, how are you? I see you found a great spot for dinner," Stephen said, sliding onto the barstool next to Robert's.

"Yes. I like it here," Robert replied.

Stephen turned to the bartender. "Leon, please get me a martini and another glass of wine for my friend."

Robert looked surprised. "You know the bartender?"

Stephen laughed. "John and I come here all the time. The food is good. The people are interesting. John knows the owner, of course—another hedge fund guy with too much money, like Lenny. The guy invested in this place just so he can tell women he owns a restaurant."

Robert still hadn't met the infamous Lenny of the masquerade party, but he suspected he wasn't missing much. He had met other "hedge fund guys with too much money," and such people seemed more or less interchangeable.

"So how do you like the city so far?"

"I'm loving it," Robert said.

"Sorry I didn't have much time to talk to you this past week. The market's been crazy! If this continues, we can all retire in a couple of years."

Robert laughed. "No worries. And yeah, retirement sounds like a plan."

"Have you started dating yet?"

"I had a couple of dates with this woman I met at the party."

"Nice.."

Leon brought the drinks. The two men raised their glasses, and Robert spoke. "About that party. I've been meaning to ask you what the big deal was with the color codes. What happened on the second floor?"

"That was months ago. What took you so long to ask?" Stephen said with a grin.

"Well, you and John never so much as mentioned it again, so I assumed it was something hush-hush, something I shouldn't ask about. But I'm asking anyway."

"Well, it is something you can't repeat. I'm not supposed to know either, but John told me." Stephen took a sip of champagne. "Lenny has parties like that masquerade ball every month. Different themes. Different locations. Sometimes at his place. Sometimes some place he's rented. He *always* has a VIP section. He knows a lot of women, and he invites a select few to the VIP section."

"So, the blue and yellow bracelets were VIP guest passes."

"Yes. I had to call in a favor to get one. Lenny is *very* particular about who he lets into his entourage. Especially men. But John is one of his trusted friends, and he got me invited."

"John does seem to know everyone."

Stephen nodded. He leaned toward Robert so he could whisper. "Those Saturday parties? Those are nothing. Lenny throws some *wild* parties at his place on Sundays. I've never been, but John has attended a few times," said Stephen. "He says that there are always three to five girls and four or five guys. The girls are all models, or they *could* be models. Lenny has one or two servers in French maid costumes serving champagne and food. At one point Lenny starts the party by choosing one of the girls and undressing her down to her underwear. Then he invites a guy at random to come caress her in front of everyone. I am told it's just like a porn movie. At one point the girl undresses the guy, and they go at it. The rest of the night continues with lots of alcohol and sex."

Robert stared at Stephen in shock. "And the girls are okay with that? Do they know what's planned when they accept the invitation?"

"I would guess Lenny pays them a good amount to be there."

"He pays them?" *A good amount*, Robert thought. He was astonished by the surreal world of obscene wealth and all the pleasures it claimed as entitlements. Was this decadent circle of hedonistic bankers and brokers really in New York—or ancient Rome?

13

VANESSA

ROBERT HAD DATED Vanessa a few times, and he truly liked her. She came from a wealthy family in Seoul. Her father was a prosperous business-man who had been able to send her to a top school in the United States. She had come to America to study ballet, and after graduating had started working at the American Ballet Theater while pursuing a fine arts degree at NYU. She performed as a ballerina until a career-ending neck injury just a year after she graduated from NYU. As it did for many of its top dancers, the ABT offered her a teaching position at the company ballet school. She'd been teaching there for six years.

Vanessa had enjoyed a very comfortable life in the city, with her modest teacher's salary supplemented by her generous father's fre-quent gifts. Her father had passed away three years ago, and when the gifts stopped coming, everything in her life had changed. Even though she was working for the one of the top ballet companies in the world, her life as an artist remained challenging, especially in a city as expensive as New York.

Vanessa was a smart, stylish woman. Many of the women Robert had known in Boston readily sacrificed style for comfort, happily walk-ing in winter boots or sneakers to the office and only then swapping them out for heels at the office. In New York, more women seemed disinclined to the practicality of comfortable shoes. For his part, he preferred watching women walk in heels, their calf muscles tensed, their bodies swaying. With her graceful dancer's style, Vanessa looked particularly lovely in heels.

Robert had grown attached to the strong-willed woman. Her dedication to ballet and hard work impressed him. Vanessa had strong opinions and always spoke her mind in true New York style. In one way, Vanessa was particularly interesting and clearly different from Nicki; his instincts told him he could actually trust her. She was honest and genuine. She was also very different from Robert himself, and he appreciated the differences. She was artistic and creative; he was logical and methodical. She trusted her instincts and intuition; he trusted rationality and facts. She always knew how to share her emotions; he wished he could do the same.

Vanessa liked Robert, too. Typical, jaded New York men had disappointed her, and she found Robert was refreshing. He wasn't a player like most men in the city. As a rule, she hadn't liked the men she knew who were in finance, as they tended to be childish, self-centered, and arrogant. Robert seemed different; he was modest, attentive, and he didn't talk about money all the time. She knew he was doing well financially, but he never showed it off. He was old-fashioned, which was probably why they had not been intimate in the first few weeks of dating. They had seen each other more than half a dozen times, but he had yet to invite her to his apartment. Most New York men gave up on anyone they couldn't take to beds after the second date.

Robert had finally invited her to his apartment for dinner. She wondered if she might be sleeping over, and she was actually looking forward to the possibility.

Robert had chosen a Thursday evening for that first dinner at his apartment. He had been planning the evening for several weeks, wanting everything to go just right. It was just a few days before Christmas. He enjoyed cooking and thought of himself as an excellent cook. He had done a lot of experimentation in college to sharpen his skills. That evening he planned to serve one of his specialties—veal scaloppini with a tomato sauce and grated cheeses served with risotto and asparagus—a meal that he considered a secret recipe that could make any women fall in love with him. He imagined that the magic concoction would be so overwhelming that no woman who tasted it could ever live without him again. He knew the fantasy was a bit far-fetched, but he liked to think it worked anyway.

Robert had stopped at the grocery store that afternoon to make sure that everything he needed for dinner would be as fresh as possible. He also bought flowers, candles, and massage oils. Massage was another skill he had perfected in college, and it had proven quite useful on numerous occasions to get girls to sleep with him.

The evening was special to Robert. He hadn't invited anyone to his apartment since he moved to New York. He wanted the evening to feel warm, cozy, and intimate. Although he had had sex with other women breaking things off with Nicki, they had been just that, sex. Meaningless affairs. With Vanessa, he felt a true connection, and he expected the night to be something special.

When Vanessa arrived at the apartment building, she explained to the guard that she was visiting Robert. He said, "You're all set. Just take that elevator to the top floor." When she did, she found a private foyer with just one door. She knocked.

When Robert opened the door, delicious smells wafted out as he stepped aside to let her enter. "Come on in." He smiled and kissed her on the lips, then took her in his arms. "I'm really happy to see you. You look great as always."

"Thanks." She smiled.

"Let me take your coat and show you around." Robert hung her knee-length leather coat and cashmere scarf in the entry closet, and then took her hand to lead her to the living room. "This is my favorite room."

"Wow! Great view," she said, gazing out into the clear night at the illuminated city. The Empire State Building was lit up for the season in green, white, and red. From there, he led her to the kitchen. "Mmm, something smells good."

"I'm making a very special dinner," he said as he pulled a bottle of Bouchard Pere & Fils 2007 from a large wine rack, that was mostly empty. "Do you want a glass of red wine?"

"Yes, please. Special how? I hope you're not going to poison me."

"Well, I am rather hoping it will put you under my spell. It's my special recipe to make women fall in love with me. No poison."

Vanessa laughed. "Cute. We'll see if it works on me."

He poured two glasses. He put down the bottle, gave Vanessa her glass, and then took his. "Welcome to my home. Cheers." He took a sip. "I know you aren't available for Christmas next week, but I wanted to ask if you had anything planned for New Year's Eve."

"Not determined yet. Some of my friends and I usually get together every year, but I've put them off so far. I wanted to talk to you about it first."

"Some colleagues of mine, John and Stephen, are organizing a New Year's Eve party. I'd love to take you there," he said.

In fact, he was a little nervous about the idea. He had not yet introduced Vanessa to any of his colleagues or friends, and this would be an important step for him. He was starting to think of her as his girlfriend.

"A party sounds fun."

"It's a plan, then?"

"Sure."

"Great. Are you hungry?"

"Yes, and I'm curious about your love potion."

They walked to the dining room. He lit the two long candles and moved the fresh-cut flowers away from the middle of the table. He put his champagne glass on the table and said, "I will be right back." He left for the kitchen.

"Do you need help?" she called after him.

"No. I'll be fine."

The extent of Robert's preparations impressed Vanessa, and the attention flattered her. He had obviously tried to create a romantic setting, with a dozen white roses on the table, soft lounge music, candles, and a table setting worthy of the best restaurant in the city. There was cutlery for all the courses planned, red and white wine glasses, and crystal water goblets, all on a brilliant white embroidered tablecloth.

Robert brought in two small bowls of soup and a bottle of white wine on a tray. He introduced the first course. "Leek soup with a touch of cream, served with a white Burgundy, this 2007 Chassagne-Montrachet Les Caillerets."

"Did you prepare dinner all by yourself?"

"Of course. Just for you."

Vanessa smiled.

"*Bon appétit!*" Robert said.

Robert's cooking skills impressed Vanessa. A chopped salad followed the soup, and then came the main course—the famous love potion. The dessert was a chocolate mousse. For each course he selected a wine to complement. The white Burgundy was for the soup, a Pinot Noir went with the entrée, and a Malbec accompanied the cheese plate.

"Robert, I have to admit that this was an excellent potion."

"Thank you. Cooking for me is a labor of love, something I got from my mother. She loved to combine everyday, fresh ingredients to prepare great dishes. She is a great cook. I guess you should thank her," he said, clearing away her dessert plates. "Do you want coffee? Cappuccino? My espresso machine makes great coffee."

"Cappuccino would be great. I'll use the bathroom first, though, if you don't mind."

Robert was pleased. The evening was going perfectly. He prepared the coffee and carried it on a tray back to the living room, setting it down on the polished onyx coffee table. He sat on the couch facing the window. He saw Vanessa's reflection approaching him.

"Thank you for a lovely evening, as always," Vanessa said, sitting close to him on the soft leather sofa.

He looked into her eyes, leaned forward slowly, and kissed her. He could taste the minty toothpaste. He grabbed her hair to keep her close to him. His other hand slowly surrounded her waist to bring her closer to him. He continued to kiss her intensely for a few seconds and then slowed. He kissed her repeatedly on the lips softly. He stopped and pulled his head back so he could see her face. After a few seconds of silence, he said, "I think you should spend the night here tonight."

She smiled. "You do?"

Robert understood her sense of humor. She was always a bit sarcastic. He simply said, "Yes, I do."

Robert had found a woman to finally help him move forward. Vanessa had brought him back life.

14

OLGA IN RUSSIA

OLGA HAD BEEN back in Russia for a few weeks. She missed America, but she was happy to be back to her routine—and to be able to save as much money as she could in expectation of her next trip to New York. A few month of work plus some cash extorted from her remorseful husband would ensure that she could live comfortably for a few months in New York until she found a job. Working in the United States without the proper visa would be difficult, but Masha had explained that there was always some type of work available for an attractive woman, such as hosting or serving at a Russian restaurant. Finding something would be relatively easy with the right connections, and some of Olga's new friends would certainly be able to help.

Since returning from New York, she had seen her Frenchman just about every day, and enjoyed every moment with him. She loved him, but knew her mother was right: he was not the right man for her. And she certainly didn't want him or any other man to stop her from going to America. That was her dream. She frequently remembered the lyrics of the song "New York, New York," and it brought her back to the city. "If I can make it there, I'll make it anywhere." She would find a way to make it. She would help her mother run away from her father.

Olga had every intention of going back to New York in early March. François was leaving in late February to return to France for an undetermined period, and she would no longer have any reason to stay in Krasnoyarsk. She would have sufficient savings by that time to go back to the United States.

She wanted to focus on Christmas at the moment, which was celebrated on January 7 per the Eastern Orthodox liturgical calendar, based on the modern Gregorian calendar. Christmas was one of the most important holidays in Russia, and she wanted to celebrate it with François and some of her friends.

Oksana, Olga's best friend, had warned her not to get too close to the Frenchman, but Olga was certain she would be fine once she left Russia for good. She had no intention of maintaining contact with him once she returned to New York; he had served his purpose, both as an important step in the visa process and as a personal diversion and companion. Olga was ready to replace him with an American man who was willing to help further her dreams.

Oksana arrived very early the morning of the party to help Olga prepare. There would be more than a dozen people at the holiday party, so the two women prepared a great amount of food, including traditional Russian salads; an Olivier salad with eggs, potatoes, apples, pickles, green peas, and a few other vegetables combined with a generous amount of mayonnaise; a Mimosa salad with smoked salmon, potatoes, carrots, sour cream, and more mayonnaise; a beet salad; and a carrot salad. The main dishes were as copious as the salads. They served traditional beef Stroganoff made from Olga's family recipe; a stack of blini served with smoked salmon, sour cream, onions, eggs, and white caviar; and finally a goulash, a meat soup combined with noodles and potatoes.

The Christmas party was a great success, and it wasn't until just past three in the morning when Oksana left. She was the last guest at the party and knew it was time to leave her friend and the Frenchman alone.

"You can stay here," Olga said to Oksana.

"You know me. I always want my own bed. I'll stop by to help you clean tomorrow," Oksana said, with a quick look around. There were empty alcohol bottles everywhere in the dining and living room. The fifteen guests had found a way to empty a dozen vodka bottles and a few bottles of champagne—a sign of a great party by any standards.

"Okay. I'll see you tomorrow," Olga said, and she walked her friend to the door. Back in the living room, Olga grabbed François's hand and pulled him off the couch. "Come to the bedroom."

He followed her to the bedroom. François took off his clothes as quickly as he could and climbed into the bed, but Olga stripped slowly to tease him. She pushed him onto the bed, and took him in her month. After a few minutes, she reached for the drawer, grabbed a condom, and put it on him. She looked at him and said, "Do me from behind."

She set herself up on all fours. François obeyed and slipped himself into her slowly. Then he increased the pace. After a few minutes, he screamed, "Olga, I'm going to come."

She replied quickly. "Come for me. Fill me up, *babitchka.*"

He climaxed, slowly caught his breath, and pulled out of her. He looked down. "Fuck. The condom. The condom is still in you."

A moment of great pleasure suddenly turned to panic. Olga turned around. "What?"

"Baby, I think the condom slipped off. It's in you," he said with alarm.

Olga got up and ran to the bedroom. François sat on the bed. He combed his thick hair nervously with his two hands. *Shit, shit, shit!* he thought. *She put it on wrong.* He could not believe this was happening. *She did this on purpose,* he thought.

She came out of the bathroom a few minutes later. "I got it out. I washed up. It should be okay. I mean, I won't get…" She did not continue.

"No, positively not. It should be fine. Just fine."

⸎

"Oksana," Olga said. "That happened on Christmas. I was supposed to have my period two weeks later. I'm now one month late."

"I think we need to get a test from a pharmacy. Maybe you're just stressed."

"Maybe."

"We should go now."

The two women got in the car. During the short drive to the closest pharmacy, there was an uncomfortable silence. Oksana could not say anything to calm the fears of her friend. Olga was thinking about being pregnant. She could not and would not keep the child.

When the two women returned to Olga's apartment from the pharmacy, Olga quickly went to the bathroom. She came out a few minutes later. "I'm pregnant," she said emotionlessly.

"What are you going to do?"

"I can't have this in my life now. I'm leaving for New York in a few weeks. I know a doctor who will help me with this."

"Are you going to tell him?"

"François? Certainly not. His stupidity got me into this. My plans are all fucked up because of him."

"I understand."

"My mother warned me. She told me not to get close to him. I should've listened. He fucked everything up."

She avoided François for a few days, making up excuses not to see him. She said she was sick for a few days. Then she said that she was taking a trip to see her parents. François must have known she was avoiding him, but not why. He tried to contact her every way possible, but he received no answer. He sent text after text.

Oksana, as always, was there for Olga. Her best friend had offered to accompany her to the procedure, which was scheduled for just a few days away.

"You'll need to tell him," Oksana told her friend repeatedly. Olga did not agree. She could not and would not tell him. It wouldn't have made any difference anyway. She had a dream to go to America, and that was the only thing that mattered to her.

After a week of avoiding him, Olga finally sent François a text message, *"Baby, don't worry. I have something to take care of this coming Thursday. You can come after that, maybe Saturday. Olga."*

François received the message that evening and was relieved she had finally reached out to him. He decided not to ask any questions. He had been thinking about Christmas night, worrying, but he assumed she would have told him if she had become pregnant. That Saturday, he went to Olga's apartment as she had suggested. Oksana was there, too. She opened the door for the Frenchman and said, in broken English, "Hello, François."

"Oksana—nice to see you." François was surprised to see her there.

"Olga's in living room."

Oksana walked with François and let Olga know in Russian she would be in the guest bedroom. François walked over to where Olga sat on the couch. "Baby, are you okay? I haven't seen you for over two weeks."

"I'm okay. I wanted to tell you earlier, but I've been very sick. I had to go to the hospital."

"Are you okay?"

"Yes, I'm okay now. I was sick, but now I'm fine. I just need a few days to recover my strength, that's all."

"Whatever you want, my *babitchka*." He kissed her. "Don't get up. I'll leave now, but I'll be back. I'm leaving for France in two weeks. I want to see you as much as possible before I leave."

She smiled and said nothing. He got up and walked out of the apartment. He was sure that her "illness" had been related to what had happened on Christmas night, and felt great relief. Her silence in the past few weeks could not have been just a simple flu or virus. He was glad she had been sensible. He was only twenty-five, and not at all ready to abandon his liberty. He liked Olga a lot, and he felt very close to her, but he was not ready for any kind of commitment. Especially one that involved raising a child.

15

ROBERT AND VANESSA

EVERY MOMENT ROBERT spent with Vanessa was great. She was beautiful, intelligent, open-minded, adventurous, and simply fun. After Nicki, Robert hadn't thought he could ever fall in love again, but he cared for Vanessa. He thought he might even be able to fall in love with her.

Robert had been planning his Valentine's Day with Vanessa for a few weeks. He had decided to make it a true New York event. He made dinner reservations at what was widely considered to be one the most romantic restaurants in the city.

He picked up Vanessa that evening. In the taxi, she kissed him. "Thank you for the flowers. It was very thoughtful of you."

"My pleasure. You look great."

"So do you, Robert. Where are we going?"

"You'll see soon enough."

As the car took off, the couple made small talk until they arrived at their destination in the Village. Vanessa said, "Wow, Robert. I'm impressed. One if by Land, Two if by Sea—what a great choice for Valentine's Day. I have heard about it but never had the chance to come."

Robert was proud he was able to impress his girlfriend. "You see? I'm becoming a New Yorker very quickly."

"You are."

As soon as Robert entered the restaurant, he understood why it had earned its reputation. The restaurant, which looked like an old tavern from the Revolutionary War and had once been Aaron Burr's carriage house, was warm and cozy. Candlelit rooms, flickering fireplaces, and soft music set the mood for a romantic meal.

Robert looked at Vanessa and thought how fortunate he had been to meet this woman. *She is a great catch,* he thought. *She had been prone to lose her temper, but she's honest, genuine, kind, and very caring.* She had been the perfect companion since he had arrived in the city. Thanks to Vanessa, Robert had discovered many things the city offered—fantastic restaurants, relaxing lounges, and trendy nightclubs, as well as opera, theater, and ballet.

After ordering dinner, Vanessa said, "Robert, I want to ask you a question. If you don't feel comfortable, though, you don't need to answer."

Robert was intrigued. "You can ask me anything."

"I know you don't want to talk about Nicki, so I'm afraid my question might annoy you." She paused. "But I'm just curious. You try to hard to be such a very romantic guy. So how did you propose to her?"

Robert smiled and took a few seconds before answering. "You really want to know?"

"Yes, if you don't mind. It doesn't matter—I'm just curious."

Robert explained that after dating for over two years, he and Nicki had taken a one-week vacation to Paris. Robert found what he thought was for the perfect setting to ask the question. One warm, spring day in early May, Robert had taken her to the Eiffel Tower. They walked to the Pont de l'Alma, a bridge near the tower. They stopped to look at the city. After a few minutes, Robert got down on one knee and pulled out a little, velvet box from his pocket. When Robert put the ring on her finger and stood to give her a long kiss, a few passersby who had witnessed the scene applauded and shouted, "Bravo! Bravo!"

Robert recalled the moment vividly while he was telling the story. The memories brought mixed feelings. He could still feel the great joy of that moment, still see Nicki's smile and tears, and still hear the sound of her voice as she said yes. But he could also remember the hurtful moment he had discovered her betrayal and the great pain of the breakup.

He took a few deep breaths, sitting in silence, looking at Vanessa. He was lucky to have her in his life. He would be fine.

Vanessa said, "That's a beautiful story." Vanessa thought of all the men she had dated. As a beautiful woman of independent means, she'd had lots of men chasing her over the years. Commitment and monogamy had seemed like a foreign concept to them. They were always looking for something new, carelessly moving from one woman to the other. Robert was different. She had been with him since he moved to the city. He had everything she had always been looking for. He seemed willing to commit. He had taken some time before they slept together, which she took as a sign of respect. He didn't have "cheater's blood." *This Boston boy might actually be a great match for me,* she thought.

16

OLGA'S SECOND TRIP TO NEW YORK

MARCH WAS ALMOST gone, and Olga was still in Krasnoyarsk. The recent events had changed her timeline. She would be leaving soon, though. François was returning to Russia from France to start the new rugby season around Easter, and she wanted to make sure she was gone at least a week before his arrival to ensure that they wouldn't cross paths. She was still very upset with him, as it was clear to her it was his stupidity that had gotten her pregnant.

Olga called Sergey from the agency to set up the second trip to New York; he had done an excellent job for her first trip, and she was sure he would do it again. She asked to stay with Elena again, but Sergey told her that the room would not be available.

"Don't worry," he said apologetically. "You'll be as comfortable at this new place as you were during your first trip. Plan to leave on Friday, April 18, and arrive in New York the next morning."

The timing was perfect. She could stop by her parents for one last time before her departure—and before the return of the Frenchman.

17

ROBERT IN THE CITY

ROBERT HAD ESTABLISHED a Saturday morning routine in the city since moving there four months earlier. He got up by seven thirty and headed to the midtown gym near his office. After a one-hour workout, he ran two miles from the gym to his home to complete this session. He had been maintaining that strict workout schedule since he graduated from business school.

Robert had returned from his workout and run, showered, was getting dressed to meet Vanessa for brunch. It was a sunny, spring day, perfect weather for a walk to the restaurant. As he always did on his walks, he put on his headphones, turning up the pop music as loud as his ears could tolerate. Thus isolated from the noise of the city, he enjoyed walking. That morning he walked from his apartment all the way to SoHo, passing by Madison Square Park and the Shake Shack, where tourists patiently waited in a long line for what a tour guide magazine had called the best burgers in the city. He passed Union Square where chess players took on challengers and artists showed off their work. He strolled past Grace Church on Broadway where he sometimes went to escape from the city by listening to the choir there.

Finally he arrived at Delicatessen, one of his favorite brunch spots in the city. It had good atmosphere, great food, and a "beautiful" crowd of A-list models, celebrities, and movie stars. Just as he checked in with the host, he received a text.

Vanessa: Running fashionably
late. Will be there at 1:45.
Robert: No problem.

He knew the host well. "Hi, Catherine. We'll be two, but my friend isn't here yet. I'll wait at the bar."

"Okay, Robert. Come see me when you are ready."

He appreciated the benefits of being a regular. The restaurant was packed as always, but he would be able to circumvent the wait. He found the only open seat at the bar, ordered coffee, and pulled out his BlackBerry to check his e-mails. At ten minutes before two, Vanessa came in and found Robert at the bar.

"I am so sorry, but I was on the phone with my brother."

Robert kissed her. "Is everything okay?"

"I'll tell you when we get our table."

Robert checked in with Catherine, and then returned to Vanessa at the bar. "We'll get our table shortly. How was rehearsal?"

"Okay," she replied, her voice flat, her face expressionless. It took all Robert's restraint not to ask again what was wrong. Finally, the host approached the couple and led them to a table. The moment Catherine left, Vanessa opened up. "I'm sorry. I guess I'm in shock. My brother took my mother to the hospital a few hours ago when she said she wasn't feeling well. They think she has a heart problem."

"I'm really sure she'll be fine."

"I hope so, but she's almost seventy now," said Vanessa. "I'm not so sure."

After a few seconds of silence, Robert spoke. "Do you think you should go to Korea to see her?"

"I have to. I'll talk to her doctor later. My brother is very busy with his job, and I don't want to leave her alone in the hospital all day. I should go take care of her."

"Of course you should go. Do you need anything from me?"

"No, I'll be fine. Thank you for your support. I appreciate that."

He smiled and took her hand.

"I'll arrange to take some time off from teaching, and I'll probably be gone for three, maybe four weeks." She sadly looked at his reaction. "Of course, if it's very bad, it could be longer."

"You should take all the time you need. This is important."

"I know." The rest of the brunch was much less animated than usual. Vanessa had been choreographing a special ballet for her class's annual summer recital, and usually she entertained him with anecdotes from her morning rehearsal, but not that morning. Robert understood her preoccupation; Vanessa had been living far away from home since high school, but she remained very close to her family.

Before the week was out, Vanessa had organized her trip. She found a substitute to take over her ballet classes. She easily found someone to sublease her apartment, which would to alleviate the financial burden of the trip. The following Saturday morning, Robert picked her up and drove her to the airport. Vanessa came out of her apartment building with a large suitcase.

"Good morning," he said, kissing her and placing her bag in the trunk.

"Good morning. I could've taken a cab, but I really appreciate this."

"My pleasure," he said. "My car needed a spin anyway. The battery died a few weeks ago since I hadn't been using it at all, so I'm happy to have a reason to take it out."

They reached JFK in less than thirty minutes, as there was little traffic that morning. Robert found a spot in short-term parking and pulled her bag from the trunk.

"Thank you for driving me," she told him. "And you could have just dropped me at the terminal."

"You're my girlfriend, and I'm not going to see you for a month. I want to spend as much time as I can with you. Of course I'm going to walk you to the terminal." He walked hand in hand with her, pulling her rolling suitcase behind him. He stopped at the security checkpoint. "I guess this is it," he said, and he looked into her sad eyes.

"Thank you. I'll e-mail you when I get there. We can Skype, too, but it's not going to be easy with the time difference."

"Don't worry about me. Take care of your mother."

Robert kissed her, and he walked back toward short-term parking. He trusted Vanessa, but he felt uncomfortable being separated from her. He tried to fight his doubts, but images of Nicki came back to haunt him. *What if Vanessa finds another man during her trip? What if she cheats on me, like Nicki did?*

18

BACK IN NEW YORK

OLGA'S SECOND TWENTY-TWO-HOUR flight to New York seemed longer and more painful than the first, but she was thrilled to be back. She got off the plane and walked slowly through the terminal to the luggage carousel. After what seemed an eternity, the carousel began to spit out the luggage from her flight. The very last bags to come out were her two large red suitcases. *The last bags,* she thought. *Really? Not a good sign.* She hauled them off the carousel, put them on a small trolley, and got in line for passport control. The agent asked her more questions than last time—her marital status, the purpose of her trip, the address of her room in America, her itinerary, her budget, and her date of return. After ten long minutes of questioning, he finally let her go. She was relieved. Sergey had prepared her to answer the questions correctly. It was at least easy to find her driver, who held up a sign with her name on it. He grabbed her bags and led her to the car.

She sat back in the black sedan and finally relaxed. She smiled. She was on her way to her new home. The car took off for Brooklyn. After twenty minutes the driver turned onto a side street from highway. Small houses lined the street. He finally stopped in front of the smallest one. "We are here," he said in Russian, and he got out of the car.

The white paint of the house had lost its luster after years of neglect. One broken window had been patched with tape. The screen door, wide open, flapped in the breeze.

"Here? Are you sure?" Olga was confused.

The driver said, "It's better inside. Come in." He carried her bags to the house and rang the doorbell. An old Russian woman came to the door. She greeted her visitor in Russian.

"Olga Kotova. I am Karina. Welcome to my home."

"Nice to meet you, Karina."

The driver dropped the luggage inside the entrance and left Olga without a word.

"This is a very humble home, but it is comfortable," Karina said. She guided her visitor to a small room. "This is your room."

Olga walked into the small bedroom. It was musty and dirty, just like the outside of the house. The walls had not been painted for in several years, and the once-white walls were now as gray as a rainy sky, mottled with pale shapes where mirrors or pictures had once hung. The red bedcover had faded unevenly to a salmon pink closest to the window. The lingering dampness in the room made Olga nauseous. Dust bunnies had accumulated in the corners. *This is totally unacceptable. I will have to find another place,* she thought.

The old woman asked, "Do you like it?"

Olga thought, *Like it? There is nothing to like. This is a disgusting place to stay.* But she said, "It will do."

"Do you want to shower?"

Olga was scared to discover the state of the bathroom. "No. Thank you. Maybe later."

Olga didn't want to stay in this rathole. She needed to find another place to stay as soon as possible. Olga continued, "I want to go see a friend who lived on Brighton Thirteenth Street. Is it far?"

"It's just a few blocks away—about a fifteen-minute walk."

"Can you give me directions?"

Karina drew her a small map on the back of an envelope. Olga left the house with a key to the dilapidated house. Although she was tired and discouraged, it was a warm, spring day, and she was happy to be back in America, despite this setback. It was only ten in the morning; she had all day to find another place to stay. She was sure that Elena or Masha could help her. If nothing else, she could find a cheap hotel until she figured out her living arrangements.

After about a fifteen-minute walk, she found Elena's apartment building. She tried to remember the apartment number. She rang the number she recalled, and when someone buzzed the door open, she walked in. She smiled, remembering all the great moments she had spent with her two friends. After a short elevator ride, she walked to apartment 1214 and knocked on the door.

A young woman, no more than eighteen, opened the door and asked in Russian, "Who is this?"

Olga replied in Russian. "I'm sorry. I'm looking for Elena and Masha."

"Wait a second." The woman closed the door.

Another woman opened the door again. She said, "Elena doesn't live here anymore. Masha moved to Washington a few months ago."

"Do you know where I can find Elena?"

"Not really. I have an old phone number you can try."

"I'll take that please."

"Okay. Let me get it."

Olga was upset. Everything seemed to be going wrong, unlike her first trip. She was mad that Sergey's agency had put her in such a horrible situation. Elena was her only hope. She and Masha were the only people she really knew in America. She'd met others, but never even learned their last names. Her two friends were her only hope of getting help in the city.

She took Elena's phone number and walked away from the building. She pulled out the cell phone the driver had given her and tried to dial the number. The phone was dead. Olga was furious. She had just paid another thirteen hundred dollars to Sergey's agency, and for what? For nothing!

She walked back to the busy road and found a public phone. Using the quarters she had kept from her first visit, she called the number, but there was no answer. She couldn't think what to do next. She needed a place to stay. She had enough money to get a cheap hotel room in the area until she found something more suitable for the next few weeks, so she flagged a taxi.

In a few minutes, she was back at the little gray house. She asked the taxi driver to wait. She knocked on the door, then opened the door with her key and walked in to fetch her luggage. She called out hello a couple of times, but there was no response.

In her room, she found her suitcases wide open and her clothes spread all over the floor. She couldn't believe it. She put everything back in her bags and dragged them outside. The taxi driver got out to help her and put the heavy bags in the car.

"Where ya headed?" he asked in English.

She had tears in her eyes and took a few seconds to answer in her heavy Russian accent. "Any cheap hotel not too far. Can you drive me there?"

"Of course." He noticed the tears. "You okay?"

"I'm fine. Just tired," she replied in a small voice.

She *was* tired. Exhausted, in fact. She had been up for more than twenty-four hours, she could barely think straight. She suddenly realized that more than half the money she had brought with her had been in her suitcases. With a panic, she thought about the five thousand dollars in her cosmetic bag. *The bag I put the money in was still there. It seemed untouched. The money is probably still there.*

"How far?" she asked.

"We'll be there in five minutes. You want the Comfort Inn or the Best Western? I think they're both good."

"Whichever one is closest."

Five minutes seemed like five hours. Olga wanted to desperately to get behind closed doors so she could check to see if her hard-earned money had disappeared. Finally the taxi pulled into a hotel parking lot. Not wasting any time, she pulled a twenty-dollar bill out to pay the driver.

"Please give me back five dollars," she said after checking the meter. She thought the four-dollar tip would be sufficient to entice the driver. "Can you help me with my suitcases?"

As he gave back her change, he shrugged and said, "Okay." He pulled the two heavy bags out of the trunk and rolled them up to the hotel door.

"Thank you," she said. She pulled the two suitcases into the lobby of the Best Western. It was obviously a no-frills hotel, but anything would be better than the gray house with the thieving hostess. She even spotted two computers by the elevators. *Perfect*, she thought, *I will be able to e-mail Mama later.* First, she needed a shower and a quick nap.

She checked in and rushed to her room, locking the door behind her. She quickly kneeled down in front of one bag, opened it, and searched for the small cosmetic bag. *Is it in the other one?* she thought. She moved closer to the second suitcase. She quickly unzipped it and found the small bag. She opened it.

She fell back. The money was gone. Her five thousand dollars was gone. Someone at the house had to have taken it. She wondered if she should go back to confront the old woman. If America was like Russia, though, the money was gone forever. She decided to try, even though there was no chance of getting it back.

Olga got up after her alarm went off twice. She sat on the bed and looked at the alarm clock. It read 4:15 p.m. She felt light-headed. *Food*, she thought. *I need to eat something.* She would visit to the old woman after a quick shower. Later she would try calling Elena again, and try to find Masha via e-mail or VK. She would also look online to find an affordable room. At $125 per night, even the Best Western would quickly deplete what was now a small cash reserve.

After a quick shower, she got dressed and put on a minimum amount of makeup. She would normally have taken up to an hour to get ready, but there was no time to waste. She needed to go back to the house to get her money. She opened the minibar and took a can of soda and a couple bags of nuts with her. She left the room, took the elevator, and ran out of the lobby. She was fortunate to find a taxi right away. She gave the driver Karina's address.

"I do not think this is too far. Correct?" she asked the driver in decent English.

"No. We'll be there in five minutes."

Olga thought that confronting Karina might be dangerous. She might need a quick way out if things became violent. She didn't think the old woman would try to harm her, if she tried, but there might be others. Still, she asked the driver, "Can you please wait for me outside for a few minutes when we get there?"

"I can't. I could get a ticket," the driver said.

"I won't be long. I'll give you a twenty-dollar tip." Money always convinced people to do things in Russia.

Apparently it helped in America, too. "Okay, I can drive around the block. Give me the money before you go."

"You promise that you'll wait for me? I'll be back soon."

The taxi driver nodded his head in agreement. A few minutes later, the taxi pulled up in front of the shabby house. Olga handed the driver some money and got out of the taxi, and then walked to the house. She knocked at the door. There was no answer. She turned the knob. It was unlocked. She pushed it open and entered. "Hello? Hello?"

She walked around the house, but there was no one there. She walked out of the house frustrated. She had lost her money, and there was no chance of getting it back.

As promised, the taxi was waiting for her, and she got back in.

"Can you drive somewhere near where I can eat?"

"How about Emmons Avenue? There're a lot of restaurants there."

"Okay. Where do people go to eat?"

"I take a lot of people to Liman. It's a Turkish place."

Liman, she thought. *Like the Suleyman.* On a day where everything seemed to be going wrong, maybe this was a good omen. Olga sensed her luck was about to change. It could not, after all, get any worse.

The driver dropped her off at the restaurant, and she approached the host. It was 6:00 p.m., and the restaurant was still pretty empty. She said in English, "One, please."

"Okay. You can sit anywhere," a young woman replied in accent-free Russian.

Olga chose a table, sat down, and said in Russian, "Thank you."

"Menu in English or Russian?"

The request surprised Olga. "Russian."

A man at the bar noticed Olga from the moment she came in. Olga looked like a typical Russian to him—tall, model thin, with bangs neatly trimmed to the middle of her forehead, a style popular with young women in Russia. He walked over to her table.

Olga noticed him walking toward her with a beer bottle. He was in his late thirties or maybe early forties. He was half bald, unshaven, and in very good shape. He was wearing a blue Adidas gym suit. His long pants matched his jacket, and he had sparkling, clean, white sneakers. A gold medallion hung around his neck. He might have been handsome when he was younger, but Olga didn't find him attractive.

"*Privet*," he said in flawless Russian. "I don't think a beautiful woman like you should be eating alone. Are you waiting for someone?"

"No, I'm not," she replied in Russian.

"Can I sit down?" he asked as he put his beer on the table.

"Yes," she replied, though he was already sitting.

"So how long have you been in New York?"

The question surprised her. *Is it so obvious I am new to America?* "I was here once before, but I just got here today."

"Okay. My name is Mikhail Sokolov."

"Nice to meet you, Mikhail. My name is Olga. Olga Kotova."

"Olga, tell me about you."

Olga was apprehensive. She didn't know who to trust in this country. Mikhail was a bit too forward for her tastes, but she was alone and in desperate need of help. She wanted to trust someone. She explained that she had come to New York with great hopes, but that things had gotten off to a difficult start. She withheld most of the details, though, saying only that her living arrangements had fallen through.

"Well, you could stay at my place if you want. I have a spare bedroom."

Olga took the offer as a good omen. *Maybe things are going to get better,* she thought. "I don't know you."

Mikhail said that the arrangement would only be to help her out— an offer made from the kindness of his heart, with no other expectations. He told her his story. He had come to New York to play ice hockey, but after five years with the New York Rangers, he had suffered a career-ending injury. Now he worked as a trainer for the team. He traveled frequently to Russia to scout potential players for his team, and he also coached a couple of minor junior teams in Brooklyn. He enjoyed working with kids.

His story sounded legitimate. Olga thought Mikhail seemed like a nice, generous man. "Mikhail, I think I will accept your offer."

The server had purposely stayed away from the couple until Mikhail signaled him. At Mikhail's nod, he stepped over to the table.

"May I help you?"

"We'll order now. Please bring us two glasses of vodka. We need to celebrate the arrival of this ambitious woman from Russia," he told the waiter in Russian.

Olga enjoyed Mikhail's company. He spoke amusingly of his difficulties adapting to the city and to American culture, of his cross-country travels with the team, and of the friendships he had developed. He enjoyed his experiences, he told her, but he still missed Moscow. If he returned, though, it would be as a visitor, as he was now an American citizen—a status he obtained during his tenure as a hockey player.

After dinner, the waiter brought the check. Mikhail paid. *Lucky,* Olga thought.

"When do you want to come over? I can pick you up at the hotel tomorrow. Around eleven in the morning?" Mikhail asked.

"That would be lovely."

"My car is parked outside. May I drive you back to your hotel?"

"That would be nice."

Olga returned to the hotel. She felt tired but happy. Things were already starting to turn around. The day had started in the worst way but ended on a good note; she had found a free, short-term place to stay, which would give her time to find Masha and Elena. She felt so alone. She missed her Frenchman. She decided to write him. She wanted to make love to him. She had forgiven him.

19

BANKERS' NIGHT OUT

AFTER ROBERT TOOK Vanessa to the airport, he felt antsy. He didn't feel like being cooped up in the apartment, and he felt very anxious for the first time in months. It was the first time since he'd moved to New York that he had faced a Saturday without plans—without Vanessa—and he felt suddenly and uncomfortably alone. He wished he could talk to Carl. *I need to talk to him about this.*

After his workout, he showered and changed, then walked to Barbounia for a late brunch. While he sat at the bar, he received a text.

Stephen: Any plans for tonight?

Robert: No.

Stephen: Join us for dinner. Drinks at

Barbounia, dinner at Meatpacking.

John is bringing a few friends.

Meatpacking was a new clubbing spot in New York, an area of restaurants and exclusive nightclubs that that had recently become hip. Robert had been a few times with John and Stephen, and they had ended up spending a few thousand dollars on table service. That bought them the rights to a tiny coffee table with a small couch and a couple of minuscule ottomans, as well as the privilege of having a dedicated attractive woman to serve as their personal bartender for the duration. As long as there was alcohol left to pour, the scantily dressed woman was there to serve.

Robert: K.

Stephen: 8:30 at Barbounia.

Robert: Gr8. See you then.

That evening, as Robert looked through his bedroom closet deciding what to wear, he pulled out a Dolce & Gabbana shirt Nicki had given him the year before. Tears suddenly rolled down his cheeks as sorrow overwhelmed him. He sat down on his bed, took his head between his hands, and sobbed uncontrollably. He had not experienced such a deep feeling of loss in a long time, and he could not understand what had triggered it. *Vanessa leaving? The shirt? That seems so silly,* he thought. As he went to the bathroom and splashed water on his face, he noticed the song that had been playing on the radio: "Summer Love," sung by Justin Timberlake—the song Nicki had selected for their first dance at their wedding. The wedding that never happened. Robert was surprised. *Was that what caused the sadness? If so, I should be mad, not sad.*

He got dressed and he left the apartment. Normally on such a warm spring night, he would have walked to Barbounia, but tonight he walked to Park Avenue South to catch a taxi because he was running late. Robert got out of the cab, entered the restaurant, and saluted Leon as he stepped up to the bar. He quickly found Stephen.

"Robert, how are you? Glad you could make it."

"I'm glad too. I needed to go out," Robert replied.

"Vanessa left this morning?"

"Yes, I dropped her off at the airport this morning."

Stephen caught the bartender's attention. "Leon, please give us a couple of martinis." He looked at Robert. "Martini okay with you?"

Robert nodded.

"John changed the plans. We are not going to the meatpacking district after all," Stephen said. "After you and I have a few drinks here, we're meeting John at Tao for dinner. He's getting a table. Then we'll hit Lavo just across the street. Have you been to Tao?"

"I don't think so."

"One of my favorite spots in the city. John's bringing four of his friends. Lavo's a club owned by another one of John's clients."

Leon brought the two glasses, and Robert raised his glass. "Cheers." After a couple drinks, Stephen received a text from John.

Stephen texted back, then said to Robert, "John's on his way. Getting to midtown at this time will be a pain, so we should go now."

"Got it. Let me get the bill," Robert told his friend.

The two men walked into Tao, passed the hosts, and wandered into to the lounge area, where they quickly located their friend. John had taken care of everything. He had arranged the perfect setup for the small group in the crowded bar. He sat on a couch with two girls, with two more girls on another couch facing them. He had ordered a two bottles of champagne for the group. He hugged Stephen and welcomed Robert.

"Let me introduce everyone. Ladies? This is Stephen and Robert," John said. He pointed to the platinum blonde. "This is Irina." He pointed to the brunette. "Natalia." He pointed to a black-haired woman. "Katia." He pointed to another blonde. "And Anna."

Robert recognized Anna from the masquerade party, but decided not to mention their initial encounter. The three other women were also very beautiful, but Irina especially attracted his attention. Perhaps he'd attracted hers, too, as she seemed a bit warmer than the others and had smiled when John introduced him, holding his gaze for a just a few seconds.

Robert and Stephen joined Irina and Natalia on the second couch. John grabbed a bottle of champagne and filled everyone's glasses. He put the bottle back in the bucket and raised his glass. "To a great night."

Everyone raised their glasses. Robert was used to John's toasts. John was a player, and he always wanted to impress women with money. This would be just the beginning.

The music in the lounge was so loud that Robert had to lean close to Irina to hear her speak. She said that she was originally from Moscow and had been in New York for three years. After completing her college degree, she had signed with a New York–based modeling agency. She had done mostly print and some runway shows in the city.

Although she had studied ballet in Russia, she knew that was not for her.

At the mention of ballet, Robert thought of Vanessa, who would still be on the plane to Korea. He felt somewhat guilty, wondering what Vanessa would think of him chatting it up with four beautiful, single women, but then he shrugged. He and Irina were just talking. And Irina was interesting, and not at all like most of John's airhead model friends.

Irina noticed his momentary lapse of attention and stopped. "I talk too much. Tell me something about you."

Just as Robert started to tell his story, the restaurant pager started flashing, calling the group to their dinner table. While John took the device to the host, Stephen tested the bottles of champagne. One was empty, and the other was almost empty.

"God. All gone," he told the group.

John returned to the group with the host, who led them to their table on the second floor. The restaurant was spectacular. Robert continued to be amazed by the people, places, and things he kept discovering in the city. Tao's owners had converted a movie theater into another New York monument. It was huge by any measurement. The main room could have easily fit a three-story building. There were three floors. It was impossible to miss the thirty-foot Buddha statue at the center of the wall on the first floor. The second floor, the U-shaped former balcony section, was large enough to accommodate over two hundred patrons. The top floor, the former the projection room, had been transformed into one very private dining room. Four large, white banners filled with Chinese characters hung from the ceiling over the open area. Asian sculptures and paintings completed the decor.

Robert sat beside Irina so he could continue the conversation they had started in the lounge. He looked around, and everyone had found a seat. He noticed Anna was paying particular attention to John. She had kissed him a few times on the cheek already, held his hand on the table, and whispered in his ear. She was clearly more than a casual friend. Stephen entertained the other two women. They seemed to be enjoying themselves.

John took charge of ordering food for what would become a copious dinner. John indulged to the point of gluttony, with double servings of most of the dishes, while the four women nibbled sparingly on every dish, clearly thinking about maintaining their tiny waists. The other two men enjoyed the food. Alcohol was flowing again. John had ordered three large bottles of sake and five cans of Sapporo beer. When they finished the meal, everyone ordered cappuccino, and John decided to get dessert for the table. He asked for three of Tao's special fortune cookies. He explained these were not the typical fortune cookies, and ordering them was a must. Besides, reading each person's fortune would be amusing.

After the waiter left with the dessert order, Anna got up, kissed John on the lips, and said she was going to freshen up. When she signaled her intention to the other girls, they got up in unison and followed their friend to the restroom. Irina took longer than the other two girls. She kissed Robert on the lips and told him, "I like you." Then she left with the other girls.

After the women disappeared from view, John looked at Robert. "Nice!"

Robert enjoyed the kiss. He was feeling the effects of the alcohol. He thought again of Vanessa. *Nothing will happen tonight with Irina,* he thought.

The dessert arrived just as the four women returned to the table. John asked the waiter to place one dessert between Robert and Irina, one between him and Anna, and the third in front of the three other guests. The fist-sized fortune cookie could easily feed two or three people. Vanilla and chocolate custard filled each cookie, and cups of fresh fruit surrounded each. John instructed Robert to open his cookie. When he pulled out the piece of paper and read it, he laughed out loud, then gave it to Irina. She smiled.

John asked, "What's your fortune?"

Robert read the long piece of paper. "For once, you will get lucky tonight."

Stephen pulled his fortune out. The two women started giggling. He then shared with the group. "One, two, three. Your lucky number is three tonight."

John pulled his fortune from his cookie and read it to the group. "You will be in many positions tonight." He laughed. "I guess we're all going to have a great night tonight." He checked his watch. "Ah, just past eleven. Perfect time to go to Lavo."

After John took care of the bill, the group left and crossed the street to the nightclub. Irina grabbed Robert's arm while they walked down the stairs, and she did not let go until they hit the line at the nightclub. He realized he had not told her about Vanessa. It would be awkward to do so now, though, and he convinced himself that it wasn't really necessary, even though Irina seemed rather interested in him.

There was a long line outside the nightclub. People waited patiently to be invited in. Getting into Lavo had more to do with looks and money than anything else. Like most hip clubs in New York, having beautiful women or reserving expensive table service were a sure way of bypassing the line.

John approached one of the bouncers to let him know he had reserved a table. The large man pointed John toward one of the hostesses. She took a few steps forward and spoke with him briefly, then led them into the club. A server greeted them and led them down the stairs into the dimly lit club. The music was blaring. The server guided them to a C-shaped couch with a large, round table. Everyone took their places as if seating had been assigned: John with Anna, Robert with Irina, and Stephen with Katia and Natalia. John ordered a couple of bottles of vodka. The party was getting started.

"I love this song," said Irina. "Let's dance." Irina stood and pulled Robert up from the couch.

Robert looked at Stephen as if for approval, and Stephen smiled. Soon Robert and Irina were dancing. Robert looked intensely at Irina. He wanted to kiss her. He let himself go, followed his impulse, and kissed her. After a long kiss, he pulled back. He was fully aware he had just crossed a line, but he did not feel remorse or guilt. He just felt good. Irina looked at him and smiled. She seemed happy about the turn of events.

The group partied in the great tradition of New York bankers, beautiful women, and unlimited alcohol money could buy at one of the hippest nightclubs in the city.. As the night progressed, the alcohol continued to flow, and everyone at the table was showing the effects. John was openly making out with Anna. Stephen was lavishing attention on Natalia and Katia equally. Robert, too, had lost all sense of restraint; he kissed Irina every moment he could.

It was about three o'clock when John said, "I'm outta here, guys. We're heading home," John said with a wink, his arm around Anna.

Stephen hailed a taxi, and both girls climbed in with him, leaving Robert and Irina standing on the sidewalk in front of the bar. Robert looked at Irina and said, "I think you should come home with me."

She kissed him. Robert hailed a cab and the two got into the taxi. Robert gave his address to the driver. He started making out with Irina in the cab, overcome with lust and desire. He wanted a woman. He wanted Irina. Irina moved onto his lap, and they continued to kiss passionately until they arrived at Robert's apartment building. Robert paid the driver, tipping handsomely, and led a giggling Irina to the elevator. He pressed the PH button; they kissed all the way to the penthouse. When the doors opened, Robert opened his apartment door with one hand while he held Irina close with the other, fumbling with her blouse. The two of them bounced drunkenly off the walls as they left a trail of discarded clothes to the bedroom.

Robert woke up at 6:18 a.m. He turned to find Irina sleeping beside him, naked, only half-covered by the blanket. He got up to use the bathroom, stepping over three used condoms on the floor and several articles of clothing. He had had sex with a total stranger. He was still far from sober, and only vaguely remembered what had happened after they'd arrived at his penthouse. When he returned to the bed, Irina stirred, turned to him, put her arms around his waist, kissed him on the neck, and stopped moving. Robert closed his eyes and fell back asleep, too.

Noise from the bathroom woke Robert. When Irina sat on the edge of the to bed, he opened his eyes. "I'm sorry, Robert," she said softly. "I didn't mean to wake you up. Here's my number. Text me."

She kissed him on the cheek and left before he could get out of bed. The clock read 9:03 a.m. When he heard the door close, he slipped out of bed and wandered toward the kitchen to make coffee. While he was waiting for the coffee to be brewed, he walked down the hallway to pick find his jacket and pull out his BlackBerry. He looked at his clothes on the floor. The trail could not have been more obvious. His jacket was near the door. His shirt, shoes, sock, other sock, and pants led toward his room. *What a crazy night.* He grabbed his BlackBerry and checked his texts. There was a text, only a few minutes old.

John: Brunch at 2 at Essex, LES. K?

Robert: Maybe. Will let you know.

Robert had been to Essex in the Lower East Side and knew that part of brunch was unlimited champagne. He wasn't sure he could stand another drop of alcohol. He checked his e-mail. Vanessa had written him a short note.

Hi, Robert.

I have arrived safely, and I am already by my
mother's side. She seems to be doing okay. She is
happy to see me. I am exhausted because I did not
sleep on the plane at all. I will write more later.
Kisses, Vanessa.

As he finished reading, he got another text.

John: You have to come. Lenny will
be there. You have to meet him.

Lenny, the infamous man of mystery, had many connections in the city—the kind of people who could help Robert in his work. There was also the curiosity factor. Robert wanted to know the man behind the parties and Sunday debauchery. He swallowed a handful of aspirin, grabbed a cup of coffee, and stumbled toward the shower after texting John that he would be there.

GOING BACK TO work on Monday morning was a relief after the wild weekend. Sunday had been filled with as much alcohol as Saturday night. Robert had met John and a few of his friends at Essex, and as he'd expected, the champagne had not stopped flowing. Robert had indeed met the mysterious Lenny, who stopped by their table at the Essex for a few minutes to talk to John. John had promised Robert that he would have another chance to meet Lenny over lunch later that week.

After an uneventful day at the trading desk, Robert walked the usual route to his therapist's office, mulling over the events of the past few days. He tried to remember the feelings he had experienced. There had been anxiety right after Vanessa left and sadness when he heard the familiar song, then lust when he met Irina, and, most surprisingly, no guilt or remorse, even after having sex with Irina. This last reaction puzzled him, and the session with Carl was well timed. He had many things to talk about.

As usual, Carl said nothing at first. When Robert failed to fill the silence first, the therapist finally spoke. "So, how was your week? You seem a bit preoccupied. Did Vanessa leave on Saturday as planned?"

Robert nodded. "I guess I am a little...preoccupied. A few things happened this weekend. And yes, one of them was that Vanessa left on Saturday morning."

Carl asked, "How did you feel about her leaving?"

"It was fine."

"You told me recently that you like her a lot, and that you have a positive feeling about the possibility of building a meaningful relationship with her."

Robert nodded. He didn't want to talk about her just then. "Um, yeah... But something else happened. Actually two things happened. First, I started crying on Saturday afternoon. It happened when I heard a song that Nicki had selected for the wedding."

Carl nodded. After a brief silence, he said, "For several months after you cancelled the wedding, you saw no one seriously. Then you moved to a new city and immediately began spending a lot of time with one woman, Vanessa. Just when you start thinking about how well things are going, she leaves. You know she'll come back, but it's a loss, nonetheless. You have some difficulty handling loss."

Robert thought about this, but he wasn't sure Carl was right about Vanessa's departure triggering his sadness. "I don't know. It happened so suddenly. I thought I was doing well…feeling good. Then *that* happened."

"Robert, you have been dealing with Nicki's adultery, over which you experienced strong, negative feelings. Now you are getting close to Vanessa, so even though the circumstances are different, you might be feeling some of the same feelings as those you had when Nicki was suddenly no longer in your life Nicki. Once again, you've gotten close to a woman and once again, for reasons that have nothing to do with you, she's suddenly gone. It might feel to you as though Vanessa has left you."

Carl paused. The two sat in silence for a couple minutes, with Carl waiting for Robert to comment further. When he did not, Carl said, "You said that a few things happened this weekend."

"Yes. I went out with a few friends on Saturday night. I got a bit drunk. I brought a girl back home…and I slept with her."

Carl's face showed no expression, but he waited a minute before replying, apparently choosing his words carefully. "Given how you reacted to Nicki's infidelity, I find this news, and the timing of it, somewhat surprising. Can you tell me what was going through your mind that night?"

Robert laughed grimly. "Ha! Martinis! Sake! Beer! Champagne!" Carl smiled, but Robert knew he was waiting for a real answer. "I don't really know what I was thinking, if anything. It all happened so quickly—dinner, dancing, drinking…lots of drinking. I just let my physical impulses take over."

"So you didn't consciously choose to sleep with someone other than Vanessa?"

Robert shook his head. "Of course not."

"And how do you feel about it now that you've done so?"

Robert understood what Carl wanted to know. He wanted to know if Robert felt guilty or remorseful, given how he'd spoken about his feelings for Vanessa over the past few weeks. He had grown attached to Vanessa, and he felt…something…but it wasn't guilt. After a few seconds, he replied, "I don't feel guilty. I don't feel any remorse. It happened once, but it won't happen again."

As he said the words aloud, Robert knew he was lying to Carl and himself. He wanted to see Irina again. He had her phone number, and he had already texted once today. If he had the opportunity to have sex with her again, he would not resist.

"It seems that Vanessa's departure has triggered a lot of buried feelings. We talked about the fact that you might have felt...abandoned. Have you considered that maybe some part of you felt that it was your turn?"

"You mean like paying Nicki back?"

"It's never that simple. But you felt that someone you loved—Nicki—betrayed your trust. While you and Vanessa are not engaged, you've used the word 'committed,' yet now you've acted in a way that is not dissimilar," said Carl. "I'm merely wondering if what you did Saturday night changes how you feel about what happened with Nicki last summer. Does it lessen your sense of pain, or increase your understanding of what she did?"

"Like I've evened the score somehow? No, I don't think so," said Robert, shaking his head, but in truth he wasn't sure what he thought.

"I'm wondering, too, if this changes how you feel about Vanessa, and if this was a sort of preemptive strike—a way to 'abandon' her back before she could somehow betray you."

Robert shook his head again. "No, no, I really miss Vanessa. I wish she were back here in New York. Wait...are you saying that what I did was wrong?"

"There is no right or wrong in this: two consenting adults had sex. One of them is my patient, and my only concern is how this affects your emotional health. We've talked about the difficulty you have dealing with loss and abandonment—both real and perceived. What happened with the woman over the weekend is not coincidental. By your own admission, Vanessa's sudden departure left you feeling vulnerable. Sleeping with another woman was just one of the myriad ways you might have dealt with your feelings."

"But you don't think it was the right way?"

"Again, if there were black and white answers to emotional questions, no one would need therapists. We could fix everything with a computer program," said Carl. "I'm not interested in passing judgments. I'm interested in helping you heal."

Robert did not reply. They spent the rest of the session talking about Nicki, Vanessa, and Irina, and how abandonment related to each. Carl wanted to bring his thoughts about Robert's parents into the conversation, but the session was already running a few minutes late.

"Robert, I think we've made great progress this week." He said. "I'd like you to think about what we talked about today so we can talk it up again next week."

Robert left Carl's office thinking about his empty apartment. He pulled out his BlackBerry and sent a text.

> Robert: Hi there. Any fun plans
> tonight? Want to have dinner?
> Irina: Love to. Tell me when and where.

Robert felt no remorse about his behavior.

20

THE HOCKEY PLAYER

OLGA HAD BEEN living with Mikhail for two weeks. He had been a generous host. He had taken her out a few times to the local Brooklyn restaurants, and they had traveled to Manhattan together a couple times. She paid no rent; Mikhail took care of everything. Things were becoming a bit too intense for her, though. Despite his repeated assurances that he wanted nothing in return and was content with the platonic relationship, he was clearly hoping for sex.

Olga knew the signs. The innuendos were getting so frequent she had stopped listening. Mikhail had become physical with her a few times, too, trying to kiss her on the lips. Once he invited himself to her bedroom. It was only a question of time before hints became actions. The man was looking for a physical payment for his generosity.

Olga felt very uncomfortable. She didn't consider herself to be the type of girl who offered herself to just any man, and she understood that it was time to leave Mikhail before he moved forward with his advances. Once she started looking seriously for a room in Brooklyn, she quickly found what she was looking for. A Russian woman named Katrina had a nice, clean apartment to share, and she was looking for a new roommate.

Katarina had been in the United States for only a few weeks. Sharing an apartment would give them the chance to explore the city together and become friends. The apartment was just one block from Elena's old house, so Olga knew the area, and that would certainly be helpful. The price was right, too. Five hundred a month was not very expensive by Brooklyn standards.

She planned her escape from Mikhail. He kept telling her that she would need help from someone like him to succeed since she had no status in the country, and she agreed with his assessment, but she believed that he was planning to take advantage of her. One morning after he left for work, she packed her bags and left. She left a short note to thank him. She did not leave her new address.

After Olga had been at her new home for a day, already things seemed to be looking up. She now had a clean room in a nice apartment with friendly people. Katarina was a quiet girl from Saint Petersburg who had traveled to New York to study accounting. The landlord was a gay Turkish man in his midforties who had no sexual expectations of his two young tenants.

Olga had worked out a budget based on her remaining funds and figured that her money would last for at least ten weeks. Nevertheless, she intended to start looking for work to build up a financial cushion. She was certain she could find some work in one of the local Brooklyn restaurants. After all, she had worked in the best Krasnoyarsk restaurants as a server.

Two days later Olga found an Internet café from which she could send e-mails back home. She wrote a quick message to her mother to let her know things were going well. She wanted to write to the Frenchman, but she decided to follow her mother's advice and ignore François. She kept in touch with her husband in case she needed more money. In her e-mail to Vladimir, she said she loved him, although she knew they were empty, fake words as she wrote them.

After e-mailing she walked down Emmons Avenue to look for work as a server in one of the many restaurants there. She started first at Liman, the Turkish restaurant where she had met Mikhail. With luck that could be her only stop.

Luck, however, was not with her that day. Although Olga stopped into about ten restaurants, and all of them agreed that she was highly qualified, none of them would hire her without papers. *Papers.* The word haunted her every time she heard it. She understood after that first day that finding work in America without papers would be a major undertaking.

By midafternoon, she decided to return to the Internet café to search the local Russian ads. She had found her room using a local site, and she assumed that the site also had job ads. She soon found a few server positions, one of which described itself as an upscale bar looking for beautiful women to serve drinks. It said that no experience was required; reading between the lines, Olga took that to mean that they would consider people without work visas. That seemed like a perfect fit. She found a few more interesting job possibilities and wrote down the contact information so she could call from her room later that day.

At the apartment, she went directly to her room to make the calls. Katarina was still at school and wouldn't return for another hour. Olga called the first number, and someone picked up after a few rings.

"My name is Olga. I'm calling about your ad in *Rusrek* for a server job," she said in English.

"You speak Russian?" the man asked.

"Yes," Olga replied in Russian.

"Do you have papers?" the man asked in Russian.

"I don't," she replied.

"Well, that's not really an issue for us."

Olga was surprised. "Great."

"Have you worked as a server before?"

"I worked as a server in some of the best restaurants in Krasnoyarsk, in Siberia, including the Suleyman."

"Good. How tall are you? Tell me your weight and hair color. We need attractive women here."

"Well, I am one hundred seventy-three centimeters, fifty-five kilos, and I am a blonde. I am told I am beautiful."

"Okay, so you're about five eight and about one hundred twenty pounds. Thin. Good. Can you come tonight? I may have a job for you."

"Yes, of course."

"Okay. A beautiful woman can make more than two thousand a week here, easy. The work is not so hard. You serve alcohol. I will explain more when I see you. You just have to work at least four days a week. Are you interested?"

Olga replied with enthusiasm. "Yes."

"It's four twenty now. Can you be here by six o'clock? We are in Brooklyn. I'll give you the address. What's your name again?"

"Olga."

"Okay. Ask for me when you come. My name is Mark. I'll give you money for your taxi. One hundred dollars. Is that okay?"

"Of course."

She wrote down the address. She was happy to have been offered a chance to work after just her first call. She went to the bathroom to get ready, taking time to redo her makeup and hair to look stellar for her interview. She removed the jeans she had worn all day and opened the minuscule closet choose a dress. Katarina had set aside a small space where she was able to hang six of her best dresses. She settled on a tight, black top and a red skirt that had been one of François's favorites. After putting it on, she walked back to the bathroom and looked at herself in the small mirror. *I look fabulous,* she thought. *Things will be just fine.*

21

LENNY

VANESSA HAD BEEN gone for more than two weeks, yet Robert barely thought about her anymore. He found that he didn't really miss her. He had spent a few nights with Irina and he enjoyed her accompany. She was sexy, sufficiently intelligent, and very affectionate. Robert had replaced Vanessa with Irina.

On Saturday as he was getting ready to go to the gym, he picked up his BlackBerry on his way to the bathroom to check his e-mails. He had received one from Vanessa.

> Hi, Robert,
> My mother is still recuperating. I am not in state of
> mind to decide what to do for myself at this point.
> I will stay here longer. I am not sure where we are
> as a couple, but I think you should not wait for me.
> Vanessa

The message surprised him. *Had she she found out about Irina or was it a lucky coincidence?* He felt free. *That takes care of that.* He didn't feel anything. He headed to the gym as if nothing happened. He would meet Irina as planned for brunch.

JOHN WALKED INTO Robert's office Tuesday morning. "Any plans for lunch today?"

"No. Why?"

"Lenny just called, and he wants to meet with me to discuss his portfolio. He's been looking to diversify, and I'd like it if you could come with us to talk about foreign currencies," said John. "I think he's willing to take some risks. This could be a very good addition for us."

"Great. What time?"

"We're meeting at the Waldorf at twelve thirty."

The two men walked from the office to the hotel. As he approached the host of the hotel restaurant, John indicated Lenny at a nearby table with a subtle nod of his head to Robert. Robert tightened his tie and buttoned his jacket before he and John approached the client's table. Lenny got up to greet his two guests.

"Lenny, let me introduce Robert Thompson—one of the best FX traders in New York," said John.

Robert shook hands with the old man. "Nice to meet you. I've heard a lot about you."

"Only good things, I hope," said Lenny, and the three men sat down.

Lenny, just past sixty, was short but gave an impression of power. Unlike many men his age, he had a full head of hair, white and professionally styled. He wore round, tinted glasses with heavy, brown-spotted, plastic frames that, combined with his white pencil moustache, gave him an artistic look; he could have easily passed for the creative director of a theater company. He dressed impeccably. His navy pinstripe suit fit him perfectly, accentuating his broad shoulders and effectively hiding his expanding middle section. A red silk tie, precisely knotted, bisected the front of his flawlessly pressed, custom-tailored white shirt. His black wing tip shoes shone like polished marble.

At Lenny's request, Robert began with an overview of his background, skipping quickly past his childhood to his Harvard credentials, his experience in Boston, and his stellar performance in recent years. He ended by mentioning his recent move to New York, which prompted a few questions from Lenny.

"How do you like the city?"

"I'm really enjoying myself. I've met some great people, and of course there is always so much going on, so much to do," said Robert. "It's a great city."

"I've heard that you know how to find a good party," Lenny said, winking at John.

Robert hesitated. "Yes, John has been very helpful in that department."

Lenny said, "Please take a look at the menu. We'll order before we talk business."

After the waiter left the table, John led the discussion, explaining that Lenny was looking to leverage some of his assets and put them to work in high-risk, high-return investments. On cue, Robert replied that foreign currency trading fit that profile exactly, and offered a quick overview before the salads arrived. He delved into greater detail over their entrées, and by the time they ordered coffee, Lenny was nodding and smiling.

"Well, this seems very promising. John will work with my team, and we'll put two to work. Robert, I'll be looking for you to manage this— and, as you said, to create wealth."

Robert was not quite sure what Lenny meant by two. *Two thousand...too small. Two hundred thousand? Possible. Two million? Could he have meant two million?*

"I'll text Conrad about the meeting," said Lenny, sipping his espresso. "By the way, John tells me you are a man of great discretion."

Robert answered quickly, "Of course."

"As you might have guessed, I relish the benefits of privacy. I have never enjoyed the spotlight. That is very important to me."

Robert listened, not understanding why the older man was stating what should have been obvious. *Confidentiality agreements bind interactions with all my clients,* he almost said. Just before he spoke, it dawned on him that Lenny was not talking about business.

"I'm having a private event this Sunday at my home—a small gathering with a few friends. I wondered if you'd like to join us? John, you are welcome, too."

Robert hesitated, but curiosity took over. "I'd be honored."

John looked genuinely crushed. "Damn. I'm away at the Vineyard this weekend."

"I see. Robert, I'll have my assistant put you on the guest list. John, another time, absolutely," said Lenny. "Well, you gentlemen will have to excuse me now. John, this is on me," he said, reaching slowly for the tab.

"No, on me this time," John said, covering the tab before Lenny's manicured hand was halfway to the table. It was clear to Robert that the choreography had been perfected over years of practice.

Lenny excused himself and left the table with a nod to both men. When he was out of earshot, Robert leaned close to John and whispered, "What just happened? What's two? Two hundred thousand?"

John laughed. "Two hundred million."

Robert took a deep breath. "Two hundred million...wow. John, this is...wow."

"I know. He obviously likes you. We're both going to make a lot of money with this. Lots of money."

"I knew he was wealthy, but I had no idea," said Robert. "So, this 'private event' on Sunday...that's one of those parties you told me about? With the women?"

"That's how I know the guy likes you. Of course, I told him he could trust you, but even I don't have that kind of power. Lenny makes up his own mind about people, and once he does..." John grinned. "One thing, though. You can't tell Stephen you got invited the party. In fact, you can't tell anyone, but especially Stephen. It would kill him. He's been trying to get in, but it just hasn't happened." John shrugged.

"Got it."

Robert sat back in his chair, smiled and thought, *I misjudged him. I guess John is a good guy after all.*

22

THE NIGHTCLUB

OLGA ARRIVED AT work that afternoon as she had every afternoon for the past week. It hadn't gotten any easier. She still felt very uncomfortable each time she walked into the club, knowing what was coming. She was a proud woman, but the lure of quick money was too appealing, so she was determined to stay as long as it remained tolerable—providing the money improved. She had worked five days in the past week and made only a few hundred dollars—far from the thousands Mark had promised.

She walked into the poorly lit club. The disco balls and Christmas lights hanging off the dark ceiling were the only sources of lighting. The cleaning crew was finishing up, and there was still a residual smell of bleach in the air. She entered the dressing room. Two Russians and two Poles were already there getting ready for the evening crowd. Like Olga, the women had been lured by promises of quick, easy money. She sat down near her small locker in silence to change into the small bikini that Mark had sold her. She turned around so the other girls would not see her naked. As she put on her five-inch pumps, the DJ started his set. Mark would come soon to call the girls out as the first clients arrived. Olga sat on the small couch in a corner, making small talk with Dinara, her only friend at the club.

Mark came in after fifteen minutes. "Ready ladies? We have a few nice clients waiting for you."

Olga stayed seated as the four other girls slowly walked out. She was not very enthusiastic about meeting these nice clients. Mark grabbed the arm of one of the Russian girls and whispered in Russian. "Anastasia, remember I told you about the important client in Manhattan? Well, he's having a party this Sunday. You're going!"

Anastasia replied, "Okay."

"As we agreed, I get half. And I know how much he pays, so don't try to fuck with me, bitch, or else I will get you fuckin' deported. Clear?" He squeezed her arm hard enough to hurt her.

"Yes. Clear."

Anastasia walked out. Olga finally got up. Mark looked at her and said, "Princess, you could make more money, you know, if you weren't so fuckin' cold with the customers. This is a fuckin' strip club, not a fancy restaurant. Men don't come here for the snacks. They come here to be *entertained*. You need to let 'em get closer, ya know? Like Anastasia does. Now go out there and fuckin' work for once."

Olga slowly walked out of the dressing area. She watched Anastasia and understood what kind of party Mark was probably talking about. Anastasia was from Uzbekistan—an eastern republic and a landlocked Muslim country near Afghanistan and Iran. The young woman was an unsophisticated country girl with poor manners, yet she clearly understood the rules of the game at the club, and earned the handsome tips to prove it. A dark-haired beauty and a very petite woman—she stood only about five feet six in her tallest pumps— she had small but perfectly shaped breasts and a tight little ass. The white lingerie she always wore to perform seemed to glow against her tanned skin.

Anastasia was the most provocative woman in the club, and the most aggressive. Like a wildcat on the hunt, she stalked and snared the men who clearly needed attention and were willing to pay for it. She preferred bland, even unappealing men, as they were more easily captured by her charms. She purred at them, convincing them to pay for one short dance.

"Just one, baby. Just one," she teased them, all night long. Once she had a willing victim, she played with him slowly, touching him ever so slightly as she gyrated before him. Then, just as the dance came to an end, she went in for the kill. She slid her hands all around the client, ending finally by grabbing his hand and moving it slowly across her breasts, and then pulling away. The clients always succumbed, wanting more, and before long they would retreat to one of the VIP rooms, where she would give him anything he wanted, including herself.

Olga despised the girl and everything she represented. She did not understand how the Uzbek could be so brazen. Olga preferred to take a very passive approach, and she was determined to keep it that way. She waited for customers to approach her. Only then would she encourage them to buy drinks and, occasionally, a table dance. She never accepted an invitation to the VIP room.

The club grew crowded. Olga remained seated at the bar, watching the other four girls attend to the clients. A few men approached her, but when she showed no interest in talking to them, the clients moved on to the other girls. Olga had been by herself for about an hour when a man sat beside her. He looked different from the typical club patrons, who were usually blue-collar types looking for some quick amusement before going back home to their wives. This one wore a nice suit and a tie. It was refreshing to smell cologne rather than beer and stale sweat.

"Mind if I sit here?" he asked. She didn't reply, but he sat down anyway. After a few minutes he said, "Can I buy you a drink?" he asked.

"Yes," she said. This would earn her a small tip from the bartender.

"Is it okay if I sit here?" he repeated.

"Maybe."

The man smiled. The bartender came over and took the order—a Coke for her and a beer for him. "You don't look as if you belong here."

"I really don't," Olga said.

He chuckled. "I like that. So, what's your story? I mean, where *do* you belong? I'm sorry—maybe that's too personal. I'm Edward, by the way. Ed. What's your name?"

"Olga."

"Olga. Russian, *da*?"

"*Da*."

"I also speak Russian. I've been over here for a few years now."

Olga felt comfortable with Ed, who was respectful and seemed classy, like a gentleman. In the short time they had been talking, he had kept his distance. He didn't try to grope or kiss her, which was something most men in the club felt entitled to do the moment they bought her a drink.

"I was here last fall, and everything was wonderful. This time, nothing is the same," said Olga. The loneliness of the past week came flooding out. She told him her story since landing in New York—the disgusting lodgings, her stolen money, the former hockey player who wanted to trade favors, and now this, the strip club, where drunken clients pawed every night.

Edward listened attentively. "I may be able to help you. I have a lot of connections in Brooklyn and Manhattan. Perhaps if you give me your number, I can take you out for dinner this week."

"That would be wonderful. I don't think I can work here much longer."

"Olga, I think tonight should be your last night here. I'm sure I can help you find something. How about we have dinner tomorrow night?"

"Okay," she said. She started giggling with relief. She discreetly slipped her phone number to her new friend. After he left, she stayed at the bar, ignoring all the clients who tried to talk to her. Mark noticed her lack of attention to customers and approached her.

"You're here to take care of the clients. That's your fuckin' job."

Olga answered angrily, "I don't like that job."

Mark glowered at her. "You don't like the job, then get the fuck out!"

"I will." Olga slid off the stool and walked off to the dressing room. Anastasia was cleaning herself up after another visit to the VIP room. She looked at Olga.

"Too hard for you, little Siberian princess?"

Olga was fuming, but she held back. She wanted to tell Anastasia exactly what she thought of her, and so many words filled her head—whore, slut, bitch. Instead, she just went to her locker and put her street clothes on. As she left the room, however, she couldn't resist. She turned and said to the Uzbek, "The difference between you and me is that no matter our circumstances, you will always be a whore, and I will always be a princess."

Olga quickly left the dressing room. She was proud she had confronted Anastasia and happy that she had found a way out of the rathole before it was too late. She walked past Mark, looked at him with disdain, and left the club, head held high. She vowed to never go back to a place like that.

23

SUNDAY PARTY

ROBERT HAD BEEN fantasizing about Lenny's party ever since he received the formal invitation via e-mail from Lenny's assistant. The invitation was short:

> *McLaughlin residence, 106 E 57 St., Unit PH, 7p, Sunday, May 27. Guests are expected to be on time.*

McLaughlin was the other founder of the Lenny's firm, the famous McLaughlin and Rothstein, or M&R, as everyone in the business knew it. Robert knew that the gathering would certainly be interesting: two of the wealthiest men in New York were throwing a secret party. He would soon find out whether what he'd heard about the Sunday parties was true.

On Sunday, Robert took a cab so that he would arrive freshly showered and on time. He wore a new charcoal Dolce & Gabbana suit he'd bought just for the occasion, along with a black silk shirt and tie. He added a red pocket square for a dash of color.

He arrived at the building. "Robert Thompson to see Mr. McLaughlin."

The man held out his hand. "ID please?" Robert handed the guard his driver's license and waited while the man checked it against a list.

The man returned the license and said, "Please use the express elevator. Someone will escort you."

Robert walked to the elevator where a man in a black suit ushered Robert into the car and stepped in after him. Inserting a card into the PH slot, the man spoke a few words into his sleeve. "Coming up. One." Then he stepped back out into the foyer.

Robert rode up to the penthouse alone. When the doors opened, a young woman in a short black dress greeted him. "Robert Thompson, I assume. Let me take you to Mr. Rothstein."

She led Robert through a long hallway that opened onto a living room. The room was vast, especially by New York standards. The furniture was sparsely distributed in the room, creating the impression that the room was nearly empty. The centerpiece of the room was a large C-shaped couch of bright red leather; everything else in the room was white. A quick count of the white pillows suggested that the leather sofa could easily seat more than fifteen people. Floor-to-ceiling windows framed a great view of the city.

A few guests were assembled near Lenny, who stood by the windows. The woman left Robert in the living room and walked away.

Lenny greeted him. "Robert, glad you could make it. Let me introduce my partner, Kevin McLaughlin." Lenny said to Kevin, "This is the young man I was telling to you about." Lenny turned to Robert again. "Robert, this is another business partner of mine, Bill Connors."

Robert shook hands with both men.

Kevin said, "Robert, it's nice to meet you. I don't want to talk business tonight, but let's have lunch in the next week or so. If you can help Lenny, I am sure you can do the same for me."

Robert knew McLaughlin by name, and he knew that he and Lenny had founded a very successful leverage buyout firm. M&R had made both men very wealthy. The prospect of getting another whale, as very wealthy clients were known in the business, was appealing. It could only raise his already-high stature at his firm.

Like Lenny, Kevin was about sixty, but he looked younger. He was very fit and tanned. The third man, Connors, was in his midthirties and about six feet tall. His athletic build was evident under his tailored suit. Like the other two men, he was impeccably dressed.

Another guest arrived slightly after seven. He looked similar to Bill Connors, like another reproduction Greek statue from the same classic mold—Caucasian male, early thirties, tall, athletic, square jawed, and perfectly dressed and coiffed. When he came closer, Robert recognized him as William Peterson III, his Harvard nemesis. The two had met at business school and clashed immediately. Peterson was an obnoxious braggart who enjoyed flaunting his privileges and wealth. His upbringing had been the exact opposite of Robert's, but both were very competitive. Peterson never stopped trying to prove that he was smarter, wealthier, and in all ways better than Robert.

Peterson walked up to Robert. "Well, small world. I never expected you to make it out of Boston."

"Hello, William. Yes, I made it out of Boston all on my own. Unlike some people."

Peterson sneered. "You always were a lucky SOB. Did I hear that you work for that little boutique firm Charley runs? Cute little shop. I'm at First National, of course." Peterson was as arrogant and conceited as always. Robert said nothing. "Here's my card. You know, in case you need a job. I could always use another assistant. If you'll excuse me, I must go see Lenny." William walked away.

Asshole, Robert thought. *First National fits him well.* It was the largest investment bank in New York and where everyone in business school dreamed of working. If there was a group who considered themselves masters of the universe, it was the people of FN.

It seemed as if Lenny had invited only business associates to this particular party. He saw five men and one woman, and all of them looked like they just stepped out of a boardroom. *This is a wild party?* He would have been disappointed except that he had already made some interesting business connections already, including meeting Kevin McLaughlin. And it was easy enough to ignore William.

Robert had been speaking with Bill Connors for about thirty minutes when the lights dimmed just slightly. At the same time, the background music became a bit louder—dance music. At eight o'clock, a young woman in a little black entered the living room carrying a bottle of champagne, an ice bucket, and a few glasses. She served the five men. Three more women followed. There was a brunette in a white dress, a blonde in a black dress, and a second blonde in a white dress. Their dresses were all short, tight, and barely covering the women's bodies. Lenny coughed politely for attention and then said, "Welcome dear friends. Please, enjoy the evening."

The music became noticeably louder. It was loud enough to feel its rhythm, but it was still not overbearing. The shades of the panoramic windows moved down the tracks, hiding the view of the city and isolating the room from the rest of the world. The server disappeared. Two women approached the two younger men, and the third walked over to Lenny and Kevin. Robert observed the scene as if he was not in the room.

Lenny noticed Robert and walked up to his guest. "Robert, are you enjoying yourself so far?"

"Yes, thank you," Robert replied.

"My friend, are you interested in the little brunette with the piercing blue eyes? The one talking to Kevin?"

Robert said, "Yes, she is very attractive."

All of the women, including the server, were extremely sexy and thin like models. Robert checked out the girl Lenny mentioned, a small-framed dark brunette, perhaps five feet two without heels.

"She is a new guest. I am told she can be very wild. She comes from one of those post-Soviet republics. Uzbekistan, I believe. She has a lovely name: Anastasia. I like how it rolls off the tongue. Perhaps you should taste her first."

The conversation made Robert uncomfortable. Lenny pointed to the young woman and asked her, with a gesture of his finger, to come over. She obliged and walked over to the two men.

"Anastasia, can you take good care of my friend, Robert?"

"Of course, Mr. Rothstein," she replied with a heavy accent.

"Anastasia, please. Call me Lenny. 'Mr. Rothstein' makes me sound like an old man, and I am far from that," he said in a friendly way.

"No, and you are still very beautiful."

Lenny left Anastasia alone with Robert. She said with her heavy Russian accent, "It is a pleasure to meet you, Robert."

Robert had no idea what to say. "So, how long have you known Lenny and Kevin?"

"I do not know them. My friend knows them," said Anastasia. "He arranged for me to invited to the party. Lenny likes Russian women, and I like American men. It's a good combination."

"I see. And the other girls?"

"Yuliana works with me. The other girl, Nadia, I do not know."

"Yuliana?" He smiled. "Which one is she?"

"In the red dress."

Robert noticed one of the blondes pulling William out of the room. "I think your friend Yuliana is kidnapping someone," Robert commented.

"Yuliana always wants to have fun," Anastasia replied.

"Fun?" Robert said mischievously.

"Yes. Fun," she replied with a wink. "Perhaps you would like to have fun with me?"

"Perhaps." Robert smiled.

Anastasia looked around the room and said, "Your friend is all alone."

Robert saw that Kevin, too, had disappeared. Only left Lenny, Bill, and Anastasia were in the room with him.

"Yes, the party seems to be shrinking."

"Maybe your friend would like to have some fun, too?"

Robert didn't reply, and the woman took that as a positive answer. She grabbed Robert's hand and led him over to Bill Connors. Anastasia asked Bill if he wanted to join them.

Bill responded without hesitation. "Of course."

Anastasia took the hands of the two men and led them both to another room. She clearly knew where she was going.

⨯⨯⨯

THE PARTY ENDED at just past two in the morning. William Peterson and Bill Connors had just left, followed by the two blondes. Robert, exhausted after three trips to the bedroom, walked over to Lenny and Kevin to say his farewells as all of the other guests had done. He thanked Lenny and Kevin and kissed Anastasia on the cheek.

"It was nice meeting you," Robert said to Anastasia.

She put a card in his pocket. "This is my number. You're a great lover. I would like to see you again."

Robert smiled turned toward the door. Lenny said, "Let me walk you out."

As they left the living room, Lenny reiterated the obvious. "Robert, you're now part of my circle. This privilege comes with great responsibilities. I hope you had a great time tonight and that I can count on your discretion."

"Absolutely. You can count on me."

Lenny grabbed Robert's hand firmly. Robert took the handshake as a confirmation that Lenny wanted nothing about the night to ever be mentioned. Robert knew that the repercussions of any indiscretion on his part would be devastating. Lenny and Kevin, after all, knew all the who's who of New York. As easily as they could make him, they could break him, and totally destroy his career. The privilege of being associated with the two wealthy men came with risks. Just before Robert got into the elevator, Lenny said, "Robert, one thing. Be careful about Russian women, especially women like Anastasia."

Robert nodded. He'd gotten used to the fact that any encounter with Russian women generated a warning. He rode the elevator to the ground floor and walked outside to grab a taxi, thinking about the evening. He had enjoyed many sexual encounters since Vanessa left for Korea, but nothing like close to the events of that night—the threesome with Anastasia, an intimate session with the brunette, and a threesome with the two blondes. He couldn't believe it had all happened in one night. He couldn't stop thinking about the two sessions with Anastasia. He remembered what Stephen had told him about Lenny paying the women to come. It was clear she was more than a server. Robert had never had sex with a prostitute, and he had mixed feelings about it.

―⦿―

THE NEXT DAY was Monday, and that meant another evening session with Carl. Despite Lenny's request, Robert needed to talk about the events of the weekend with someone,. He had experienced so many feelings during and after the evening as his feelings of pleasure had slowly been tainted by remorse. Lust had turned to guilt, and happiness had changed to sadness.

"Robert, how are you? How was your week?"

Robert smiled and took a few moments. "The week was fine, and I had a good weekend. I went to a party. A very different kind of party. A…a swingers' party," he said, looking out the small window. "It was like a movie. I participated along with everyone else there. The girls were all so beautiful, but I think…no, I know that they were paid to be there."

Robert paused and waited for Carl to speak. His question was as expected. "And how do you feel about all that?"

"I think I liked it, but I'm not sure I would do it again. When I got back home, I felt disgusted. It was so primal. So emotionless. Fucking for fucking," he said. "And the girls…I don't know. They act like they enjoy it, but I'm pretty sure they were only doing it for the money. Nothing else."

"How did you feel about the women at first? And did those feelings change after you realized they might be prostitutes?"

As usual, Carl had zeroed in on exactly what was troubling him. Robert thought about the women's behavior. He had always thought of prostitution as a system in which male pimps exploited young, vulnerable women for their own economic gain. But these three women had not fit into that image somehow. Anastasia especially seemed to actually enjoy the sex, including the threesome, and Robert was confused.

"I always thought that prostitutes were, I don't know, *forced* into it. Now I'm not sure. Why would a woman want to have meaningless sex?" he asked.

The therapist said, "Why would a man?"

Robert sat back in his chair. "I guess it depends on the people…and if there's money changing hands, on who's paying and who's earning."

"People become sex workers for many different reasons. Traditionally it was thought that those who did out of choice were more likely to have been abused in the past and, as a result, to suffer from poor self-esteem. Some researchers assert that many female sex workers actually hate men, and become prostitutes as a way to control them, consciously or subconsciously. Other researchers take that a step further and say that there really is no such thing as 'choosing' to be a sex worker—that bad experiences, unfortunate circumstances, and lack of choices make it inevitable for some people."

"And what do you think, Carl?"

"I think it's like many professions: some people choose it, some people fall into it, and others are forced into it. No matter what, however, I think it's a mistake to think of what they do as 'meaningless' sex," said Carl. "It may not be about romance, attachment, or personal connection, but it means *something*. You said the women you met seemed to enjoy it, and I think the operative word there is 'seemed.' Sex can be a very powerful tool, and when the amount sex workers get paid depends on how much they appear to enjoy what they're doing, you must realize that what you're seeing might not be genuine pleasure but superb acting skills."

For the rest of the session, Carl tried to focus on Robert's negative feelings after the event, trying to seek out the trigger of the remorse, guilt, and sadness. The session came to an end without a clear resolution. Carl asked Robert to think about what made sex meaningful to him, or meaningless, and about the progression of his feelings from before the party to the aftermath.

After Robert left, Carl made his usual notes about the session. Most men saw sex as a form of pleasure, yet part of emotional maturity was understanding the importance of balancing that physical pleasure with true intimacy—emotional connection. Robert had experienced what he called meaningless sex, and though the experience had been physically satisfying, the emotional aftermath had not.

Carl was not at all surprised. He knew that much of Robert's distress could once again be traced to his childhood with the abusive father and his mother's way of reclaiming her independence through serial dating rather than forming close attachments. She had trust issues of her own. And Robert might possibly be fixating on these questions about the possible exploitation of the sex workers because of some echoes from the mistreatment of his mother in the past. Robert had trouble with loss and abandonment. Did he see the women as kindred souls, lost and abandoned? Or did he see them as a way to exert his own power?

ROBERT FOUND ANASTASIA'S number in his pocket. She had written it on the back of Lenny's business card, and made him promise to call her. *Maybe I should,* he thought. *The sex was really, really good.* He felt the vibration of his BlackBerry and checked for new text messages.

> Irina: Baby, will I see you later tonight?
> Miss you soooo much. xoxoxo.
> Robert: Irina, baby, going home after
> long meeting…need to shower and
> change. Mari Vana later tonight? 9p?
> Irina: Da!

He held the business card with Anastasia's number. Vanessa. Irina. Anastasia. *I love New York.*

24

EDWARD

EDWARD TOOK OLGA to a sushi restaurant in Manhattan for dinner. He had not been able to find her work, but he had given her three or four hundred dollars every time they met. This was the fourth time in a week. She enjoyed spending time with him.

"Well, I could take you to my apartment, but it's still being renovated. I know a nice place where we can go."

"Okay," she replied.

He drove to Manhattan Beach in Brooklyn. "Come. I want to show you something," he said.

They both got out of the car and walked about fifty feet until they got to the beach.

"Isn't it beautiful?" he said.

"Yes, but though it is a bit chilly."

"You're right. Let's sit in the car." He opened the back door on the passenger side of the four-door sedan. She climbed in and he closed the door behind her, then walked around and got into the backseat on the other side. "Warmer?"

"Yes, thank you."

"Have you ever done it in a car?" he asked.

"No," she replied.

He started kissing her. "Let's do it here."

After the relatively short session, they dressed and returned to Olga's apartment. Edward was usually talkative, but for once he didn't have much to say. Olga was also lost in her thoughts. He parked in front of her apartment.

"I had a lot of fun tonight," Edward said. "It was exciting to do it in the car."

"Yes." Olga sounded unconvinced. "Thank you. Ed, I have to ask you something. I need to buy something on the Internet, but I don't have a credit card. I hate to ask, but I wonder if maybe you can buy it for me."

"Well, maybe. What is it?"

"I hate to trouble you. You could just give me your card number, and I could order it myself."

A flicker of surprise crossed his face. "My credit card number… Can I trust you?"

Looking somewhat offended, Olga replied, "Of course! I'm a proud woman. I will pay you back later."

"Okay, then. Let me write it down," he said reluctantly. "Text me when you have the amount, so I know how much it is."

"Oh, thank you so much." She kissed him on the lips. "I will go to the Internet café tomorrow morning. The cost is about one hundred fifty dollars, but I will tell you the exact amount after I place the order."

"I called my friend about finding work for you, but he has not gotten back to me yet."

"Thank you. You have been so good to me! I'll talk to you later," she said. She stepped out of the car and blew him a kiss as she walked up the steps to the apartment. She wasn't sure how she felt about Edward anymore. He had been good to her, but something did not feel right. He had told her that he was a highly successful businessperson, yet he drove a Honda Accord, a very common car. He could never see her on weekends, and he never invited her to his place. He had not found her work as he had promised, yet he continued to say that he was a well-connected man. She liked that he took her out to nice restaurants and helped her out financially, but she had not found much else to like about him.

NOT LONG AFTER the evening at the beach, Edward came to pick up Olga at seven o'clock and they went to a restaurant in Queens. It was far from Brighton Beach, where they both lived, but Edward explained that he wanted to show her the real New York. The restaurant was nice but nothing luxurious, not like the fancy ones in Manhattan he had taken her to on a few occasions.

"Do you like this place?" he asked.

"It is nice of you to take me out to nice restaurants, but I hope that you can invite me to your place soon. I would like to see it. Is it close to being finished?"

"Actually, it's taking more time than I thought. The Italian marble is not here yet, so the kitchen is still a big mess. I have to live with one of my friends."

"Well, that's fine, but I don't want to do it in the car again. We have been there three times now. Maybe we can go to a nice hotel." Olga was determined to ask him for a few more favors.

"That's a great idea. Maybe tonight," he said, smiling.

"Maybe." She smiled back. "I really need a computer. It's getting difficult for me to talk to my parents. They are worried. I could talk to my mother every day if I had a computer at home."

"Hmm," he replied. "Do you know how much it costs?"

"I found one when I was at the Internet café. A nice red laptop."

"How much is it?"

"It is about two thousand two hundred dollars," Olga said carefully. "But it's exactly what I want."

"Olga, that's a bit difficult for me right now. My renovation is costing me a lot of money. You will have to wait."

"I can't wait for too long. You make a lot of promises—work, travel, moving in together. Nothing is happening, though. If you can't help me, I have to find another way. I need to find work."

"Okay, I'll see what I can do."

"Okay."

They started eating, but the conversation had put a damper on things. Dinner was unusually quiet. When they left the restaurant, Edward asked if she wanted to go somewhere else. She understood the underlying question. Should we go somewhere and have sex? She was in no mood to give him anything he wanted that night. She asked him to drive her home.

"Next time. Promise," she told him.

Edward was a nice man, but he meant nothing to her if he couldn't follow through. She needed real help, not empty talk. He had made a lot of promises, but continued to fail to deliver. She had only planned to see him until she figured things out on her own. It seemed that might be sooner rather than later. She still had some money, but she would need to find work soon.

She went to the Internet café the next morning to look for jobs posted in the Russian ads. She checked her e-mail. Her mother had written a short note to ask once again for help. A few hundred dollars would be very helpful, she explained. She also said that Vladimir had been seen by family friends escorting another woman to some event; she was probably his new mistress. The news left Olga indifferent. She sent a short reply:

> Mama,
> Things are going well. And yes, I will
> send money as soon as possible.

She searched the ads for work. The nightclub continued to post ads on the site. *Not for me. Never again.* A spa was looking for a reception-ist, which seemed perfect to her since they were looking for Russian women. No experience was required, as training was provided. Olga wrote down the phone number and continued her search.

She called the spa as soon as she got back to her room. After a short conversation, the spa owner asked her to come to the spa on Saturday morning. *That's a good start,* she thought. She continued making calls. Some positions needed experience, and some needed papers. She needed to find a way of getting papers if she wanted to stay in the country. She remembered what Sergey from the agency had told her about marrying an American and thought of Edward. She might be able to ask him to marry her at some point, but she didn't find the thought very appealing.

Saturday was two long days away. She didn't want to stay in the small apartment, and she knew Edward would not call that night. He said he was traveling again. She wanted to go out, do something, and get out of the room. She wanted to go into the city. *Manhattan,* she thought. *I want to go to Manhattan.* She asked Katarina to accompany her. Her shy roommate hesitated, but eventually she accepted Olga's invitation.

"I'm not as beautiful and stylish as you," Katarina said.

"Let me help you. You're the same size as me. We can get ready together. We can go to a place I have been with Ed—Mari Vana. I had fun there. We need to help each other, Katarina. It is difficult in this country for people like you and me."

"I think it is difficult for everyone," said Katarina. "But you are right. It would be easier if we all helped each other. Still, I really should be studying, not partying."

"Come on! You are always studying! You never go out. This should be fun!"

"Yes, it should be."

25

THE MEETING

ROBERT HAD DECIDED to stay in for the evening. It was unusual for him to stay home alone, but Irina was not available, and Stephen and John were in Boston meeting with clients. He ordered food to be delivered from his favorite sushi place. He also ordered a few bottles of champagne. His reserve was running low. New York continuously amazed him. He could literally get anything delivered in the city; it was just a phone call away.

Perfect evening to stay in, he thought. *Good food, a few glasses of red wine, and one of my favorite movies on cable TV.* He sat down in his living room, settled in, and started watching the movie. After about twenty minutes of watching the movie, he grew restless and decided that he needed to go out. He felt uncomfortable. He wasn't lonely, but he felt the need to be surrounded by people. He couldn't stand being alone.

It was just before eight—the perfect time to go to Barbounia. He finished his glass of wine and changed to go out, then walked the few blocks to Barbounia. He knew all the staff there and most of the other regulars at the bar. Leon behind the bar gave him a sense of comfort. As expected, the bar area of the restaurant was packed on Thursday.

Great decision, Robert thought.

Leon extended his hand over the bar and shook Robert's hand. "Nice to see you again. I'll have a spot here at the bar in a few minutes, if you want to sit. I'll keep it open for you. What can I get you?"

Robert answered, "The usual."

OLGA AND KATARINA arrived in Manhattan after a ninety minutes subway ride. They got off at the station at the corner of Twenty-Third and walked down Park Avenue South towards Twentieth Street. As they turned onto Twentieth Street, they could see that the restaurant on the corner of the street was especially busy.. Olga crossed the street without hesitation. "Let's try this place."

The two women walked into a place Olga had never tried before. Barbounia was a Mediterranean restaurant that reminded her of the Suley. Olga had always been very superstitious. She welcomed anything that could be seen as a sign of good luck. *This is a good sign,* she thought.

The host greeted them and asked, "For dinner or drinks?"

Olga replied, "Drinks."

"The bar area is right there. Have a good evening."

The two women went to the bar to order. Olga asked Katarina what she wanted to drink. "I usually don't drink. Maybe I will have whatever you are having."

Olga tried to get the attention of one of the three bartenders. Leon saw the attractive blonde and walked over. Olga asked, "Can you recommend drinks for us?"

"I have a great drink with champagne. Let me prepare one, and you can tell me if you like it."

Olga signaled for two with her fingers.

Leon quickly walked down the bar a few steps and spoke to Robert, who was checking his e-mails. "Robert."

"Yes?"

Leon pointed with his head at the tall blonde. "Two hot women down there."

Robert turned and looked at the woman. She was at the other end of the bar, about twenty feet from him. Leon was right. She was very attractive: model thin, tall, and very feminine. She had hot, red lips, and she wore her pale blond hair past her shoulders. She looked taller than he was, though she was wearing very high black pumps. She wore a red and black dress, very tight from the shoulders down the waist, that showed off her small, perky breasts. The red bottom opened up to the knees. She turned toward him and glanced his way for just a few seconds.

Robert smiled at her. She looked familiar. He had the vague impression that he had seen her before, and started thinking about all the spots where he might have encountered her. Then he remembered: Lenny's masquerade party. She had taken her mask off while they were talking.

Now that Robert had the perfect reason to talk to the attractive woman, he made eye contact once again. Then he started making his way through the crowded bar toward her. He kept an eye on his target. As he approached, she and her friend were talking in Russian.

"I've been trying to remember where we met," Robert said when he finally reached her.

Olga looked at him. "We have met before?"

"Yes. Were you at a masquerade party in October? At Lenny Rothstein's party?"

"I was." Olga tried to remember the man. *One of the many bankers there, maybe,* she thought.

"I think we spoke at the bar. My name is Robert."

"Yes, Robert. Now I remember." He was handsome and well dressed, so she pretended to remember him. "I'm Olga, and this is my friend Katarina. She doesn't speak English very well."

Robert didn't care about Olga's friend. She was not as pretty as Olga. He said hi to Katarina to be polite and focused again on Olga. "I think you were visiting New York. Still visiting?"

"In October, yes. I returned to Siberia for a short time, but now I am here to stay."

"Your English is excellent, especially for someone who just arrived recently."

"Thank you. My mother was an English teacher, so I grew up reading English books and listening to English music."

"So, you learned English at a young age," he said. "Maybe you're a Russian spy?" He smiled.

"Me? A spy?" she looked frightened. "No. Why would you say such a thing?"

"I was trying to make a joke. I guess it wasn't funny. During the Cold War, people from each of our countries were taught the others' language so they could infiltrate and be spies."

She smiled politely. Robert could tell that she did not get his humor, so he changed topics quickly. "What do you do here in New York?"

Olga took a few seconds before she answered. She wanted to give the right impression. "I'm looking for a job now. I want to go to school."

"School. Interesting."

"Robert, what you do?"

"I work on Wall Street. I'm a banker." He didn't feel the need to explain to her the intricacies of foreign exchange trading.

As he pronounced the word, she remembered him from the party. He was the man who lived in the penthouse. He had given her his card, but she had lost it. She recalled what one of the Russian girls had told her. In New York City, bankers were the kings—the gods of the universe. She thought he might be a great replacement for Edward, who was less than useless.

"I see you need another drink. Shall I order us another round?" Robert said.

"Yes," Olga replied.

While Robert was talking to Olga, Katarina was really getting bored. Olga looked at her friend and said in Russian, "After this drink, we will go to Mari Vana. Okay?" Katarina shrugged.

Robert and Olga continued talking for another ten minutes, and then Olga told him they were leaving. Robert said, "Please. Give me your phone number."

"Perhaps you can give me your business card instead," Olga said.

Surprised, Robert pulled out his wallet to oblige. He gave his BlackBerry to Olga and said, "Here is my card, but you need to give me your phone number. Please." Robert thought about his upcoming obligations—Irina on Friday, Anastasia on Saturday. "Maybe we can meet on Monday. Mari Vana down the street is usually fun on Monday."

She typed in her number. "Yes. I like Mari Vana. I have been there before, though. Maybe you can take me somewhere else."

"Okay, I will."

"It was nice seeing you again, Robert," said Olga, handing him back his phone.

"Likewise. Until Monday night, then?"

Olga told Katarina in Russian, "He's a handsome banker. I will text him for sure."

Olga was happy with the thought she would be upgrading soon from a cheap man with a Honda Accord to a handsome banker with a penthouse.

26

THE SPA

OLGA SET UP an interview at the spa on Saturday morning. After many phone calls, she had understood that finding any legitimate work without the proper papers would be nearly impossible, but she believed that the receptionist job would be a great start.

It was a warm, spring day, and Brooklyn residents descended in masses to Kings Highway, the busiest shopping area of the borough. Mothers walked with kids in tow to get their groceries, young women wandered in and out of clothing stores in search of the latest fashions, men stopped by the barbershops, and elderly folks slowly strolled the sidewalk in search of bargains.

Olga got out of the taxi and joined the crowd on the busy street. She was early for her eleven o'clock interview, so she decided to do some window-shopping a few blocks away from the spa. She spotted Edward coming out of a store across the street. As she was about to wave to him, she saw that he wasn't alone. He had a woman and two children with him. Edward took one of the two kids in his arms. Olga was shocked. Edward was married with kids. Everything became clear—the business trips, the apartment renovation, and the out-of-the-way restaurants. She quickly turned around before he saw her and headed to her interview. She was fuming and felt cheated. She had been taken advantage of. She could not trust anyone in this country. *He will pay for this*, she thought. *I will make him pay.*

After a ten-minute walk, she found the spa in a small apartment building. As the manager had told her, the spa sign was barely visible from the street. A minuscule sign reading "Little Moscow Spa and Bathhouse" hung on the door. Olga took a couple of deep breaths to regain her calm, and then opened the door. An older woman greeted her.

"Can I help you?" the woman asked in Russian.

"I am here to see Boris, the manager," Olga replied, also in Russian.

"One moment." The woman left the reception area.

The reception area looked like a doctor's office. Six chairs were pushed against the wall, and popular Russian and US magazines covered a small, square coffee table. Olga took a seat. It was simple but clean.

Boris came out after a few minutes. He was a typical Russian man. He had an Eastern European round head, and he was short and bald. He wore a dark sweater tightly wrapped around his strong belly.

He shook her hand. "Olga, nice to meet you. Let's go to my office."

As they walked down the short hallway, Boris said, "I will show you around in a few minutes. We have three floors. The first two have the massage and spa center. The basement has the *banya*—the Russian bath."

Boris walked into the office and asked Olga a few questions.

"As you can see, I can't have an old woman at the reception desk. Most of our customers are men, and it's better to have an attractive woman there."

Olga took this as a compliment, but she wondered what exactly would be expected of this "attractive woman."

Boris continued to explain how things worked at the spa, as if she had already been hired for the position. He discussed the money and her schedule.

"So, are you interested?"

"Yes, of course," she replied. She wondered why he did not ask questions about her work status.

"You will start Tuesday at 6:00 p.m. and your shift will end at 1:00 a.m., okay?" She nodded. "I'll introduce you to Alina. She will help you here at the desk, just as you'll need to help out in the back occasionally as needed."

Boris led her to a locker room. There, he introduced Olga to another young woman. "Alina, this is Olga. Can you show her some of the things she will need to do? The towels. The table. Everything."

Alina was short and curvy, with large breasts, a small waist, and a round butt. She got up and walked with Olga around the spa, giving her a more detailed tour. Alina explained that she was originally from Moscow but that she had moved to Israel in the late nineties during the Russian emigration. She had come to the United States as a student and decided to stay. Like Olga, she was not authorized to work in America, so the spa was a good place for them. After her long monologue, Alina asked, "Where do you live now?"

"I live in Brighton Beach," Olga replied.

"A room? Shared or alone?"

"A shared room. Very small."

"I'm asking because one of our roommates is moving out. I live with two other girls in a big, three-bedroom apartment. The rent is seven hundred fifty dollars a month. It's very clean. We need a third roommate right away."

"Maybe... I can move any time I want, so if it's nicer..."

"It's very nice. Maybe you could move next Saturday? It is the last day of May. You can start June with us."

"If it is very close by, I will trust you. I don't need to see it, and Monday would be perfect."

Olga walked out of the spa smiling. She could not believe it. She got the receptionist job without any papers. The pay was not great— only ten dollars an hour—but she could make more from the tips that customers regularly left. She had also found a new place to live that sounded much better than her minuscule room, and was very close to her new job. As she walked to the subway station, she thought about Robert the banker. She also knew exactly how to get back at Edward. She had a perfect plan. The vengeance would be complete.

27

THE FIRST DATE

Robert finished work and headed to Carl's office. He had been seeing his therapist for close to six months, and he was starting to wonder if there was anything left to talk about. It had now been close to one year since he left Nicki, and he was doing fine.

"Robert, how are you?" Carl asked.

"Doing fine. Busy at work. Good busy."

Carl asked, "What about relationships?"

Robert said, "I'm dating."

"Anyone special? I know you liked Vanessa. Any news from her?"

"I ran into her in SoHo. She's back in New York. I was with a friend for brunch. She looked great."

"How did you feel about seeing her?"

"I was happy to see her, but nothing more than that." He paused for a few seconds. "She told me that I had changed."

"What made her say that?"

"I'm not really sure. I just know that after we talked for about five minutes, she said that she missed the old Robert. She was very blunt. She went on a rant about me being full of shit, and said I was a conceited, arrogant SOB who couldn't see reality. She told me to remember I was better than the projection I had created. I think she meant that she thought I had become a player."

"So you saw this as an indictment. How did you feel about that?"

"She's wrong. I haven't changed. And I'm certainly not a player."

"What's being a player mean?"

"Why do you ask?" said Robert, raising his eyebrows. "You know."

"I know what it means to me, but not what it means to you."

Robert thought about it, and then gave the first definition that came into his head. "A man who dates and is looking for sex without commitment, as there is always someone better out there. That's not me."

Carl said, "I see. I'm curious, then, about why you interpreted what she said as you being a player."

"Ah. Okay, I told her I was dating several different women and I think she took that to mean…you know…that I was playing around."

"Are you? Playing around?"

"No. Not really."

He thought about his weekend—Irina on Friday and Anastasia on Saturday. He would be seeing someone new, Olga, that evening after the session with Carl. He had given an update to Stephen earlier in the day, and Stephen had said, "Nice! Dorothy is no longer in Kansas." He had laughed. "Robert is no longer in Boston. You're a real player now."

Robert said to his therapist, "Carl, I think you're asking me if I'm ready to have a relationship. I'm if the right person comes along, I'm absolutely ready to have a serious relationship. Right now I'm dating. There's no one special. I would like there to be, but there isn't."

"I see. Tell me about the women you are seeing."

Robert told him about Irina, the model, Anastasia, the server, and Olga, who had just moved to New York. The rest of the hour was spent talking about the three women, why Robert was attracted to them, and why he enjoyed being with them. Carl asked if these relationships were based on substance or if they were simply about sex.

Robert answered, "Of course there's something more." He wasn't sure he believed it, though. They were all gorgeous, sexually alluring, and available. He was not dating them for their intellect or accomplishments.

As Robert left the office, he thought again about his answer. Maybe there was nothing with the women but sex. Irina was a great sexual partner, and very beautiful…although she was smart, too. He had invited Anastasia to dinner so he could take her home. She did not need to be persuaded; they had not discussed a single memorable topic. He didn't know Olga, but already he had imagined having sex with her; she was beautiful.

Sex was important to him, but he needed more. He wanted to find a woman with great intellect and a fun sense of humor. He wanted someone career-oriented, feminine, and very sexual. He was indeed ready for a true relationship, yet always his first criterion was that she be beautiful. *Was that so wrong?*

He remembered the feelings he had had for Nicki. She had been everything he wanted in a woman. She had been his best friend, confidante, partner in crime, and number one supporter as well as a great lover. He missed being in love. He hated not being able to care for a woman.

Robert had decided to take Olga to a small, cozy French restaurant in SoHo. He had been a few times and had gotten to know the owner, Jacques. He arrived just before nine and was at the bar drinking a glass of water when Olga came into the restaurant.

"I'm so sorry I'm late," she said. "I came from Brooklyn, and it seems there is always so much traffic coming into Manhattan."

"Olga, you are only ten minutes late. So, you are fashionably late."

"This is a very nice restaurant. The colors remind me of a restaurant I saw in Paris."

"So, you've been to Paris, too?"

"I loved it there."

The host seated them and left them with menus. Robert asked, "How long were you in Paris?"

"Four days. I was also in Prague for four days," Olga said. For some reason, she felt compelled to add, "I traveled with a friend."

"I've been to Europe a few times, but I've never seen Prague. I hear it's very beautiful."

"It is."

Robert said to Olga, "I was thinking of a few fun things we might do tonight. There is a nice rooftop on the corner of Fifth and Twenty-Eighth Street. It has a great view of the city, and it's always hopping. Especially on a warm night like tonight."

"That sounds like fun."

Robert realized over dinner she was more than a pretty face. Yes, she was very feminine, sexy, and classically beautiful, but she was also smart and very articulate, especially given that English was her second language. She was opinionated—in a good way—with a fun a sense of humor. He realized he had set his expectations low and been pleasantly surprised. He was enjoying himself.

After dinner, Robert took Olga to 230 Fifth Avenue—the rooftop bar he had mentioned. He'd discovered it during one of his long walks in the city. Riding up in the elevator, Robert explained that the bar had become one of his favorite spots because of its spectacular view. The elevator opened in the bar area, and they walked up as set of stairs to the rooftop.

The view stunned Olga. The Empire State Building was all lit up like a gleaming statue in a sea of sparkling lights.

"How do you like it?" Robert asked.

"It's fantastic."

"Isn't it? Look, over there you can see there the Chrysler Building. That was the tallest building in New York for a short time, until they built that one," he said. He pointed to the Empire State Building.

"This is such a big bar, and it's funny to have palm trees here."

"Yes, the palm trees remind people of summer. Have you been anywhere else in the United States? I mean outside of New York."

"No. Only New York."

"Well, maybe I should take you to South Beach and Vegas."

"Maybe," she said, but she didn't really believe his words. She wondered if he was like Edward—all words and no action.

They spent the next couple of hours talking about themselves, their childhoods, their families, and how they had come to be in New

York. Robert took great care not to get too personal. He didn't want to talk about his fiancée. Olga also filtered her stories because she wanted to impress the banker.

Robert was surprised how comfortable he felt with her. It was very late when he finally noticed the time. "Wow. It's getting late. We've been drinking a lot, and you have to go all the way back to Brooklyn." He realized, too late, that what he had said sounded like a invitation to go home with him. He wanted to see her again, and he didn't want to jeopardize that by being too forward on their first date, so he quickly added, "Olga, I had a great time. I'd love to see you again."

She smiled. "Me too. Thank you for tonight. I like to discover new things in the city. The rooftop was a fun idea. I loved it."

"Maybe we can get together again sometime this week after work. I'll text you."

"Okay."

"Do you need cab money?"

"Cab money?"

"Sorry. I would have taken out my car to drive you to Brooklyn, but I don't think that's wise given how much we've had to drink. So I'll take care of your taxi fare, okay?"

"Thank you. That is very nice."

They walked to Fifth Avenue and Robert flagged down a taxi. He took Olga's hand and put a bill in it. Then he kissed her on the lips just as the yellow taxi pulled up to the curb. Robert opened the door and ushered Olga into the car.

"Text me when you are home safely, okay?"

"Okay," she answered as Robert closed the door.

She opened her hand and looked at the folded bill. One hundred dollars. *He is a generous and thoughtful man,* she thought. *And very handsome. Plus, he is one of these bankers, a king of the universe. Robert is perfect for what I need.*

28

THE FIRST DAY AT THE SPA

OLGA WOKE UP very excited. With a new job, a new place to live, and a rich man, she was finally on track, and looking forward to being busy. She had been feeling frustrated because she had had no money either to enjoy herself in New York or to help her parents. Shopping had been out of the question. Going out for dinner or drinks had only been possible if she had someone else pay for it. She was in New York, which offered so much—as long as you had money to enjoy it. Olga had been a prisoner in her little room, but things were looking up. And now she had met Robert.

As Olga was getting ready for work, Katarina came back from school. Olga told her she was moving.

"I'm sorry to lose you. You're my only friend in America," Katarina said.

"Don't worry. We can still be friends. I'll give you my new address so you can come and visit," Olga replied.

"That'll be nice."

"I'll be getting a package in the name of Edward Weisman...the friend I talked to you about? He was so nice to me. I wanted you to know just in case I'm at work."

Olga took the subway to work. She found the New York subway system very dirty, unlike the one in Moscow, and in America men apparently felt free to stare at without end. Some even ventured to come forward and talk to her—usually the older, uglier ones. She hated riding the subway, but it was only for now. Once money started coming in, she could abandon the subway for good.

Olga finally got to work and got settled in behind the desk in the reception area. After an hour at the desk, she finally got to greet her first client, a man in his late fifties.

"Hello. Can I help you?" she asked in English.

"Well, yes. I wanted to know who is working tonight."

Olga pulled out the list of massage therapists and read the names of five women. She added helpfully, "We have pictures on our website, if that helps."

Boris had explained that clients sometimes preferred to get a massage from a specific woman. If the client didn't have a preference, Olga should try to distribute the clients evenly among the girls.

The man thought for a few seconds. "Alina. I want to see her. Yes, Alina."

Olga asked, "How long do you want to see her? A thirty-minute massage is ninety dollars, and a one-hour massage is one hundred fifty dollars."

The man pulled out his wallet and gave her ninety dollars. "Thirty minutes."

She took the money, put it in the cash deposit box below the desk, and led the man to one of the massage rooms.

"Have a seat here. What's your name?"

"Mike."

"I'll go get Alina for you."

After that there was a constant flow of clients to the spa. Olga noticed that all the customers were men. Some were old, some were young, and most were married. She assumed they needed massages after long days at work. As the day came to a close, Boris came out to talk to Olga. "One of the clients would like to see you."

"See me? I don't know how to give a massage."

"Yes, I know. He's one of our best customers, though. He specifically asked for a massage from you. Go see Alina in the women's locker room. She'll give you some quick tips. He's going to give you one hundred dollars as a tip if you do it. I'd like you to treat him well."

The appeal of making additional money was strong. It was one hundred dollars for a quick massage. She told Boris she would do it.

She walked into the locker room and talked to Alina. "So, what do I do?"

"First take off your clothes. Keep your underwear on and put on this white lab coat. You can keep your heels on. We all do. You're seeing Oleg, right?"

Olga replied, "I think so."

"Give him a massage, just as you have probably done with one of your boyfriends. It'll be fine. I will show you more techniques tomorrow."

Olga followed instructions and put on the white coat. It was really short and barely covered her bottom. She bent over in front of the mirror, and she was right. Everyone would see her butt. She walked out of the locker room and went into room number seven where a man lay on his back on the massage table, naked except for the towel across his hips. She blushed as she came in, feeling uncomfortable at the sight of the man.

"Hello. My name is Olga. I'm afraid I'm not very good at giving massage," she said in English. "I mean…"

"It's okay. I'll help you by telling you what to do," he said in Russian. "To start, you should take off your coat."

She hesitated for a moment. *One hundred dollars.* She took the coat off, exposing her pale body. Her lingerie barely covered her. She hung the coat behind the door, feeling a chill. She took a massage bottle, poured some oil on her hands, and walked to the table.

"Start with my feet, and work your way up. Don't worry. I just took a shower."

She followed instructions. She clumsily massaged his feet, worked her way up to his calves, and then massaged his quads. As she moved up to his quads, she could see some movement under the towel. He was getting excited. The man took her right hand and tried to guide it under the towel. She pulled her hand away.

"Listen, baby, I'll give you two hundred dollars. No one will know."

She still resisted, pulling her hand away. Feeling he might be losing, he said in a stern voice, "It's very simple. You do what I say or I call my friends at immigration. They'll arrest you, put you in a disgusting jail, and then deport you. You'll never come back to this country. Never. So, take the money and do it."

Oleg took off the towel with his free hand and guided Olga's hand to his erection. As she started touching him, he stared at her almost-naked body. At that moment, she felt her entire being disappear. All of what she was and all of what she believed in melted away in a mere second. He growled as she moved her hand mechanically just a bit faster.

"Kiss my nipples," he said. "Kiss them, I said."

Olga moved her head forward as she continued to touch him. As she kissed his nipples, he emitted a loud sound of relief. She immediately let go of his penis and walked to another table to get a clean towel and quickly wiped her hands. She then gave him a towel. He sat on the edge of the table. As he took the towel from her hand, he said, "Can you get me a warm towel?"

Olga nodded and put her white coat back on. She walked out of the room and went to the locker room. She washed her hands mechanically a few times, trying to erase the feeling of repulsion, then gave up and picked up a hand towel. She rinsed it in hot water, wrung it out, and carried it back to the massage room. She gave the towel to Oleg without a word. After he washed up, he put on his clothes and pulled out two crisp one-hundred-dollar bills. "Here you go. As promised. Not so difficult, no? I like you. I'll be back."

He left the room.

She stayed in the room, felt numb. She could not believe what had just happened. Would it always be like this—men trying to take advantage of her? She remembered her first days at the nightclub when men kept trying to grab her. All they wanted was to use her for their own selfish pleasures. She thought that working at the spa would be different, but the spa owner had manipulated her. He had made her do the unthinkable. She didn't know what to think. She was mad and upset with him, with herself, with everyone. She felt dirty and disgusted. She tried to justify her actions; she needed the money, and the faster she got it, the sooner she could stop. Yes, money was the only reason this could happen. She walked out of the massage room and went to the locker room to put her clothes back on.

Alina saw Olga's face. "Are you okay?"

"I think so."

"Is this your first time?"

Alina understood that the silence meant yes.

"You are like me. No status. It's difficult to get real work without papers. One of my friends is working at a spa in Manhattan. It pays a lot more money for the same…services…and the clients are much better. More class. She is saving money for a paper marriage."

"I don't understand."

"Yulia knows an American guy who will marry her just so she can get papers. He has a girlfriend, and they have two kids together. He needs money, and Yulia is paying him fifteen thousand dollars—five thousand dollars before the marriage, five thousand dollars when they get married, and then five thousand dollars when she gets her green card. She is making between two thousand dollars and three thousand dollars a week at the spa in Manhattan."

Olga remained silent. She was still processing the events with Oleg. Olga needed to get papers somehow. She didn't want to be a massage girl for long. Maybe she needed to find a man. Not Edward; he was out of the picture. Robert was single, but she barely knew him. Was this the answer? A fake marriage? She was ready for many things, but that felt so wrong.

"So a paper marriage is a fake marriage, then?" Olga said.

"Of course. You know there are many people doing it to get papers. And it works."

"You said she's working in Manhattan. Doing what?"

"Working in a nice, classy spa…doing what you just did. I know it's your first time, but it's easier if you imagine you are a nurse, and just massaging a foot or a hand," Alina said.

"A nurse. Massaging a foot."

"Yes. Men in Manhattan will just pay a lot more than the men here to be with a young, beautiful woman like you. You decide what you want to do there. Here, Boris will start telling you what he wants you to do. I was going to tell you tonight anyway, but I'm leaving this place. Come with me to Manhattan! I promise, it will be much better."

"But I don't want to…"

"What do think Boris will do after today? You think that's the end of it? He'll tell you to do more."

"He will?"

"Of course he will. We're nobodies here. He doesn't care about you, me, or the other girls. He cares only about money. He'll give the clients what they want, and they want sex. That's why he hires girls with no papers—so you won't have a choice. He'll threaten you. He's not lying about reporting you to immigration, either. He's done it before. Manhattan will be much better than anything in Brooklyn. You won't do anything more than what you just did."

"I understand. I guess I can try."

Alina got dressed. "We're done for the day. Let me get ready, and let's go to Tatiana. It's usually busy there on Tuesday night. We need drinks."

Olga sat down and waited for her friend. She grabbed her phone from her purse. She had received a text from Robert earlier that evening.

> Robert: I hope you didn't already for-
> get me. Are you available on Friday?
> I would love to take you out.

She looked at the time. It was just past one in the morning. She decided to text him back, even though it was very late.

> Olga: Of course I haven't forgotten you.
> Tell me when and where on Friday ;)

The text from Robert had been the only good news for Olga that day. After, Olga and Alina walked out of the spa, Boris locked the door after them. Olga was not sorry at the thought of leaving it forever.

29

OLGA AND ROBERT

ROBERT HAD BEEN looking forward to seeing Olga again. Their first date had been a pleasant surprise, and he realized with a shock that it wasn't just her beauty that he'd appreciated. He could actually recall their conversations, a joke she'd made, a comment she'd offered about the view. True, she was very beautiful, but it was also much more. She was fun, intelligent, and somewhat naïve—a quality he found very attractive.

Robert had been planning their second date for a few days. Wanting to provide her with a great New York experience, he took her to Tao, one of the most spectacular restaurants in the city. Then they went up the Empire State Building. It was a warm, clear, spring night, and it provided a great opportunity to see the greater New York area. They stood on the outside observatory deck on the eighty-sixth floor.

"So, what do you think?" he asked her.

"Robert, this is amazing. I'm having a great time. The restaurant was nice, too. Sushi is my new favorite food. Now I am at the Empire State Building. This is so wonderful."

Robert put his arm around Olga and pulled her close. He turned his head and kissed softly on her lips. He pulled his head back just a bit and looked her in the eyes. Then he kissed her deeply. After a long kiss, he said, "Olga, I really like you."

"Robert, I like you too," she said. "But it is getting late, and I should be going home."

Robert checked his watch. It was just past midnight. "Maybe you should come to my place."

"Another time. It is too soon," she said softly. "I do not know you very well."

"Well, can I see you tomorrow? Have you been to the Met? The Metropolitan Museum?"

"The big museum near Central Park?"

"Yes. They have a great collection. Would you like me to come and pick you up? Maybe around one tomorrow?"

"Tomorrow I am moving. I will try to finish early."

"Well, text me tomorrow morning to confirm. It will take me about thirty minutes to get to Brooklyn."

"Great."

They walked to the street. Robert hailed a taxi and put a bill in her hand. "I'll see you tomorrow."

He started walking home alone. *This Russian is not so easy,* he thought. Irina and Anastasia had both ended up in his bed on the first date. He had been out with Olga twice now with nothing more than kisses. Rather than bothering him, it gave him a better appreciation for Olga. She was a woman of principle, and he respected her for that.

As he started walking home, he pulled out his BlackBerry and saw that he had received a few text messages from Irina.

> Irina: 9:15 p.m.: Baby, where
> are you? Are you busy?
> Irina: 10:30 p.m.: Baby, I'm going out
> with my friends to Lavo. Come. Kisses.
> Irina: 11:45 p.m.: Getting
> drunk. Need you. Kisses.

Robert could not resist. He wanted to have sex, and Irina was so very easy. He replied.

> Robert: Going home now. Will be there
> in 10 minutes if you still need me.

Maybe Vanessa was right, he thought. He had become a player. He was taking advantage of every situation to have sex with a beautiful woman. This was far from the man he had been in Boston.

He kept his phone in his hand, waiting for a reply. It came a few minutes later.

Irina: Coming.

30

THE FIRST TIME

OLGA STARTED HER day early on Saturday so she would be able to meet Robert at one for a third date. She got up at seven and finished packing, and then called a taxi to move out of her small apartment. Moving was simple. She had just her two large, red suitcases and a couple of overflowing duffel bags. That was the extent of her worldly possessions in America. *So sad,* she thought. By eleven, she had moved into her new room and had already unpacked almost everything. She sent a text to Robert.

> Olga: Robert, I finished moving early this
> morning. I can meet you at one. Do you
> still want to come and pick me up?"
> Robert: Great. I can be there at one. Text me
> the address. I'll text you when I leave the city.

She pulled out the new computer that she had received the day before, thanks to Edward's credit card. She was sending e-mails to Russia when the familiar Skype ringtone rang once, twice, three times, and then four times. It was François. She decided to answer. His face appeared on the screen.

"Baby, how are you? What a great surprise! I've not heard from you for so long! Are you okay?" François said in his broken English.

"*Babitchka*! I've missed you so much. It has been difficult because I didn't have a computer. I am borrowing my friend's right now. I can't use it too long, though. I'm so happy to see you."

"You look great. Beautiful as always. How is New York?"

"New York is great. I really can't talk with you for long. I am meeting a friend for lunch soon. We are going to Manhattan."

"No problem. Good-bye." Just before he was going to hang up, François could not resist. "How are the men in New York?"

"*Babitchka*, you ask the silliest questions. I don't know, as I have only one man in my life. You. I love you."

"I love you too. We'll try to talk again soon?"

"Yes. Soon."

"Bye, my princess."

Olga hung up. She walked out of her room and went to the kitchen where Alina was making coffee.

"Would you like some?" Alina asked.

"No thanks."

"Did I hear a man in your room?" Alina asked with a smile.

Olga laughed. "Ha, yes! I was talking to a French guy I know on Skype. He was a good friend of mine in Krasnoyarsk."

Olga looked at the clock. It was eleven thirty. "I need to get ready. I'm meeting a friend who is taking me to the city."

Alina asked, "A guy?"

"Yes, and he's a nice guy. A banker."

"Mmm, a banker," Alina said enviously. "You know they have money."

"Yes," Olga said proudly. "He has a penthouse."

"Have you seen it?"

"Soon. Very soon.

THE DATE WITH Robert was wonderful. He arrived a few minutes before one in his black BMW, which provided Olga some relief after Edward's

Honda Accord. Robert seemed to be the real deal. They went to the Met, and then Robert took her to a fashion exposition. After that, they took a horse-drawn carriage around Central Park and ate a late afternoon snack at the Mandarin Hotel lounge, which overlooked the park. They had a few drinks at the nearby Hudson Hotel, enjoying the warm weather on its rooftop terrace. Finally, they grabbed dinner at Lavo, the hip midtown restaurant. It was just past nine when they left the restaurant and headed south on Madison.

"Did you enjoy the day?" Robert asked.

"This was fabulous day. Thank you."

"It's still early. You could come to my apartment for a drink."

Olga hesitated for a few seconds, and then said, "Maybe."

"Maybe?"

"Okay…yes!"

She was enjoying Robert's company and was very curious to see his apartment. She wanted to confirm he was really wealthy…and single.

"Let's take a taxi. We've walked all day, and I am sure your feet could use a rest, too," he said, looking at her high heels.

"I'm okay. I've been wearing heels since I was thirteen years old. But a taxi would be nice."

After a short taxi ride, Olga found herself in one of the most amazing apartments she had ever seen. *Wow,* she thought, *he has to be very rich.*

"You have a great view of the city."

"Yes, I do."

"This is really lovely. I love your apartment. It's so big."

"I'm very lucky. I like it, and I had been hoping to buy it, but the owner will probably move back in when my lease expires. I have it until November, at least. After that, I'll have to find somewhere else to stay."

"I see."

Robert felt the need to add, "Naturally, it will have to be just as comfortable and big as this. With a view."

"That will be difficult. This is *very* nice"

"Yes, it is pretty amazing," he said proudly. "So, what would you like to drink?"

"Champagne, please."

Olga looked out the panoramic windows. *This is the life I want,* she thought. *A great apartment, a great husband, a great family, and a great future.* She thought of her Frenchman. He could not have offered her all this. Only a man like Robert, a banker, could offer her all she wanted and deserved.

Robert came back with two glasses of champagne. "Here. Welcome to my home."

After the toast he put his arm around her waist and kissed her. They put their glasses on the coffee table and kissed passionately.

Olga said, "Perhaps you should show me your bedroom."

Robert took her hand, and she followed him.

31

MR. LOWENSTEIN

THINGS SETTLED DOWN for Olga over the next month. She now had real stability in her life. She had a comfortable home, friends, a job, and a banker boyfriend. Her living arrangements suited Olga. Her room in Alina's apartment had a small, half-filled walk-in closet, a queen-size bed, a worktable, a small television set, and her new computer. The rest of the apartment was perfectly set up to accommodate the three women living there. The kitchen was very functional, and two of them could use it at the same time without bumping into each other. The living room was at the end of the apartment and far enough from the bedrooms that they could watch television or listen to music without disturbing someone sleeping.

Olga was friendly with her roommates. Alina worked with her in the city, and the other girl, Yuliana, was also very nice. They were all in the same situation—three Russian women without papers trying to figure how to get great lives in America. Yuliana was in the process of arranging her fake marriage. She was working at the spa to earn fast money while doing some modeling on the side. When anyone asked for details about her work as a model, she avoided the topic altogether. Her two roommates suspected she was a high-end escort in the city, but they never dared ask the question directly. Alina was thinking of arranging a fake marriage of her own when her student visa expired.

Olga wasn't convinced. She didn't want another loveless marriage. Robert might be a great prospect for a real marriage, but she couldn't think about that yet. She still had a husband in Russia.

Olga saw Robert a few times a week. She enjoyed his company. He was a man of class, good taste, and wealth. He always had something planned for them to do and seemed eager to give her a taste of the life she craved—a life where money did not seem to be a problem. They went to a multitude of restaurants in Manhattan. They attended a few ballet performances. They danced in the hippest nightclubs. They attended gallery openings and charity events. They even visited the Hamptons, the summer playground of well-off New Yorkers. Best of all, he took her shopping as much as she wanted.

Work at the spa was not too bad after all. Olga followed Alina's advice and tried to imagine she was a nurse with an unusual specialty, and treated the male organ no differently than she would a foot or a hand. As for any other interactions with her clients, she was very strict. There was no touching her of any kind. Adventurous hands were quickly put back in place. The massage never lasted a full hour and always included a "happy ending" for the client, provided with a firm hand and lots of massage oil. She accepted the work without further complaint, as the money was good. She regularly made four to six hundred dollars a day.

One day as she was at work, sitting in the back room with Alina, Yuliana, and one of the other girls awaiting clients, Olga's phone rang again and again. She looked at the number on the caller ID and didn't answer. "Idiot!" she said.

"Who's that?" Alina asked.

"It's Edward calling. I told you about him. I saw him with his wife and kids. When I confronted him, he denied it. Now he's complaining about the computer I bought with his card. He keeps calling and texting me, whining that I took money from his family."

"You bought a computer with his card?" Yuliana asked.

"Yes. The asshole told me a story so I would have sex with him. 'Oh, I'm going to get you a job. Oh, I'm going to help with your future. Oh, we're going to move in together. Blah, blah, blah.' Promises, promises!

I got my revenge. I bought a computer with his credit card, and I refuse to pay him back," Olga said proudly.

"Yes, you're right. They use us! The least they can do is help us and treat us right. If Edward didn't help you, then you did right," Yuliana said.

Alina nodded.

The spa manager came into the waiting room. "Olga, Mr. Lowenstein is here for you. Room three."

Olga stood up and looked at Alina. "He's the old guy who keeps trying to grab me. I spend more time pushing his hands away than I do giving him a 'massage.' He's so ugly, too, with his hairy white body and a belly like a whale." She made a disdainful face.

"Well, you know he's not getting any at home," Alina said. "And he has money to burn."

Olga left the waiting room and headed to room number three. She knocked and walked in. The naked man on the massage table could have used a larger towel to cover his bulk. It seemed to barely cover his hips.

"Hello, baby. I missed you. I haven't seen you here lately," Olga said in English.

"I've been busy," he said. "But I've been thinking of you."

"You are so sweet. I'm really happy to see you. Do you need to take a shower?"

"No, I just took a shower. Olga, honey, I want to ask you something."

"Ask, baby."

"I want to have sex with you. Real sex, I mean. I have two thousand five hundred dollars right here for you. Cash."

He showed her an envelope filled with bills.

Olga was stunned. Her mind started spinning quickly. She thought about what she could do with that much money. She could cover her expenses for several months and still be able to send some to her parents. She knew that without her husband's help, her parents were struggling financially. Vladimir had ignored her repeated requests for more money. She seemed to have lost control of him. She hesitated. "Sex. One time, right now, for two thousand five hundred dollars?"

"One time. Today. And we tell no one."

"No kissing."

"No kissing," he replied.

She took the envelope. "Okay. Do you have protection?"

"Yes, of course."

The entire session lasted less than fifteen minutes. The old man finally climaxed, and Olga put her white lab coat back on. She picked up the used condom and told the man she would be back in a few minutes with a warm towel. She stopped by the bathroom to clean up and dispose of the evidence; the spa rules were very strict. Though "happy endings" were commonplace and tolerated, the girls were told that full intercourse was prohibited. Olga doubted many followed this rule.

After a few minutes in the bathroom, she walked back to the room with a hot towel. The old man was already dressed.

"Thank you. I have to go now. I'll see you soon."

"Yes, baby," said Olga. "I hope to see you very soon."

Olga walked out of the room and went to the hostess. She told the woman that she wasn't feeling well and wished to leave early. The woman verified the schedule for the day.

"You don't have any more appointments booked. Yes, you can leave."

Olga left the spa. She texted Alina on her way out. "*My period started. Leaving now. See you at home.*"

She walked along Madison Avenue and headed north to Saks. She had plans for her pussy money. She was going to spend some of the dirty money today. Saks seemed like the perfect place to spend a thousand dollars. She would also send some money to her parents. She had been sending a few hundred dollars whenever she could, and her mother's hints that more would be appreciated were getting less and less subtle. She would wire them some money, and save the rest.

As Olga walked down the street, she saw that men were noticing her, as they always did. Most times, she reveled in the attention. Today she totally despised the men for it. A stare that would have been flattering in the past was today a reminder how men wanted her only for their own selfish physical pleasures. She was livid. She hated all men.

∽∾∾∾∽

OLGA HAD TAKEN three days off work after her encounter with her hairy client. Alina had noticed something different in Olga—the absence from work and the long periods in her room alone. She could only guess what might have happened on that day. She did not dare ask.

Olga thought of that day again and again, trying to make sense of her actions. *What was I thinking? The moment he made the offer, I lost myself. Money*, she thought. *I was so desperate that I sold myself.* She had been rationalizing it for the past few days. She figured it was a onetime event, and she was determined it would never happen again. It had been too difficult. The memory of the disgusting old man rutting away on her was too vivid. She remembered every touch and every word of the session. She knew Alina suspected something, but she also knew that neither of them would speak of it.

Olga found comfort in an e-mail from her mother that confirmed that Vladimir had completed their divorce. It was now clear why her repeated appeals to him for much-needed financial help for her family had gone unanswered. She also caught up on news from her friends on VK. They asked her how she was doing in New York. Robert had been texting her a few times a day inquiring about her health—she'd feigned tummy troubles—and all the attention eventually helped her get over the trauma. She decided to text Robert.

> Olga: Baby, I'm much better. When can I
> see you? It has been too long. Kisses.
> Robert: So happy you feel better! I have an invita-
> tion to a charity event tomorrow. Would love it
> if you could come. Wear that little blue dress!
> Olga: I can meet you at your place
> after my shift tomorrow, k?

Robert: Gr8. Tomorrow's Friday, so I can
be done early. Home about 5. When you're
done, I'll be there waiting for you.

Olga: Perfect ;)

Olga had been purposely vague about her line of work. The other girls at the spa had told her that American men often visited the spa to get some satisfaction, but that they would never marry a woman who offered "happy ending" massages. The double standard was the same in America as it had been in Russia. Fully aware of Robert's potential rejection, she told him she was a receptionist at a high-end spa in mid-town. He didn't ask any more questions.

Olga put her phone down and walked out of the room to see Alina, who was reading in her room when Olga interrupted.

"Alina, I want to go out tonight. Let's celebrate. I am now a divorced woman. My asshole husband filed for divorce without me, and I got the papers from my mother today. Dinner is on me. Let's go to Tatiana. I want Russian food, Russian music, and Russian people."

Alina smiled. Her friend Olga—the ambitious vibrant woman, the dreamer, and the adventurer—was back.

32

THE MOVE

ROBERT INVITED OLGA to dinner on a warm August evening. On Saturdays they usually went out, but he wanted to make the evening special. He had been seeing her exclusively for a few months now, and he had developed strong feelings for her. He believed he was in love, and he wanted to tell Olga. He also believed the feeling was mutual, but he wanted to hear it.

Olga had been to his place for dinner on a few occasions in the past, but tonight would be special. He had a few dozen roses delivered for the day—red for the bedroom, white for the dining table, and pink for the living room—and spent the day preparing Mediterranean chopped salad, leek soup, stuffed chicken with spinach, mushrooms, and feta cheese, an assortment of French cheeses, and a chocolate mousse dessert. He stocked up on champagne and wine.

At just past eight, the guard buzzed Robert's apartment. Robert was annoyed. Olga had been to his apartment many times, so there was no need for her to be stopped by the guard. Olga knocked at the door. Robert greeted her and led her to the living room.

"Wow, *babitchka*. Is this a special occasion?"

Robert liked his Russian nickname. It seemed so personal to him. "Come. Sit down. I would like to talk to you."

They both sat on the couch. He removed the bottle of champagne from the ice bucket, popped the cork, and poured two glasses. He raised his glass. "We've been seeing each other all summer now, and I was thinking…I was thinking that maybe you should move in with me."

Olga stared. The offer was unexpected.

"I like the idea, but I could not come before September."

"That's no problem. I can wait a couple of weeks." He smiled. "I wouldn't ask you if I didn't feel the way I do. We've spent a lot of great times together." He took a sip of champagne and then set the glass down. He took her hand, looked in her eyes, and said, "Olga, I love you."

He was relieved after telling her how he felt.

"Baby, I love you, too. I've wanted to tell you so for such a long, long time. You are the most wonderful man in the world—the best thing that has ever happened to me." Olga told Robert exactly what she knew he wanted to hear.

"So, the answer is yes? You'll move in?"

"Yes. The answer is yes."

33

A SURPRISE

Robert had been a bit secretive about the evening. He had told Olga only they were going to a special event and that she needed to dress up. She was more than happy to oblige. She always enjoyed fancy evenings with him.

"Olga, are you ready? I told you to be ready by six, and it's almost six thirty."

"*Babitchka*, I'm ready." Olga finally came out of the master bedroom.

"Wow, you look fabulous! I love that dress on you."

"Thank you, Robert. It's a present from my boyfriend. He is such a great man."

"I have to tell you again. You look great. Simply amazing!"

"Come." She took his hand and guided him to the bedroom. They stopped in front of the mirror. She said proudly, "We both look good. Let's take a picture. I want to send it to Mama so she can see how wonderful we are together."

Robert found Olga stunning in the Dolce & Gabbana dress he had bought her. The long, black dress wrapped her body tightly. Open in the back, it stopped just before her hips, exposing her entire back. The front showed her cleavage, revealing the round shape of her small breasts. The bottom part enveloped her legs, with the exception of a wide opening that stopped just above her knees.

"Okay. Then we have to go. It's 6:45, and the car is waiting downstairs."

They snapped a photo, and then left the penthouse.

Just outside the main entrance, a black sedan was waiting for them. A chauffeur stepped out. "Mr. Thompson?" He opened the rear passenger door and helped Olga into the car. He held the other door for Robert.

Robert asked, "Do you know where we are going?"

"Yes, sir. We'll be taking Sixth Avenue."

Olga looked at Robert and kissed him. "Thank you, baby, for everything you do for me."

Robert was excited. He had planned the evening thinking of Olga. He was sure she would love what he had in store. After a short ride, the car pulled up to the curb behind a stretch limousine. The chauffeur got out to open the door. Olga looked outside and saw a large, white tent in Bryant Park. "Are we going into that tent?" she asked.

"Yes, baby. I am taking you to the opening show of New York City Fashion Week. Dolce & Gabbana is presenting its spring collection tonight."

Olga shrieked with joy and kissed Robert. "You are the best."

Olga stepped out of the car and walked to the red carpet, hoping to catch a glimpse of some of the celebrities. Robert handed a pair of tickets to a host. She spoke into her radio, "Two VIPs."

Another woman greeted the couple. "Please, follow me."

As they walked up the stairs, flashes from dozens of photographers went off. One yelled to Olga, "What are you wearing?"

A bit surprised, she replied, "Dolce & Gabbana."

Robert let go of her hand, and Olga stood alone on the stairs, turning slowly. For a few seconds, she was the center of attention. A photographer stopped her so he could snap pictures of her.

"What is your name?" someone in the crowd called out.

She replied proudly, "Olga Kotova." The attention overwhelmed her. She was a star.

The host asked Robert to come into the tent and he grabbed his girlfriend's hand. They entered, and an usher showed them to their seats in the second row.

Olga was overjoyed. She could not believe it. She kissed Robert again and said, "I love you. You are the best man in the world."

Robert replied, "Olga, I love you too."

"This is the best thing anyone has ever done for me. Thank you. Thank you!"

"I thought we needed something to celebrate our four months together."

"Four months already?"

"Well, we met at the end of May. So, yes, four months."

It was one of the happiest moments in Olga's life. She was surrounded by movie stars, pop musicians, and local New York celebrities. The beautiful people. And she was one of them.

As the show finally started, Olga looked at the models walking down the runway wearing the most recent designs of famous Italian designers. After the show, Domenico Dolce and Stefano Gabbana came out in person to salute the crowd, and everyone in the tent stood up and clapped. The applause continued for several minutes as people called out, "Bravo! Fantastic!" At that very moment, Olga knew exactly what she wanted to do. She would become a famous fashion designer.

Olga could not remember the last time she had been so excited. She had finally found her calling. Fashion was a natural path for her. She had always admired the high-end clothing stores in Moscow. She recalled the moments when she imagined the fancy dresses she wished she had. She thought of the hours she'd spent with her grandmother making clothes.

Her eternal question had been finally answered. She would become a rich, famous fashion designer.

For several days after the fashion show, Olga searched the Internet to find the best fashion school in New York City. She had an innate sense of style, but she knew that she would not be able to become a designer without going to school. She found what she was looking for, the perfect choice: Parsons The New School for Design. One of seven divisions of The New School, Parsons had an excellent reputation, it was located within walking distance of the apartment, and the next semester started in January. Tuition was the only issue. It cost over twenty thousand dollars per semester. For the first time since she had been with Robert, she would have to ask him directly for financial help.

It seemed a simple matter. Robert had money and she did not. He loved her, so he should pay her tuition. That was what Olga would expect from any man who had the privilege of calling her his girlfriend.

Robert returned home after another meeting with Carl. "It smells good in here," he said as he walked into the apartment.

Olga greeted him. "*Babitchka*, I have prepared a fine dinner for you. Some traditional Russian salads, blini with smoked salmon, caviar, and a few other goodies."

"That sounds great. Do I have time to take a quick shower?"

"Yes, of course."

After they sat down for dinner, Olga said, "Robert, I wanted to ask you a few things."

It was unusual for her to call him Robert. She always said *babitchka*. Robert noticed. He looked at Olga, and she looked uncomfortable. "Yes. You can ask me anything. You know that."

"You know that I really liked the fashion show. I want to be a fashion designer. I found the perfect school. It's called Parsons, and it's close to here. I want to know if you could help me with the tuition."

"Of course I will Olga. How much is it?"

She replied, "It is the best school in the city. I think it is expensive, but I'm sure it will be worth it." She paused. "It costs twenty thousand dollars per semester."

"No problem."

Olga was shocked. "You're the best! I love you," she said, and she kissed him. "I have to get prepared for school. I would like to stop working if that is okay with you."

"Olga, I love you, and I will do everything to help you."

"*Babitchka*! You are the best man in the world."

34

THE CRASH

THE COMPUTER MONITOR had been shouting the news all morning, even before the trading day started. As Robert read the words scrolling past, he thought this was going to be a rough one. The US government had taken over Fannie Mae and Freddie Mac, two giant financial institutions, the week before. Bank of America had purchased Merrill Lynch, one of the oldest investment banking firms in New York, the day before. Lehman Brothers was rumored to be in serious financial difficulty.

When the market opened, Robert couldn't believe what he saw. The market had dropped at the open by 15 percent and seemed in a free fall. He felt panic from the trading desk, as the traders were trying to make sense of the events. The phones wouldn't stop ringing, and the firm's brokers struggled to calm their clients. The stocks of all major banking firms were dropping like rocks, and his firm was no exception. Brewster shares kept trading down, and stockholders kept selling as if the shares were cursed. First it was fifty-five dollars, followed by another ask at fifty dollars. There were no takers. The prices kept sinking lower and lower. Forty dollars, thirty dollars, twenty dollars. There were no takers at any price. Then the news came across the wire: Lehman Brothers had filed for bankruptcy protection. Brewster shares dropped again.

Robert called the Boston office. He had lost his usual calm. He hoped Charley might provide some answers. Charley would know. He had to know.

"Kathy, it's Robert in New York. I'm trying to reach Charley."

"He's not in the office today. He flew to New York last night for an early meeting."

"New York? He's not at our offices." Robert kept an eye on the firm's shares. They were at five dollars a share and still dropping.

"I'm sorry, Robert. If he's not there, then I don't know where he is."

That was a bad omen. Charley's assistant *always* knew where he was. There were rumors that the major investment banks were supposed to meet with the US Treasury in the coming days. Charley would have to be there as the managing director of Brewster.

At just past eleven in the morning on September 16, the news flashed on the computer screen: "New York Stock Exchange has suspended the trading of the Brewster shares." The share had reached seventy-five cents, down from a high of sixty-two dollars a few weeks ago. Robert was in shock. He sank into his chair.

Seventy-five cents a share.

He had kept all his investments in his firm's stocks except for some minimal emergency funds. Now the world had collapsed around him. He was losing…had lost…everything. Five million dollars had just disappeared. Five million of his hard-earned money had vanished.

Stephen came into his office. "What the fuck is happening, man?"

Robert's eyes were still fixed on the screen, which glowed red—the sign of decline. There was no hint of green, or even a slight shade of yellow. Another news flash came across the screen: "US Treasury Secretary, Fed Chair, Meet Today with All Major NY Banks."

Robert finally answered Stephen. "This is not a market correction. This is a market crash. A fucking crash. Like 1929. Charley must be at the Fed meeting trying to save Brewster."

"John just ran out of the building. He didn't say a word. He has all of his cash in the firm. All of it in Brewster. Like me."

"Same here," replied Robert.

"Let's get out of here. I need a drink."

"I need more than one drink. Believe me."

Both men walked past the trading desks. There was little point in standing by waiting for more news. The early turmoil had given way to an uncomfortable silence, and employees gathered in small groups trying to understand the events of the day. Robert thought, *It's easy to understand. We are all screwed.*

IT HAD EASILY been one of the worst weeks in Robert's life. He had lost his job and all his money. Everything was gone. He couldn't just find another job in banking; there weren't going to be any new jobs in banking any time soon. Two days after Lehman Brothers filed for bankruptcy, the regulators had come in to take over Brewster. His company suffered the same fate—bankruptcy.

Robert had been very distant with Olga lately. He just wasn't ready to tell her that he had lost just about everything he had. He had some savings, but that was less than one hundred thousand dollars—a pittance for someone who had been a millionaire a few days before. He left Brewster with little to no employment prospects.

Olga was getting ready to go out to meet Alina at Mari Vana. Robert stood next to her. "Olga, can we talk for a few minutes?"

"Of course, *babitchka*."

"You heard what happened this week on Wall Street, right?"

"Yes, I think some banks are in trouble."

"My company, too. Baby, I lost my job."

"*Babitchka*, why didn't you tell me earlier?" she said compassionately, throwing her arms around him. "You'll find another. There are plenty of banks in America. And you are the best banker ever!"

"It's not just my job. I lost a lot of money. Just about everything I had. I can't…I won't be able to help you with school. At least not right away."

Olga's face was blank. "I will be okay. And as I say, you will find a new job. Everything will be okay. This is America. They love bankers here."

"Yes. Yes. Everything will be okay. I love you, Olga."

"I love you too, *babitchka*. Do you want me to stay home?"

"No. You have plans. Go out and have fun tonight. I need to get things organized."

"I won't stay out too late. I will come home to comfort you, *babitchka*."

Olga left the apartment. It took all her strength not to slam the door behind her. *Damn! Damn! Damn!* Robert couldn't afford her tuition after all. She couldn't trust anyone in this country! Now she would have to find another way to get what she wanted.

At Mari Vana she found Alina at one of the high-top tables near the entrance. Alina hugged her. "I'm so happy to see you. I haven't seen you for a week. I've missed you."

"I'm happy to see you, too," said Olga, struggling to maintain her composure.

"Are you okay? What's wrong?"

"I'm fine. You look great," said Olga.

"I'm not as beautiful as you, and never will be, no matter how hard I might try," said Alina. She put her hand on Olga's and stared into her eyes. "You know you can't lie to me. What's going on?"

"Robert lost his job, and he's not going to be able to pay for my school."

"The fashion school you told me about? What are you going to do?"

"I don't know yet. Men here are useless. We can't count on anyone in this country."

"I know you. You will find a way. You can always come back to work."

"I never thought I would have to work again. I really don't want to play nurse anymore, but I do need money. I have no other choice."

When Alina excused herself to go to the restroom after dinner, a woman walked up to Olga.

"Olga, how are you?" the woman asked in Russian.

Olga looked at the young Russian woman and barely recognized her. It was Dinara. She had worked at the nightclub with her. Dinara had been so totally transformed from head to toe that it took Olga a few seconds to recognize her. From a peasant girl fresh off the boat, she could now be compared to any stylish New York woman. Her clothes, shoes, and everything had changed for the better. She had traded her cheap off-the-rack, Chinese-made clothes for designer apparel.

"Dinara, I didn't recognize you. You look great."

"Thank you."

"How did you—? I mean, your clothes… Do you still work at the club?"

"Yes, I'm still there." She lowered her voice. "You were always nice to me, so I'll tell you. Anastasia took me a few times to this party in Manhattan. We go and have fun with rich guys. When we leave, the man who invited us pays us. I make seven thousand dollars each time I go. I think Anastasia gets more because she does more."

Olga clearly understood that the combination of Anastasia and fun could only mean one thing: sex. Now that she knew that she couldn't count on getting Robert's help with school, she was desperate. She was ready to do anything necessary make fast money. She knew that Anastasia would never invite her to the party, so she asked Dinara.

"Can you invite me? Without Anastasia."

"Well, yes. That's what I did. Anastasia had me go to a photographer at first. Then I dropped off my pictures with the guard. A few days later, Kevin called me."

"Kevin?"

"Kevin is the man who has the parties."

"Can you help me? Maybe with the photographer and Kevin's address? I would like to go."

"Well, don't tell anyone I told you. I want to go back, too."

"Of course not. I would never tell. You can trust me."

Alina came back to the table. Olga introduced Dinara as a girl she had worked with in the past.

"I should be going. My friends are here," Dinara said.

"Dinara, here's my phone number. Text me."

Dinara texted the information right after she left.

Dinara: Photos Boudoir NYC 212-555-1212. K. McLaughlin, 106A East 57 Street, Unit PH.

Olga: Thank you!

Olga had not yet decided to use the information, but now she had an option. The appeal of quick money seemed to trump anything else, as she had a very clear goal. Nothing would stop her.

Alina asked, "Should we stay for another drink?"

Olga looked around. The bar was crowded on that Thursday night. She looked around at the men in expensive suits. "Yes, let's stay for another hour or two. I want to have fun. We might find a nice American man ready to marry a beautiful Russian woman."

Alina laughed and asked, "Are you talking about me...or you?"

"Maybe both. My visa is due to expire soon. I was going to talk to Robert about it, but now that he has lost his job..."

35

THE ENVELOPE

ROBERT'S WORLD HAD turned upside down. He needed to adapt quickly to his new circumstances. He was an unemployed banker with few prospects, and he would be homeless in the coming weeks. On his way back home from the gym on Saturday morning, he called the real estate broker who had gotten him his apartment, figuring that she would be able to find him something again. She agreed to meet him that afternoon and try to help him although she made it clear that his rental budget was a lot less than the high-end apartments she usually showed.

The next item on his list was finding work. That would be a challenge. The banks continued to lay off hundreds of people like him, so his prospect of finding any banking work in the city was low, despite his top-notch credentials. He hoped that Lenny and Kevin would be able to help.

In all this turmoil, Robert remained optimistic. He'd started from nothing. Money could be replaced. He would find work at some point, and he would be making a lot of money once again. For now the penthouse would be replaced with a furnished, one-bedroom, three-thousand-dollar rental, but it would still be home. The most important thing in his life was keeping Olga happy. She was the love of his life. She was with him, and that was the only thing that counted. With her on his side, he could weather any crisis.

He walked into the apartment. Olga sat drinking coffee in the kitchen.

"Good morning, my love. I thought you would still be in bed. How was last night?"

"Good morning, *babitchka*. We had fun. I was happy to see Alina. I'm going to meet her and another girl this afternoon."

"Okay, but don't you want to come with me to see apartments?"

"Maybe later, after I come back from Brooklyn."

"All right. I'm meeting the agent at one. I'll keep you posted."

After Olga took her usual hour to get ready, she left the apartment for her appointment with the photographer. She still wasn't quite sure if she would actually move forward and drop off the pictures at Kevin's, but she would have the pictures taken first and decide later.

———

By MID-OCTOBER, ROBERT found a decent apartment and a temporary job consulting for a private equity firm that needed help with a transaction involving a major foreign firm. Though it was a short-term assignment—less than six weeks—it paid well. In what was being called the deepest recession since the Great Depression, any work was welcome. The number of unemployed bankers had skyrocketed. The consulting job had a relatively flexible schedule, so Robert could continue networking in the hope of finding something more permanent and more lucrative.

Robert and Olga were moving in a week to the small, furnished, one-bedroom apartment in the Lower East Side, on Thirteenth Street near Second Avenue. It was a significant step down from the penthouse. The new place was a third-floor walk-up in an older building, and the neighborhood was certainly sketchier. Homeless people regularly roamed the surrounding streets. The apartment was much smaller, just five hundred square feet compared with nearly three thousand, so everything had been downsized to fit Robert's new lifestyle. One miniscule closet that could hardly fit his clothes replaced his former matching walk-in closets. Simple ready-to-assemble products from Ikea replaced the custom-upholstered Roche Bobois furniture. The formerly vast living room and dining room were now a single room that edged into the small kitchen. It was far from ideal, but it was comfortable for the time being. Olga didn't complain.

Robert came back from work and checked the mail. He found a letter addressed to Olga. "Olga, you got a letter from Parsons."

As she heard the word *Parsons*, she quickly ran to him. "Give me! Give me!"

He handed her the envelope. She grabbed it, opened it quickly, and read it. She smiled. "I've been accepted, *babitchka!* I can start in January. I am so happy."

"That's great. We should go out and celebrate tonight. How about Cipriani downtown for dinner? We haven't been there in ages."

"Yes, great idea. I'll finish packing and then start getting ready."

Olga walked back to the master bedroom and sat on the bed with the letter in hand. She held her dream. This was what she wanted more than anything in the world. She would become a famous designer no matter the cost, even if it meant she had to sell her soul.

Going back to school would also solve her visa issue. The school could sponsor her student visa. She had been able to extend her tourist visa a couple of times with the help of an unscrupulous Russian immigration lawyer. He had explained that she had only two options—get married or become violently ill. She had not been in a position to find a husband, so she had to arrange to appear so sick that she would not be able to travel back to Russia. For two thousand dollars, the lawyer had arranged everything—a doctor's visit with a fake diagnosis, the immigration paperwork, and fees. The lawyer made it clear she would not be provided any more assistance after the second extension unless she was truly dying; she would have to find another way to stay in the country. School was a logical solution.

Olga put the precious letter in her purse. She searched for another envelope—the one she had hidden in her luggage. It contained her sexy boudoir pictures. She had written the address on it—K. McLaughlin, 106 East 57 Street, Unit PH—and thought about dropping it off as soon as possible. Robert had told her that he would find a way to fund her tuition and he meant well, but he was broke. She was on her own. As for the spa, she would never make a sufficient amount of money to pay for school without revisiting that vile day with Mr. Lowenstein. She found the envelope and held it in her hands for a few seconds, but then put it back in her luggage. She didn't want to do it. She would find another way.

—∞∞∞—

ROBERT HAD ALREADY left that Wednesday morning when Olga's cell phone rang. She woke up and stared at the number. Russia. This was troubling, as her mother never called her on her mobile phone, especially at this time. It was well past ten o'clock at night in Siberia.

"Mama?"

"No. This is your father. I have bad news."

"What is it? Mama?"

"Yes, your mother went to the hospital yesterday. She has breast cancer, very advanced cancer."

Her father paused and there was a short silence. Olga started to cry.

"Is she going to be okay?"

"They'll try to treat it in Krasnoyarsk, but it would be better if she could go to Moscow. You know they have the best hospitals there."

"Papa... That costs money. A lot of money."

Her father never spoke to his daughter about the family's financial troubles. It was always her mother who asked for help. He clearly felt uncomfortable. She heard him hesitate, and then he said, "Yes, it does."

"How much do you need?"

He hesitated again. "At least three hundred fifty thousand rubles—perhaps ten thousand US dollars. She will need to be in Moscow for at least four weeks."

"I'll get the money, Papa. Robert is very generous. I'll ask him. For Mama."

"You're a good daughter."

"Thank you, Papa. Can I talk to Mama?"

"She's asleep from the morphine now. I'll call you from the hospital when she can talk."

"Tell Mama I love her."

"I will."

Olga hung up. She no longer had a choice. She sent a text to Dinara to get some last-minute advice before she dropped off the envelope, and Dinara's instructions were clear. Include three or four pictures along with her name, phone number, a physical description of height and weight, and a short note expressing a desire to meet Kevin and have some fun. Dinara said that she would probably get a phone call within a day or two after dropping off the envelope.

Olga took a taxi to the corner of Fifty-Seventh Street and Third Avenue. It was gray and overcast, but still she wore large sunglasses to hide her face. She was nervous. She didn't know exactly what happened at these parties, but she was sure that it wouldn't be wise to let Robert to find out. When she finally reached the address, she walked past the building on purpose. She stopped about fifty feet beyond the entrance, pulled twenty dollars from her purse, and then turned around. She could feel her heart beating fast as she got close to the building. When the guard opened the door, Olga walked directly to the concierge. The middle-aged woman raised her head from behind the desk.

"Can I help you?" she asked.

Olga had been expecting a man for some reason. "Yes, I have a…a message…a special delivery for Mr. Kevin McLaughlin. Can you see that he gets this? It is very important." Olga handed the concierge the envelope, slipping her the twenty dollars at the same time. The woman took the money without hesitation. "Yes, of course. He should be in later this afternoon. I'll make sure he gets this right away. Thank you."

Olga decided to walk the twenty blocks home. She needed some fresh air and time to calm down. Her destiny was now in that little envelope.

ROBERT HAD ASKED to meet with Lenny and Kevin. He hoped that they could help him with his job search. Lenny invited Robert to join them for drinks at the Waldorf Astoria.

"Lenny, Kevin, thank you for taking the time to meet with me."

"Robert, I think I can speak for both of us when I say we certainly appreciate the hard work and the phenomenal results from our short adventure together. We know things are difficult for everyone in New York right now. In fact, we'd like to talk to you about an opportunity in Boston. We're working with a fund there that needs a guy like you," Lenny said.

Robert listened attentively. They were offering what seemed like a great opportunity, but there was only one catch. The job was in Boston. After spending the past year in New York, he wasn't anxious to return home. He knew his options in the city were extremely limited, but there was Olga to consider. Even if he wanted to go back to Boston, which he didn't, would she go with him? She was set on getting her degree from Parsons. Would she be willing to look for a fashion school in Boston? He wasn't sure, but those weren't questions he had to answer just yet.

"Well, I'm certainly interested," Robert replied.

"Great. You're the perfect candidate for the job. I'll make a couple of calls on your behalf. Then my assistant will help coordinate. Today is the fifteenth. I'm guessing they'll want to see you before the end of the month—maybe the week of the twenty-seventh," Lenny said.

"That sounds great," Robert replied.

"By the way, we're having a gathering this Sunday and we're looking for another player," Kevin said.

"I'd love to, but I have a girlfriend now and I don't think it would be…appropriate," Robert said.

"Understood. Perhaps for Halloween, then. We're finalizing the plans for our masquerade party," Kevin said.

"Yes, of course. Well, I should go now. Thank you for your help and support," Robert said.

"Our pleasure," Lenny said.

As he left the two men, Robert had mixed feelings. While he needed to find work, he didn't want to leave New York. He decided to follow up on the Boston offer but to continue looking for something in the city in the hopes that his efforts would pay off quickly.

After the meeting, Kevin headed home. As he entered his building's lobby, the concierge said to him, "Mr. McLaughlin, I have a few private correspondences for you."

McLaughlin knew what that meant. A few candidates had dropped off pictures, hoping to be invited to his private party.

"Thank you, Clara," he said. He took the three envelopes she handed to him.

He walked to the elevator, anxious to see what today's crop had brought. Back at the apartment, he sat on the couch and quickly opened the envelopes. The first envelope was definitely a no. The second was a maybe. The third was a winner. She was perfect. He dialed her number from his blocked number and a young woman answered.

"Hello," she said in English with a distinct Russian accent.

"Olga? This is Kevin McLaughlin. You dropped off an envelope at my building. Would you like to come and see me?"

"Yes, of course. I would like to."

"Well, as a matter of fact, we're having a party this Sunday at seven-thirty. I would love for you to join me and a few of my friends. Please arrive ten minutes early."

"Yes. No problem."

"See you then."

Olga hung up. She was happy. She was potentially going to make a lot of money, but at the same time, she felt sad. She remembered her time at the spa. She also thought of Robert, and the fact that she would have to lie to him…again. She started crying. Then she thought of her mother. *It was so unfair. Why must I sacrifice so much for Mama? Why and to make my own dream come true?* Then she shook herself. *You are a strong Russian woman. A very strong woman. You can do this. Everything will be fine.*

36

Her First Sunday Night

Sunday evening arrived too quickly. Olga told Robert that she had planned a girls' night out in Brooklyn and that since she would be out late with Alina, she would probably stay over there and not return until the next morning. She left their new apartment in the Lower East Side at quarter to seven to make sure that she was on time, as Kevin had requested, arriving by taxi in front of the building fifteen minutes early. The guard opened the door.

"Mr. McLaughlin, please."

"Your name?" the concierge asked.

"Olga. Olga Kotova," she replied nervously. The concierge, the same woman who had greeted Olga a few days earlier, clearly knew why the young woman was going to the penthouse.

"Mr. McLaughlin is waiting for you. You can use the express elevator to the penthouse." The woman pointed to the right.

At the elevator, Olga was met by a man in a black suit. He looked at her and said, "For Mr. McLaughlin?"

"Yes."

The man let Olga into the elevator, inserted his card key into the PH slot, and stepped back out of the elevator. The doors closed and the elevator started going up. Olga was so nervous her hands were trembling, so she took a few deep calming breaths. By the time the doors opened, she had regained a semblance of calm.

A young woman greeted her. "Olga, please follow me."

They walked down a long hallway, turned right, and walked down a few steps. The woman led Olga to a bedroom and closed the door behind them.

"There are a few dresses in the closet. Pick one, and put it on. Mr. McLaughlin would like you to wear one of those selections tonight—you get to keep it after tonight. There are clean thongs over here. If you need to change your thong again, return to this room. This will be *your* private room for the evening. You can bring your guests here. No one will come into this room without you. You can use the bathroom and shower as needed. At some point in the evening, Mr. McLaughlin will tell you discreetly that the party is ending. When he does, please return here, change, and wait for me. I will come by and pay you for your time. After that you can leave. Any questions?"

There was silence. Olga had one million questions, but she knew better than to ask. She said, "No questions."

"Please get ready. The bathroom is right there." The woman turned to leave.

"Just one question. Am I free to leave when I want?"

"Of course, but if you decide to leave before the end of the party, Mr. McLaughlin will not pay you for your time, nor will you be invited back. One other thing: always call your host Mr. McLaughlin and address all the other gentlemen here as Mr. So-and-So. Always. Even if they ask you not to. I will be back at eight o'clock sharp. You need to be ready by then. Mr. McLaughlin appreciates punctuality."

Olga chose a short dress in deep-sea blue. After she changed, she went to the bathroom to check her makeup. Then she sat on the bed, pulled out her phone, and sent a text to Robert.

Olga: Thinking of you! Love you, *babitchka*.

Robert: Love you too. Enjoy your night.

The woman knocked on the door and asked, "Are you ready? It's time."

Olga rose from the bed. She put on a fake smile and walked out of the bedroom. She had to be ready. She was doing this for her future.

———— ∞ ————

It was four in the morning when Olga returned to the bedroom. Kevin had finally called it a night. She went to the bathroom and took her fourth shower of the night, but she still felt dirty. She needed somehow to cleanse herself. She rubbed soap over every part of her body strangers had touched, washing and washing until the soap bar had just about disappeared. She finally got out of the shower, dried herself, put some makeup on, and sat on the unmade bed. She waited for the payment. Olga was there alone for about twenty minutes before the woman came back with her money. The woman finally came in. "Mr. McLaughlin enjoyed your company tonight. He said to tell you that he found you delectable, and would like to invite you again, if you want."

Olga was exhausted and revolted, but knew what she needed to say. "Yes, of course."

"This is for you. Mr. McLaughlin would like to thank you."

Olga took the thick envelope, trying not to think too much about how much was in it. "Please thank Mr. McLaughlin for me," Olga said.

"Of course. Please follow me. I'll walk you out. By the way, my name is Alisson," she said with a smile. It was the first time the woman had seemed the slightest bit friendly toward Olga. Before she had been cold and distant. When they reached the elevator, Allison said, "Remember that being invited here is a privilege. You should not talk about this to anyone. Is that clear?"

Olga nodded. In the privacy of the elevator, Olga took a quick look inside the envelope. It contained a large stack of hundred dollar bills. She had made thousands of dollars in one evening. Olga walked to the street and called a taxi. She was tired, and she needed the company of someone who loved her man. Although she had told Robert she would stay in Brooklyn, she decided to go home. She needed Robert to hold her. She needed to feel his warmth. She needed his protection. Just before she reached their apartment, she looked at the three business cards the guests had given her. They were all from bankers. She hid the cards in her wallet.

Olga arrived home at just past four thirty. She trudged slowly up the stairs, opened the door, and went into the bathroom. She hid the money in a box of tampons, then stripped naked and got into bed with Robert. She started kissing him until he finally opened his eyes.

"Well, hello there. Aren't you supposed to be in Brooklyn?"

"I missed you too much. I wanted to be with my Robert."

"Well, I'm here," he said.

He turned around and wrapped his arms around her. Olga felt safe. She lay in bed with her eyes wide open. She had done it again. She had done something that she needed to forget forever. She would put the memories in a little box in her mind and Robert would never find out. Never.

Robert woke the next morning to the sound of the alarm clock. It was like any other weekday morning. He opened his eyes and turned around to watch Olga sleeping. He smiled. She was so beautiful. She was everything he wanted in a woman. He wanted to tell her at that moment how happy he was to have her in his life. He wanted to yell as loudly as he could that he loved her. He couldn't bring himself to wake her up, though. She looked so peaceful. He kissed her softly on the cheek and whispered, "I love you, Olga."

Robert got up and started the coffee machine. After drinking a cup, he walked out of the apartment, checking his e-mail. He read the one with the subject "Boston." As Lenny had promised, his assistant had set up a meeting for him on Thursday, the day before Halloween. He would need to be in Boston early in that morning and stay for dinner. The timing could not have been better because his consulting assignment in New York was wrapping up, and he would be available for and needing work. This was a good opportunity, even if it was in the wrong city.

The sound of the door lock woke Olga. She opened her eyes; Robert had left for work. She closed her eyes again, but she could not fall back asleep. The images of the previous night haunted her. She lay in bed and stared at the ceiling. She felt an overwhelming sadness. Tears started filling her eyes. *All of this is just a dream,* she thought. *A bad dream. I will forget this very bad dream.*

Olga needed to talk with someone about what had happened, and she thought of Yuliana. Alina had said that she thought Yuliana was working for a high-end escort agency that posed as a modeling agency. Yuliana had never admitted as much, but Olga thought that if she told her what had happened last night, Yuliana might be willing to open up. She sent her a text asking if she was available to meet later that day.

Olga went to get coffee in the combined kitchen and living room. The couple had moved over the weekend to the suffocating, tiny apartment. She hated it. Things could only get better—with or without Robert. *Once I become a successful designer, I will have an apartment like the penthouse.*

Olga retrieved the envelope and sat down on the couch. She counted the money: seven thousand five hundred dollars. She smiled. The money was quickly accounted for. Five thousand dollars would go to Mama right away toward her treatment. One thousand dollars would secure Olga her spot at the school, and the rest she would spend. Since Robert had lost his job, he had not taken her shopping. Today she would pamper herself. She would go shopping and make an overdue visit to the nail salon.

She pulled out the business cards she had collected the night before. Kevin's card only included his initials and a phone number. The other two cards were from the two bankers who attended the party. She looked at one of them and smiled. She saw the III after one man's name and remembered the man as he'd introduced himself to her. She had nearly laughed out loud. *What kind of poser would call himself "the third" in this day and age, especially in America, the land of opportunity? Did he think he was some kind of royalty?* She had spent several hours with the arrogant but handsome man. He was obnoxious, but obviously rich. While she looked at his card, Yuliana finally replied to her text. The two girls would meet for a late lunch in Manhattan.

—ထဆ—

OLGA ARRIVED AT Coffee Shop, a little dinner on Union Square. Yuliana was already seated. Olga joined her at the table and ordered a coffee.

"Hello. How are you?" Yuliana asked.

"I'm okay," said Olga.

"I don't think so. What's up? I was surprised when I got your text."

"I just wanted to talk. I went to party recently," Olga replied.

"Party? Since when did you start to party?"

"I need money. A lot…for my mother. She's ill, and…"

"I get it. Where did you go party?"

"I'm not supposed to tell."

"Ah, private parties. Those are the best. First time?"

"Yes."

Olga was talking about her evening when she got a text from Robert. She apologized to Yuliana, picked up her phone, and read the message.

> Robert: A quick reminder that I see Carl tonight.
> Then I'm meeting Stephen at Barbounia.
> Maybe u can join us there around 8? ILU
> Olga: K. 8ish. Luv you 2

"Sorry—my boyfriend. He's a banker," Olga said.

"You have a boyfriend…and you party?" Yuliana said.

"Yes."

"If you want to do this, you don't want to get caught. If he finds out, you're done with your banker boyfriend. So here's what you have to do."

—ထဆ—

ROBERT WALKED TO Carl's office as he had done on so many Mondays.

"'How are you doing? There's been a lot of turmoil in your business recently," Carl said.

"I'm doing all right. I finished a short assignment this week, and I might have a job opportunity. It's in Boston, though," Robert said.

"Boston? How do you feel about going back?"

"Frankly, I'm more a New Yorker than a Bostonian now. I love this city. Then again, there aren't any real job prospects here right now for a guy like me."

"How does Olga feel about Boston?"

"I don't have the job yet, so I haven't mentioned it."

Robert explained how he felt. He felt so close to her that he could no longer imagine life without her. He had started thinking about marriage.

"Marriage is a very serious commitment. I know you had doubts about her as recently as a few weeks ago," Carl said.

"*I know marriage is serious, but I'm ready. Those doubts? Well, I was being silly. She's not Nicki. Olga woman loves me more than anything. I'm so sure.*"

After his session, Robert walked into Barbounia. Stephen was already at the bar. It was a quiet night. As always Leon, the bartender, got started on his drink, a glass of Cabernet Sauvignon, as soon as he saw Robert.

"Stephen, how are you?"

"Hey, Robert. I'm fine. How are you doing?"

"Doing okay. I'm going to Boston this week for a job interview. Mutual funds."

"Boston? Man, you can't leave the city!"

"I don't want to, but you know how it is. There's nothing here for guys like us."

"Yes, I know. John is leaving for LA in a couple of weeks—for good, he says. He's going to set up a hedge fund. His father has a lot of contacts in Hollywood, so I'm sure he can make something happen."

"That's great. What about you? Any prospects?"

"Well, you may not believe this, but I think I've found something in real estate. I got connected to a developer who needs a sales guy. I can sell securities, so why not expensive apartments? I just need to get my license, which won't be difficult."

"That's great. By the way, Olga should be coming to meet us soon. Don't talk about Boston, okay? I didn't mention it to her yet."

"No worries. How's going with her?"

"Great. Actually, *really* great. I'm thinking of putting a ring on her finger. Maybe at Christmas."

"Wow. It's serious. Congratulations!"

"I'm planning to go shopping for a ring next week after Halloween."

"Speaking of Halloween, did you get invited to Lenny's masquerade party? He's keeping it low-key this year."

"Yes, I got the invite. Should be a good time."

Olga and Yuliana got out of the taxi and walked into the restaurant. Olga quickly found Robert at the bar and kissed him.

"Hello, *babitchka*. This is my friend Yuliana. She was my roommate when I lived with Alina. Yuliana, this is Robert and his friend, Stephen."

"Nice to finally meet you," Robert said.

"Hi," Stephen said.

"How was your day?" Olga asked.

"It was fine," Robert replied.

"And your meeting with Carl?" Olga asked. She did not understand why Robert needed therapy—why anyone would need therapy. Russians believed that adults should be able to deal with issues on their own. Look at her—she'd had a difficult life, with an abusive father and a temperamental husband, but she had dealt with it without help. She thought of herself as a very strong and resilient woman, like her mother. She could get through anything.

"It was okay," Robert said.

Yuliana spoke a few words in Russian to Olga and then went to the restroom.

"Olga, I need to go to Boston for a couple days. I'm leaving on Wednesday and will be back on Friday. And on Friday we're invited to a masquerade party hosted by my friend Lenny—just like the one where we first met, remember?"

"Of course I do. Boston? Why? No—wait, don't tell me now. I need to go to the restroom."

"Okay. Shall I order drinks for everyone?" Robert said.

Olga nodded and slipped away toward the restrooms. When she was out of sight, Stephen spoke. "You need to set me up on a date with Olga's friend. She's hot!"

"Done," Robert said, smiling.

———✦———

ROBERT DROVE BACK from Boston on Friday morning. He had originally planned to return to New York on Thursday night, but he'd decided to stay over after the long business dinner. The meetings had gone very well. Although he might have to go back for a final round of interviews in November, he felt very good about his chances. The job was perfect. It seemed as if it had been purposely defined for him, except that it was in the wrong city.

Friday would have been a normal morning except that Olga had gone missing. He hadn't heard a word from her since eight the night before. All his attempts to reach her had been unsuccessful. Finally, when he was within thirty minutes of the city, his BlackBerry vibrated.

> Olga: *Babitchka*, I am so sorry. I went to
> Brooklyn, and I forgot my charger so
> my phone died. Love you. Call me.

Robert dialed her number, and she answered. "*Babitchka*, I am so sorry."

Robert was annoyed. "It is okay, but you know I've bought you three chargers since we got you your BlackBerry. Please be more careful."

"I will, *babitchka*. I will. Are you on your way home?"

"Yes, I should be there by one. How about we get lunch somewhere?"

"That would be great."

"You didn't forget about the masquerade party tonight, did you?"

"No, I did not."

"See you soon. I love you."

"I love you, *babitchka*."

The conversation calmed Robert.

37

ANOTHER MASQUERADE PARTY

ROBERT AND OLGA arrived at Lenny's place together for the masquerade party. Robert had seen Lenny a few times over the past year, but never at his home. When they checked in and received their bracelets, Robert was amused to see that he had been promoted, at least judging by his bracelet—this year it was VIP blue. Olga was still a newbie, however, with her yellow one. Robert was not about to expose his past misdeeds by going to the VIP section when Olga was there. He didn't want her to find out about his adventurous past.

The party was in full swing when they arrived. Robert found Stephen and John at the bar. While the three men were catching up, Olga looked around to see if she could find and of her Russian acquaintances in the crowd, a task made all the more difficult by the fact that most people were wearing their masks.

A white-haired man with a pencil mustache walked up to the three men. "Gentlemen! I hope you're enjoying the party," said Lenny.

"Yes. I didn't recognize you at first," Stephen said.

"Lenny, let me introduce you to my girlfriend, Olga," Robert said. He took her hand and pulled her close to him.

"Nice to meet you, Olga. Robert is very lucky to have found such a beautiful woman as you."

"Thank you," she replied in a small voice. She recognized the white mustache.

"Well, gentlemen, I should be going. Robert, feel free to come and join us upstairs. You know how much we enjoy your company. Olga will be welcome, of course." He turned to Olga. "It was very nice to meet you."

Olga was petrified. She was hoping that he did not recognize her behind her mask. *If he did, would he tell Robert?* If this was Lenny's party, was there anyone else there she might know?

Robert was not amused by Lenny's suggestion. Taking Olga upstairs would be a disaster. He didn't understand why Lenny would even extend such an invitation when he must have known that Robert wouldn't be interested. He had already declined the invitation to the Sunday party.

Olga stayed close to Robert for the rest of the evening, using him as a shield against any unfortunate encounters. She clung to his arm, held his hand, and kissed him frequently, making it very clear she was with him. She figured if anyone from the Sunday party saw her, he would not dare approach her. Apparently, the plan worked. By the end of the party, she had escaped the gathering without embarrassing confrontations.

The next morning, Olga got up shortly after Robert had left for his usual workout at the gym. She had had only a few hours of sleep, but she got up to check her e-mail.

> Dear Olga,
> I wanted to tell you again how important you are
> to me. I cannot forget our wonderful moments
> together—Krasnoyarsk, Prague, and Paris.
> It has been months since we last saw each
> other. I love you more than you think, but
> I cannot wait for you. This is difficult for
> me, and I know this will be difficult for you,
> but we have to say good-bye. I love you.
> Your Frenchman, your François

Olga deleted the message. She had no feelings left for him. Her mother had always been right. He was not the man for her.

38

THE STORM

IT WAS A Tuesday evening in November. Robert was returning from yet another networking event. He continued to go to these events because he was still unemployed. Boston remained a possibility, but he had not yet received a formal job offer. Olga had cooked dinner, and it was ready to serve upon his arrival.

She had also prepared herself for him. When he opened the door, she was barely dressed. She wore white lingerie, knee-high lace stockings, a tight thong, a little bra, and long, satin gloves. She approached him slowly, kissed him softly, grabbed his hand, led him to the bedroom, and made love to him. She was even more attentive than usual. He finally climaxed inside her. He enjoyed these moments when he felt her affection.

After the sex, however, Olga told him that she was going out with her ex-roommates Alina and Yuliana for a birthday celebration, and that she had to leave right after dinner. The event was in Brighton Beach, forty minutes from home without any traffic, which was rare. She said that she might decide to stay at Alina's. He never questioned her, but in the back of his mind, Robert knew something wasn't right. It was unusual for her to leave home alone so late—it was already nine. He offered to drive her, but she insisted on taking a cab. She seemed anxious during dinner, checking the clock several times, but he said nothing.

Dinner was done and it was nearly ten when Olga left. She said again that she might not return until the morning, and then she kissed him and left. Shortly after, he received a text.

> Olga: Good night! <3
> Robert: Have fun with your friends! I
> love you, my Olga! Good night.

⊶∞⊷

A FEW DAYS after Olga had stayed overnight in Brooklyn, Robert came home ready to take Olga out for dinner. They had made plan to go out that evening. He was sitting on the couch flipping through the TV channels while she was getting ready in the bathroom when her purse started vibrating. He knew that she had taken her phone with her to the bathroom, though; through the open door, he had seen her pink BlackBerry on the sink, so he wondered what the buzzing could be. He opened her purse and saw another phone inside—a black one. It was vibrating again. He read the text message.

> WP3: Really loved our night together. Can't get
> enough of you. When r u free again? I can't wait.

Robert didn't understand. He quickly picked up the phone. He called back the number in the text and a man answered. "Olga, baby. How are you? Olga? Olga?"

Robert hung up. A text followed.

> WP3: Everything okay? When
> can I see you? Call me

Robert was shocked. He was mad. The voice was familiar. So were the initials WP3. *Peterson? Could this be William fucking Peterson the fucking Third?* He checked his own BlackBerry for William Peterson III. He'd entered the information out of habit after running into him at Kevin's, though he had never intended to use it. It was the same number. How could this be? How did she know Peterson? Especially well enough for him to call her "baby" and say he couldn't get enough of her?

Robert put the phone back in Olga's purse. He wanted to scream. He wanted to cry. He couldn't believe it. He was living a lie. He was destroyed. Olga, the love of his life, had been with another man. And not just any other man, but one he knew and despised. She still told Robert she loved him while she was having sex with one, two, three…how many others? She was Nicki all over again!

The bathroom door was closed now. He knocked on it loudly with the palms of both hands, yelling, "Fuck you! Fuck you! Fuck you! How could you?" He grabbed his coat and ran out of the apartment, away from the pain.

As he raced down the stairs he heard her voice calling after him. "What's wrong, *babitchka*? What's happened?"

Olga ran out of the bathroom. It took her only a few seconds to guess what had happened. She found her purse, pulled out the black phone, and saw the text messages from William Peterson. She called Robert. He didn't answer. She sent him text messages, pretending nothing had happened.

> Olga: *Babitchka*, what is wrong?
> Olga: Baby, please call me <3 <3 <3.
> Olga: Baby, please
> Olga: Baby. My Robert. Please
> Olga: *Babitchka*, where are you? I worry about you.

She received nothing. He would not answer her. She called him again and left him a voice mail, sobbing into the phone. "*Babitchka*, my love. Where are you? I love you! I am concerned. Call me."

Olga decided to send a text to Stephen.

> Olga: Robert left the apartment upset.
> Is he with you? I want to know what
> happened. Tell him I love him.

Again, she received no answer.

Olga knew that Robert would probably not buy her act. Yuliana had warned her that she would lose Robert if he found out what she was doing; he wouldn't understand that it was just something she did for money. But she couldn't tell him the truth. She couldn't tell him that his failure to support her financially had pushed her in that direction. That was an impossible discussion.

Yuliana had told her to get a second phone; that way, she could avoid providing her real numbers to clients, and hide what she was doing from Robert. Olga had not followed the instructions well.

She waited for Robert, hoping to convince him there was nothing going on. She decided to tell Robert that the phone wasn't hers but Yuliana's.

Finally, after Robert had been gone for a few hours, Olga gave up and went to bed. Undisturbed, she quickly fell asleep. At around four in the morning, she heard the apartment door opening. She walked to the living room.

"Where were you? I was so worried. You never answered my texts."

Robert was still enraged. "I know everything, even the guy's name. William Peterson III. Are you fucking kidding me? Peterson. He lives downtown in a big fucking apartment with a terrace on the forty-sixth floor, and he's got a rich daddy and a brain no bigger than his dick. How *could* you?"

She looked at him and blinked nervously. "How could I *what*? I've done nothing. I don't know this man."

"Nothing? You're lying. Why do you have two phones? What the fuck? I just want to know the truth. I *might* forgive you if you tell me the truth."

"The phone is not mine. It is Yuliana's. She forgot it the other day at the restaurant when we were together."

He grew even more furious. "Fucking bullshit! I called the guy back, and he said your name. 'Olga, baby.' You're just another fucking Russian bitch. Everyone warned me. 'Don't trust a Russian woman,' they said. I should have listened."

There was silence. Olga couldn't find anything to say, so she started crying. She hoped Robert might fell guilty for being angry and forgive her. It had always worked with her husband.

"You're such a bullshitter. I had to find your marriage certificate before you told me you were married. Now this? What the fuck? What else are you hiding?"

"I told you when you finally asked me that I'm now divorced."

"I don't fucking care. I have nothing else to say. Now I know why you didn't want to come to Boston with me. I'm done with you. I was fucking going to ask you to marry me. I bought you a fucking ring. Screw that. I can't be with someone who doesn't value me. I never cheated on you. I have to be with someone loves me."

She had been caught, but she continued to deny everything. "I love you so much. I did nothing wrong. I'm not a bad woman."

Yes, you are, he thought. *You might as well be a Russian spy. You infiltrated my life and pretended to love me. You spoke words that you didn't mean and had so many secrets. Now the truth is discovered.*

He said to Olga, "Forget it, Olga. I'll sleep on the couch for a few hours, and then leave in the morning. I'll come back later to sort out how we can move forward separately."

Olga went back to bed and closed the door behind her. She was alone again without anyone who cared for her. François had moved on. Vladimir had divorced her. Edward had lied to her. Now Robert had dumped her her. She was left with only clients.

Yes…clients! William Peterson might be the answer. He said he couldn't get enough of her. *Yes, I have William still,* she thought. She fell asleep, almost smiling.

She didn't hear Robert leave. She wasn't quite sure what to expect from him, although he would probably not come back to her. He was moving to Boston anyway, and she had no interest in following him there. She needed to find another man who would provide financial help again. William seemed like the right choice. He was a handsome, thirty-something banker looking for companionship. She had been a few times to his apartment. He was clearly wealthy. She needed a rich man again. She sent William a text.

> Olga: Sorry about last night. I forgot
> my phone at a restaurant. Just picked
> it up. Want to see you soon.
> WP3: Come to my place tonight at 8. We'll party.
> Olga: K. ;)

OLGA HAD FOUND her smile once again. Robert could be replaced, but she needed one more thing from him—his apartment. She couldn't pay the rent. She had to play her cards right to find a way to make someone pay for it until the lease was up. That would give her five months to find another place to move. The apartment was small and depressing, but it was very convenient to Parsons. Most importantly, though, she needed a home base in the city so she could continue to work at those parties in Manhattan.

Olga received another text.

> Robert: I'll be by at 8 to pick up some
> of my stuff. Would appreciate if you
> were not there when I stop by.
> Olga: I love you. I do not want to lose you. Please.

Robert didn't reply. Olga forgot about Robert. Soon she would make her move on William. She would make sure that William could not live without her.

39

WILLIAM

OLGA QUICKLY FOUND the perfect arrangement after Robert moved out of the apartment. She had been able to convince Robert to let her stay in the apartment, but only if she could pay for it. William Peterson was the answer. He gave her cash every time she was intimate with him, and she had collected close to ten thousand dollars over six weeks. It was the perfect arrangement. It also meant that she could stop seeing other clients she met at Kevin's parties.

On Friday afternoon William sent a text to Olga.

WP3: Come over at 10

Olga: Of course! See you soon, my *babitchka*. Are we getting dinner?

WP3: No. Eat before you come.

Olga was puzzled. His texts that evening had been much shorter than usual. She even found them abrupt. He usually took the time to write longer texts to set the schedule for the evening. He usually invited her over earlier, too, so they had time for a long, delicious dinner followed by drinks at some famous nightspot, and still had time for sex. Tonight was different, though it didn't really matter. She would get her allowance from him. Dinner was not important.

Olga got to the apartment at ten, as William had asked. When he opened the door, she smelled the lingering scent of marijuana in the air. She hugged him. "I see you started partying without me, *babitchka*. I'm so happy to see you."

"Come in. I've invited a few friends to join us." He led her to the living room.

Two women sat on the leather couch, half-dressed. One of them was the Uzbek, Anastasia. Olga was stunned.

"Olga, meet my other two best friends. Tonight we're all going to party like Kevin," William said.

"Are you asking me to…" She could not finish the sentence.

"We all know you're not shy. You did it the night we met at Kevin's," he said. He held out a hand to Anastasia and helped her up from the couch. "This is Anastasia. I want you two to fuck each other while Polina sucks me off."

"You want me to…I thought…I thought I was your *girlfriend*. I thought you really *liked* me."

"What are you talking about? My girlfriend? I fucking give you cash every time I fuck you. Guys give money to escorts and hookers, not girlfriends. So, do you want your money or not?"

Olga felt betrayed. William pulled a bag of cocaine from the coffee table drawer. He poured out two lines on a small, framed picture and held it under her nose with a rolled-up bill touching one of her nostrils.

"Come on," he said. "Do some. It'll make you happy."

Olga had always stayed away from drugs, fearful of how they might affect her. She had done many things she wasn't proud of, but she didn't want to become a drug addict. William scared her, though, and under his persistent urging, she finally gave in. She inhaled the powder and immediately felt the effect of the drug. She could feel her heart start racing and hear it pounding in her ears.

"You see? You'll feel much better." He held up the other line, but she backed away. He shrugged and snorted it himself.

William took Olga to the couch and stood her next to Anastasia. Polina stood up and began removing William's shirt, then unzipping his pants. He grinned and he sat down on the couch.

Anastasia faced Olga and whispered to her in Russian. "I see the princess has fallen from her throne. You are no better than me, bitch. Now I'm going to fuck you *royally*."

She put her hand behind Olga's head and pulled it toward her, pressing her lips against Olga's, her tongue working to invade the unwilling mouth of her prisoner. Olga jumped back and said to William, "How could do you do this to me? I love you!"

William sat on the couch, legs splayed, ready for Polina. He started laughing. "Love? You don't know the meaning of the word. Robert's washed out, so you're moving on. You're a whore, baby. A fucking prostitute! You're only here for my money. Nothing else. You love my wallet. Not me."

William had never treated her so disrespectfully. Olga headed to the door. She heard him screaming behind her, "Baby, if you leave now, you can't come back ever again."

Olga left the apartment. This was too much. She could not take it anymore. She could not bear the thought of having sex with the Uzbek whore.

40

HAPPY BIRTHDAY, OLGA

OLGA'S BIRTHDAY WAS in one week, and her situation remained grim. She would be twenty-five on March 29. She had hoped that 2009 would bring her better luck, but so far she had been wrong. After nine months in New York, she was no closer to making her dream come true. She was on the verge of becoming an illegal immigrant. It was not possible to claim an imaginary illness for the third time to extend her tourist visa. Money remained a challenge. After leaving William Peterson III, she never heard from him again. Kevin and Lenny no longer invited her to their parties. With few other options, she joined Yuliana's escort agency to make some cash to pay for her apartment. She hoped she would find a way to fund her high tuition when the next semester started in September. She had written Robert a short e-mail.

"Do you miss me?"

He replied after a few days.

"No. I have no feelings at all for you. I was
not the man for you then. I am not the man
for you now. I have moved on. I have met
a woman in Boston and I like her. I am not
interested in seeing you again. Robert."

No one wanted her. She was alone in the city.

Olga woke around noon on Saturday morning after another long night of work. The phone rang. She stretched out of her bed to find the phone on the floor and answered.

"Olga, I wanted to wish a happy birthday."

"Thank you, Mama. I'm so happy to hear your voice."

"I have good news. The cancer is all gone for now. The doctors think I'm going to be okay, thanks to you. You're such a great daughter."

"I'm very happy to hear this, Mama."

"I wanted to tell you. Your sister saw Vladimir with his wife. An older woman, close to his age. She's ugly."

"Good for him."

"Do you have any plans for your birthday?"

"Yes, my friends are throwing me a big party."

"That sounds fun. Any nice men going?"

"No, Mama. I told you. My modeling job doesn't give me time for that."

"I'm so proud of you. Your father isn't here, but he's also very proud of you."

"Mama, I've to go now. I need to get ready."

"Okay. I'm sorry that I didn't send you a present. You know how things are here."

Olga understood the underlying message. She said, "I know, Mama, I know. It's okay. I'll send you money when I can."

"Thank you."

"Mama, I need to go now."

"I understand. You're a busy girl. Happy birthday again."

Olga hung up. She slowly got up and stopped in front of the long mirror in the bedroom. She looked at her skinny body. Work and her drug habit had taken their toll. The cocaine that kept her going, the meth when she couldn't afford the coke, the pills to bring her down… She was so thin that she could count her ribs. Her small breasts were on the verge of disappearing. When she stood on the scale, it registered ninety-five pounds. She smiled nervously. She knew she should stop everything soon—drugs, work, and entertaining clients.

Olga decided to take the rest of the weekend off to celebrate her birthday. She was alone, but she could still take herself shopping for smaller-sized clothes. She walked out of the apartment and stopped at a Starbucks. A young man opened the door for her. He wore a yellow hard hat covered with union stickers, a red jacket, torn jeans, and dusty construction boots. He smiled at her, and she smiled back. The line was long at the Starbucks, and he said to Olga in a heavy New York accent, "Hi. Lots of people needin' cawfee today."

"Yes." She thought that was a silly way to start a conversation.

"I'm just finishin' my shift around, treatin' myself for the trek back home to Queens. How 'bout you? You live close?"

"Yes. I live in this neighborhood. It's not too far."

"You got a pretty accent. Where ya from?"

"Russia."

"Cool. I'm Chris. Queens, born and raised. Third generation Italian."

Olga laughed to herself. Chris from Queens, but the Third, like royalty. He wasn't a banker, but he was a man, and he was paying some attention to her. That hadn't happened in a while, a least not with someone young and handsome.

"I am Olga."

"You got plans for the day, Olga?"

"Well, actually, it's my birthday."

"That's great! Whatcha doing? Pretty woman like you must have a lot of friends planning some big party."

"No big party."

"Small party?" He smiled.

"No party." She slightly pinched her lips. She wanted to tell him a story about a surprise party organized by imaginary friends, but she said nothing. She was tired of lying. She ordered a short cappuccino.

"Lemme pay for that," he said. "This bein' your birthday and all."

"Thank you. That's very kind."

It had been a long time since a man treated her with something that felt like kindness. They walked to the end of the counter to wait for their coffees.

"Beautiful woman like you shouldn't be alone on her birthday. Let's go across the street to the park, enjoy this beautiful day, maybe later get some dinner or something. If ya want."

"That's very sweet. Sure, why not? I'd like that."

Chris seemed like a really nice guy. With his dark complexion and black hair, he reminded her of François. He wasn't a banker, and he didn't look even close to rich, but anything was better than being alone on her birthday.

41

LOS ANGELES

ROBERT DECIDED TO leave Boston. He'd just ended a tumultuous relationship with another Russian woman. He had been in contact sporadically with Olga over the years. Now, waiting for his delayed flight at Logan Airport, he suddenly felt an urge to talk to someone. He dialed Olga's most recent number. She answered after several rings.

"Hello?"

"Hi, this is Robert."

"Robert...?"

"Thompson. Robert Thompson. Sorry. I know it's been a while since we've talked."

"No, it's just that...well, this must be a new number. I didn't recognize it. How are things?"

"Yes, this is a new number. I had to change it. It's a long story. Anyways, it's not important," he said. "I'm moving to LA, catching my flight in about twenty minutes, and I just wanted to see how you're doing."

"Well, I'm married now."

"Wow. Are you in love?" Robert asked skeptically. He couldn't believe Olga would ever truly be in love.

"Of course I am."

"Ah, so he's rich?" Robert couldn't stop himself from saying it, then wished he hadn't when he heard the quick intake of breath over the phone.

"We get by. Robert," Olga raised her voice. He had touched a nerve. "I married once for money. I told you. I want you to be happy, Robert. Can't you want the same for me?"

"I'm sorry, I assumed…"

"I have changed. I love him. He's a wonderful husband. I will go to school next year. He is helping me make my dreams come true. I will start my business after finishing my degree."

"That's great. How is your mother?"

"She's well. She's been cancer-free for some time now. I'll bring her to New York after I finish school. She'll help her with my kids."

"Kids?"

"You know that I always wanted to have my own family, but I have to start my career first."

"That's great."

"What about you, Robert?"

"I'm fine. I'm going to work with John, the finance guy from New York."

"I remember John….Robert, there's one thing that I wanted to tell you. I loved you. I made mistakes, but I really loved you. You should know that."

"Olga, you should have told me the truth when we were together. You should have trusted me. We would've found a way to help your mother. You didn't need to do…"

"Maybe. I really wanted to tell you, but…. I hope that you forgive me."

"Yes, I did, after you told me the truth, but it was too late. I was already in Boston. … Does your husband know… everything?"

"Yes, I told him. I have no secrets for him. I don't lie anymore."

"So, he must *really* love you."

"Yes, he does. He's a great man. He'll be a great father."

"I have to go. My plane is about to board."

"It was nice talking to you, Robert."

"Yes, it was nice, Olga. Good-bye."

Robert hung up. She had found a way to make it. Maybe it was as simple as that—two people truly loving each other for who they were. Robert had hated this woman for everything she had done. Now he was just happy to hear she had found what she was looking for.

42

BACK IN NEW YORK

ROBERT HADN'T BEEN to New York for a couple of years. After his short return to Boston, he had moved to Los Angeles to join his friend John to help out with a new business venture. Los Angeles was his Robert's refuge from another disastrous relationship in Boston. He had maintained contact with a few people in the city, but there was one person Robert really wanted to see—Carl.

Robert walked into the very familiar building after being buzzed in. It seemed as if nothing had changed, as if time had stopped. The lobby still needed a fresh coat of paint, and the elevator still made a cringing noise while ascending the six floors. The hall to Carl's apartment remained unchanged. Even the smell was the same.

"Robert, so nice to see you again," Carl said.

"I was really looking forward to see you, Carl. I'm sorry I don't have more time. I just wanted to stop by to say hi."

"No problem. What brings you to New York?"

"My girlfriend hasn't been to New York for a few years, so we decided to come and spend a few days."

"Girlfriend?"

"Yes, Natalya. She is Russian. Again."

"You and your Russian girls. It was never a good combination. I hope this relationship is less dramatic than your last ones."

Robert laughed. "I think I've gotten better at it. After the things that happened in Boston, I took my time."

"That's good to hear. So, you're ready to commit. Good. I wasn't sure you would be after everything."

"I know, but I took this slow. When she told me she was Russian, I freaked out." Robert started to laugh. "I was afraid I would never move on, but I did."

"So tell me about her."

Robert felt so happy to be with Carl. He smiled as he explained how the two had met and how the relationship had slowly developed. They had been talking for just about fifty minutes when Robert received a call. "Sorry, Carl. It's Natalya. Do you mind if I answer?" Carl shook his head.

Robert took the call, then said, "Natalya wants me to come to the hotel in twenty minutes. I'll need to go soon."

"Okay. Any news from Olga?"

"Yes, I called her a couple years of ago when I first moved to LA. I'm not sure why I called—just to check in, I guess. She told me she'd found love and happiness. I haven't heard from her since."

"You went through a lot with her. Good and bad. Maybe that's why you reached out to her."

"Maybe."

"I remember that you concluded, after the break-up, that she was a compulsive liar. Do you think she lied to you to hide the truth? About finding love and happiness."

Robert paused a few seconds: "I don't think so." As he pronounced these words, he wondered if she actually did lie to him. He could not understand why she would at this point, but she kept surprising him. Carl's comment left a doubt. *Maybe she did lie to me.*

"It was nice to see you."

"I really wanted to see you. And say thank you, you know?"

As Robert got up, Carl said, "You're welcomed. By the way, what happened to the Russian girl in Boston?"

"Tatiana? No clue. I went out with her friend, Yulia, a few times when I was in Boston. She told me Tatiana's entire story. It was very interesting. I'll have to tell you at one point."

"Another Russian story?"

"Yes."

Carl pulled his old body up from his chair to walk Robert to the door of the apartment. He put his hand out and said, "Good-bye."

Robert shook Carl's hand. "Thanks, Carl. Good-bye."

Robert walked down the familiar stairs of the apartment building and decided not to take a cab but to walk back to the hotel. He wanted to take in the city on that warm spring day. He took a very familiar route—Park Avenue, Union Square, Madison Square Park, Madison Avenue—until he reached his destination on Twenty-Ninth Street, the Gansevoort Hotel, a hip midtown boutique hotel. It had been a twenty-minute walk, and he found Nataliya waiting for him in the lobby. She got up as soon as she saw him come in. Robert took her hand and kissed her.

"I hope I didn't rush you," she said with her slight Russian accent.

"No, we had plans so it's okay. Plus I didn't want to stay for too long."

"Happy to see him?"

"I'm always happy to see him. He's a good friend, but things are different."

"Different?"

"I've been away for so long. I realized as I was walking back that I don't belong here anymore. I felt like a stranger."

"You're so funny. You always tell me you're a New Yorker, how New York is sooooo much better than LA. Now you tell me you don't belong here. Where do you belong, Robert?" she said, smiling.

Robert took Natalya in his arms, pulled her close to him, and looked into her eyes. "Natalya, I know where I belong." He kissed her slowly, then pulled back to look at her some more. "I belong to you, my Russian woman."

THE END

www.ingramcontent.com/pod-product-compliance
Lightning Source LLC
Chambersburg PA
CBHW071314250626
47159CB00004B/1415